SPEED OF LIFE

BY J. M. KELLY

Houghton Mifflin Harcourt

Boston   New York

LIBRARY OF CONGRESS CATALOGING-IN-PUBLICATION DATA

Names: Kelly, J. M., 1968- author.
Title: Speed of life / by J. M. Kelly.
Description: Boston ; New York : Houghton Mifflin Harcourt, [2016] | Summary:
Crystal must choose between her dream of becoming the first college
student in her family, or keeping a promise to her twin sister, Amber, to
raise together the baby one had in high school.
Identifiers: LCCN 2015037010 | ISBN 9780544747821 (hardback)
Subjects: | CYAC: Twins--Fiction. | Sisters--Fiction. | Babies--Fiction. |
Conduct of life--Fiction. | Automobiles--Maintenance and repair--Fiction.
| Family life--Fiction. | BISAC: JUVENILE FICTION / Social Issues /
Pregnancy. | JUVENILE FICTION / Family / Siblings. | JUVENILE FICTION /
Social Issues / Homelessness & Poverty. | JUVENILE FICTION / Family / New
Baby. | JUVENILE FICTION / Transportation / Cars & Trucks. | JUVENILE
FICTION / Girls & Women.
Classification: LCC PZ7.1.K454 Spe 2016 | DDC [Fic]--dc23 LC record available at https://
lccn.loc.gov/2015037010

Manufactured in the United States of America
DOC 10 9 8 7 6 5 4 3 2 1
4500611778
Permissions to use epigraph: "Dear Old Dad" written by Victor Anthony,
Commercial-free Music, SESAC

*This book is dedicated to Papa
for passing on the old-car gene.
Love, J. M.*

Cars today all look the same;
they all look like orthopedic shoes.

— "Dear Old Dad" by Victor Anthony

CHAPTER 1

JUNE

T ake her."

"No."

"Hold her for a minute."

"I don't want to."

"She needs you."

"Please, find her a family. They said there's lots of people waiting."

"But she's yours."

"I don't want her."

"You will when you're feeling better."

"I never wanted her. Please let me sleep. Don't do this to me. Please? Please? If you love me . . ."

"We're keeping her because I love you. So you don't hate us both later."

"I want to sleep."

In the silence the blackness comes again. And then . . . relentlessly . . . "I'll help you. We'll raise her together. Fifty-fifty. Just like always."

"If I say yes, will you let me sleep?"

"For a while."

"Okay. Yes."

CHAPTER 2

OCTOBER

I push a button on the iron and a little cloud of steam poofs out, sending up a whiff of clean-laundry smell, temporarily blocking the kitchen's usual odors—stale coffee, dirty diapers, and the sour tang of empty beer cans. As I press my work shirt, Amber squeezes between me and the archway, heading through the living room to our bedroom. She's got her long hair in a bushy ponytail, and it brushes my face as she goes by, almost making me sneeze.

"What time will you be done tonight?" I ask her.

"It'll be at least eleven," she answers. The dump we live in's so small I can hear her in the other room.

"I'll be there by quarter after," I say. "If you're not finished, I'll help."

"Cool. Thanks. Can I wear your old jeans?"

"Yeah, sure."

You hear about sisters swapping clothes all the time, but

we don't do it very much. Amber's job is hot and sweaty, though, and most of my stuff's grease-stained from working on cars, so my jeans are perfect for her to wear to work because they're crappy already. Usually she dresses to show off her body, and I use clothes to hide mine. Not that I'm a dog or anything. Guys think Amber's a babe — small, decent boobs, sexy red curls — which technically means I could be hot too, since we're identical twins. But I'm not interested in dressing to impress — not in this lifetime, thanks.

I hear Mom's bedroom door open, and then the bathroom one closes. The toilet flushes a minute later, and she comes schlumping down the short hallway, her slippers slapping on the bare plywood floor.

"Oh, good," she says, seeing the ironing board. "Can you do my uniform, too?"

I'm already late. Plus, Mom's shirt is . . . well . . . huge, and it takes forever to iron. I don't know why she bothers. She works the graveyard shift. No one cares. "Sorry, can't do it," I say. "I'm supposed to start at five. But I'll leave the ironing board up."

She doesn't answer, just picks up the pot with the dregs of the coffee I made before school, which means it's about ten hours old, and sniffs, trying to decide whether to reheat it or not. In the end, she tosses the leftovers into the sink. That's probably why the drain's always clogged. The box of filters is empty, and she scoops the last of the Folgers into a used one. I make a mental note to get both after school tomorrow.

Amber comes back into the kitchen, lugging Natalie in the car seat we got from our cousin. My sister's wearing my oldest jeans and a sweatshirt I don't recognize, probably from a guy she doesn't remember. "Crystal? Can we get a ride all the way to work?" she asks.

Amber washes dishes at a tavern called the Glass Slipper, and tonight I'm supposed to drop her off at the bus because I start work earlier than her. But I know it's a pain in the ass when she has to take Natalie along, and Amber pays half the car insurance. It will mean I'll be fifteen minutes late, but it's not like I'm gonna get fired or anything.

"If you're ready to go right now," I say.

"I just have to find Nat's diaper bag."

"Couch," Mom mumbles, spluttering coffee cake all over her crossword.

"Hey, Am?" I say as she goes to get it. "I put the dog in the car after school 'cause it was raining so hard. Can you get him chained up while I change?"

"If you bring Natalie with you."

"There's pizza," my stepdad, Gil, says as I go through the living room. He's spread out on the couch, a case of beer next to him and a pipe in his hand.

"Thanks."

Gil works at Big Apple Pizza when he can drag his ass in

there. Either way, he still gets paid because he kind of owns the place. He and his brother inherited it a few years ago, and he signed over his share in exchange for a weekly paycheck, whether he shows up or not. I think sometimes his brother pays him to stay away.

"It's better to lose my money once a week instead of all at once," Gil always says with a laugh.

Sound logic if you're him. In the bedroom, I hurriedly take off my flannel and put on my gray work pants and blue striped uniform shirt. Our room used to be a single-car garage until Gil padlocked the overhead door shut so we (Amber) couldn't sneak out at night. Then he cut a hole in the living room wall and built a weird little connecting hallway out of found plywood between the living room and the side door of the garage. There's no insulation or windows, so it's freezing in the winter and stifling in the summer, but we have a room of our own now. At least until Natalie came along four and a half months ago. Now the three of us are crammed in here together. But it's still better than the pullout couch in the living room, which is where me and Amber used to sleep.

The landlord had been royally pissed when he'd come around to collect the late rent, but Gil, always a charmer, pointed out that the house was now a two-bedroom and offered him twenty bucks a month more, which he took without another word.

Usually I go out the front instead of the side door when Mom's in the kitchen—in case she asks me for money for bingo—but I want the pizza, plus I have to grab the baby, so I take my chances. Mom's abandoned the crossword and is doing a word-search puzzle while eating a flattened jelly doughnut she brought home from work. She doesn't even look up when I come through.

I swing Natalie off the table in her carrier, making her squeal, which is a new thing for her. I can't help smiling. I'll take that high-pitched happy scream over whimpering and crying any day. The pizza box is open and there're only two slices left, so I grab the whole thing and go.

When I get outside, Amber's hooking Bonehead to his chain. "I'm gonna give this slice of pepperoni to the dog unless you want to pick off the meat," I say. "We can share the cheese one."

"That's okay, you eat it. I'll get something at work."

"Thanks."

She takes the baby from me, and I toss the dog the pepperoni pizza. He swallows it whole. "Don't choke," I tell him. "I need you." I nudge him affectionately with my foot because I don't want dog smell all over my hands while I eat, and he whimpers at being left behind.

While Amber buckles Natalie into the back seat, I slide in on the driver's side, and when I switch on the ignition, the radio blasts, making me jump. Amber laughs and Nat starts crying. I turn the knob down a couple notches. "Are you ever gonna get tired of that joke?" I ask her.

"Probably not," she says.

About the twentieth time she did it, I considered disconnecting the after-market stereo I installed back when we had spare cash, before Natalie, but having music is too good, so I left it. On our way to the Glass Slipper, I eat while I drive, and Amber winds her long red curls up into a tight knot on the top of her head. Kitchen regulations. No one there cares that she's breaking the law by working for cash, but the cook's a freak for hygiene. At least at the gas station I can get away with a ponytail under my baseball cap.

"Do you see my hat in the back?"

Amber leans over the seat, digging through Bonehead's blankets. "Here it is. I think the dog might've chewed on it a little."

While I'm stopped at a light, I pull on the mangled black hat. In white letters, it says *Jimmy's Gas and Auto Repair* in fancy script, and I tug at the brim, trying to make it look more presentable. Tonight I'll be working the lottery counter when I'm not pumping gas, so I have to face the public. Jimmy usually only lets me work in the repair shop on the weekends, and today's Wednesday. Three more days before I get to do the good stuff.

I drop off Amber and Natalie, and as soon as I pull out onto Eighty-Second Avenue, I hit the gas hard, feeling the power of the motor. It keeps surging, which reminds me I need to ask Jimmy about it. I don't get very far before I come to a red light, and I sit there, revving the engine, listening. Next to me, some guys in a souped-up rice burner are blasting rap music and checking out my car. The Mustang doesn't look like much yet. It's coated with primer instead of painted, and I still need to do some body work, but under the hood is a V8 that will leave them in the dust.

When the light changes, I floor it, shooting off down the street in a squeal of burning rubber. Not so good for my tires, but it's worth it because the dudes in the other car are eating my exhaust. Unfortunately, before I can really get going, I'm already at Jimmy's.

From the street, it looks like any other gas station/convenience store—brightly lit with Coke and beer ads in the windows, a couple of pumps out front, a place to get air and propane, and there's even an old phone booth that actually works over by the three customer parking spots. The real magic happens in the restoration shop behind the station. I pull into the parking lot and drive around back.

On a separate lot is Jimmy's four-bay workshop. There's no sign announcing this—we don't want to advertise what we're doing back here, because some of the cars we fix are worth a fortune. The people who need a stellar car guy already know Jimmy and where to find him. The shop's got a small parking lot with razor wire, and for years there was a watch dog, but it died of old age and Jimmy's wife talked him into an alarm to replace it. An alarm doesn't eat or rack up bills at the vet.

I always park behind the gas station, but tonight there's a 1971 red Chevelle SS taking up two spots, one of which is my usual one. Jimmy must've had some overflow and couldn't get it in the shop. I'd be pissed if it were my car. The gas station parking lot isn't safe overnight—guys in this neighborhood will steal anything not locked up. I back into my second-favorite spot, by the dumpster, and hop out.

"I'm here, I'm here," I tell Rosa, who's running the register tonight. "Sorry I'm late. I had to take Amber to work."

She waves me off without saying anything, but I can tell she's annoyed. Her drawn-on eyebrows are all wrinkled. It's getting close to the cut-off time for tonight's big draw, so there's a line of the eternally hopeful and always broke wanting lottery tickets. Because I wasn't here, Rosa had to juggle the gas customers and the lottery regulars, so she's probably been hearing some bitching. I punch in and get my ass over to the counter.

When we finally have a lull, Rosa tells me that Jimmy wants to see me in the office. Probably because it was ten minutes after five when I got here, but whatever. I've worked here since I was fourteen, and about the only thing that would get me fired is if I stole something, which I'd never do and Jimmy knows it. He's had four years to cut me loose for coming in late and he hasn't done it yet, so I doubt it's gonna happen tonight. He does like to give me a hard time, though. I stick my head out the door and yell at Raul, who's on the pumps, "Boss wants to talk to me. Can you cover lottery if Rosa gets busy?"

"*Sí*," he says. "But hurry up."

When I squeeze past Rosa to get to the office, she offers me a piece of gum, her way of saying sorry for being short with me earlier. I take it and pop it in my mouth. "Thanks."

Jimmy's door is partly open and he's on the phone, so I hang around in the hallway until he's ready. The schedule's on a clipboard above the time clock, and I flip through it to see if maybe I've got extra garage work next week. At first I think I must be seeing stuff, or not seeing stuff, because after my name, the schedule only shows two shifts. What the hell? Oregon's one of the only states where you can't fill your own tank, so I'm always guaranteed at least three nights working the pumps, plus a day or two in the bays helping Jimmy on the weekends. According to this, I'm not even scheduled to work this Sunday. That can't be right. Almost every Sunday for the past year Jimmy's had me in for training in the body shop. It's the perfect time, because the shop is technically closed, so no one pokes a head in to check up on the cars.

Jimmy hangs up and calls to me. "Crystal, come on in."

I step into the office. He's behind his desk, which is buried under paperwork and coffee cups. "Late again, huh?"

"I had to drop off Amber."

He nods and then looks over to the corner. "I want you to meet my nephew." There's a guy, maybe about my age, leaning against the wall. He was standing there so still, I hadn't even noticed him, and I startle a little.

"Uh, hi. I'm Crystal."

"I've heard a lot about you." He steps forward and holds out his hand like he wants to shake. Mine are grease-stained. When you work on a car, no matter how much Goop or Lava soap you use when you wash up, you can never get the black out of the creases in your knuckles or from under your nails. Out of habit, I wipe them on my pants first, but that doesn't change anything, so I wave his hand off, laughing a little, embarrassed. He grabs my hand anyway. He's dressed in brand-new jeans and a white polo shirt, and when he takes my hand, I can feel his skin is soft and smooth, just like him.

"David," he says.

"My sister's kid," Jimmy explains. "They moved here from Seattle last week."

"Cool," I say. "What school are you going to?"

"Jesuit High."

Figures—it's obvious he's a private-school kid. I don't know why I asked.

Jimmy comes around his desk and puts his arm around

David's shoulder, which is a big stretch. David's gotta be at least six feet tall and Jimmy's lucky if he's five foot five — he's barely taller than me. As he stands there with his light gray eyes and silver hair, he looks like he couldn't possibly be related to David, who towers over him, his hair shimmery blond, his skin tan and golden from the sun.

"Did you see David's ride?" Jimmy asks. His phone rings again, and he goes to answer it.

"Not sure," I say.

David smiles. "Red Chevelle?"

"That's your car?" My chin practically hits the linoleum.

"Yep," he says. "Restored it myself."

I raise my eyebrows, and David sees the skepticism right away. I mean, the guy can't be more than seventeen or eighteen, and without looking under the hood, I can tell that that car's worth at least thirty-five thousand. If the engine's as nice as the body, probably a lot more. Somebody bought him that car, and I'd put money on it being restored before he got it. He's way too clean and preppy to have fixed it up himself.

"I had it painted in a shop," he says. "But I did a little of the body work with Uncle Jimmy's help when I came to visit last year."

News to me. I was here all last summer and I don't remember him. I smile, but it's as fake as this guy's résumé. He's a total poseur, which doesn't really surprise me much, since he has girly hands. Also, he took up two parking spaces.

I mean, yeah, you do that at the mall, but not at a garage where space is limited. I see guys like him at car shows all the time. Mommy and Daddy buy them fifty-thousand-dollar cars, they fix one thing on it—change the air filter, or check their own oil, or something piddling like that—and suddenly they've restored the whole damn car.

"That's an amazing piece of machinery," I say, to be polite. After all, he's Jimmy's nephew. I'm actually pretty happy when Rosa yells that she needs me. "I gotta go."

"See you around, Crystal."

"Uh, sure." That's not very likely. We definitely ride in different circles.

It's not until the end of the night when I'm getting ready to punch out, and I'm whining to Rosa about not having my regular shifts next week, that she sets me straight.

"You know why, right?"

"Because I was late again?"

She shakes her head. Her eyes are made up with heavy blue eye shadow, making her look like a cartoon character.

"What, then?"

She gives me a knowing look. "David."

"What about him?" I get a sinking feeling in my stomach.

"Jimmy gave him your shifts. You and Raul have to train him."

"No way."

She nods, all eight of her gold earrings bouncing up and down.

"No fucking way," I say louder.

"Way."

I am so pissed, I make the eleven-minute drive to the Glass Slipper in six flat.

CHAPTER 3

I have to wait twenty minutes for Amber. I'm not in the mood to help her after all, so I sit in the car, steaming. I don't want to go inside when I'm pissed. Our aunt Ruby owns the place, and she lets Amber bring Natalie to work with her, but she expects us to be cheerful and grateful all the time. Which we try to be. It's not like we could afford a babysitter if Amber couldn't take her along.

By the time my sister comes out, carrying a to-go container full of scraps for Bonehead in one hand and lugging Nat's car seat in the other, I'm slamming my fist on the steering wheel. I rant the whole time she buckles Natalie in. "This is bullshit. I've worked my ass off there for four years and now he's giving my shifts to some rich mama's boy?"

"Can you be quiet?" Amber whispers. "Nat's been crying all night, and I finally got her to sleep."

The rest of the way home I rage under my breath. I drive

slower than I want to. It's late and the cops are probably out patrolling. A muscle car is a target for getting pulled over, and we can barely make the insurance payments as it is. Amber doesn't have her license because it would make our premium go up, even if she isn't on the policy.

Bonehead practically yanks his stake out of the ground, he's so happy to see us. He can probably smell all the good things Amber's brought him. He's barking like crazy, and from across the street, we hear Mr. Hendricks yell, "Shut that goddamned dog up!"

Natalie whimpers in her carrier. I rock her while Amber distracts the dog. "Shhh . . . shhh . . . Boy, sit . . . Here, have a T-bone."

He immediately clamps down on it, dropping to the ground and starting to gnaw. Natalie's whimper has turned into a moan, which makes me afraid she might start wailing, so I run her inside and set her on the table. When her little cries turn into a yawn and I see she's falling back asleep, I grab a can of dog food and go outside.

There isn't any light coming from our house. Gil hung up some towels in the living room window to make it darker for watching TV, and the porch light's burned out, but the streetlight is right in front of us. I can see enough to grab a shovel and clean up some of Bonehead's giant turds. I toss them in the mostly dead hedge.

"What else you got for him?" I ask Amber. I want to go

to bed, but I can't until he's eaten. He sleeps in the Mustang and there's no way he's taking food into my car.

"Not much," she says, tossing Bonehead a bit of burger she saved off someone's plate. He immediately drops the bone and scarfs down the beef, managing to somehow leave the lettuce and pickle. Then Amber gives him a handful of fries and something slithery and brown I don't recognize. Bonehead apparently loves it.

I pop the top on the can of no-name dog food I got at the discount food warehouse, holding my nose the whole time. When I give it to him, he inhales the whole bowl, and Amber goes inside because the smell makes her want to hurl. Not that I love it, but she really does get queasy. When Bonehead is finished eating, I lead him over to the only tree in the yard and wait for him to pee. He knows the routine and does his business. After he gets his steak bone, I open the car door for him so he can scramble over the seat and stretch out in the back. I crack the windows to give him some air. The October days are still kind of sunny and warm, but I'm freezing my ass off out here tonight.

"Don't let anyone steal my car," I tell him, like I do every night. It's win-win—I save money on an alarm system, and he gets to stay out of the rain. In the summer, there are always a few weeks when it's too hot for him to sleep in the car, and if I leave the windows down, he goes wandering off.

Next summer, me and Amber will have our own place, and I don't care how small it is as long as it's in a neighborhood safe enough to park the Mustang at night.

When I get inside, I find the usual: Mom's dirty dishes on the table, which she left behind when she realized she was late for her shift at the bakery, and Gil passed out on the couch in front of the TV. Amber's already turned it off and grabbed Nat from the table. I hit the light switch on my way to our room. Thank God Amber's somehow managed to move the baby from her car seat to the crib without waking her. A real miracle.

"Man, I'm beat," she says, getting into bed.

"Me too. But mostly I'm pissed."

"Maybe the guy won't know shit about cars," Amber says.

"I'd put money on it if I had any." And my confidence in my skills actually makes me feel a little better. But not a lot. Anyone can pump gas, and as long as David's around, those are shifts I'm not getting.

I hand Amber a birth control pill along with a glass of water. I pop one of my own, too, mostly to keep her company, since there is no way I'm having sex with anyone. When Mom heard we'd gone to Planned Parenthood after Nat was born, she'd snorted and said, "Too little, too late, dontcha think?" And then she'd laughed until she choked on the day-old lemon pound cake she was scarfing down.

Maybe it seemed like it was too late to everyone else, but it was the only way to keep Amber safe. Now that we have Natalie, we can't party together, so I'm not there to drag her home when she's too drunk to protect herself. Once she's had a couple of beers, she never can say no. There's also our family history. It's like we're extra fertile or, more likely, extra stupid. Mom had us when she was fifteen; Aunt Ruby had our cousins Jade at seventeen and Topaz at nineteen.

You'd think maybe the next generation would've learned something, but it's like babies are an epidemic in our family. At the end of our freshman year, Jade gave birth to Lapis, then Onyx fifteen months later. And her sister, Topaz, popped out Rocky last Christmas. At least by being a boy he'd avoided one family curse: the "precious stones" name thing. Everyone agreed "Rocky" was close enough.

As I get undressed, I hear Amber munching crackers so she doesn't get nauseous from the pill. I don't need to eat them—if I go right to sleep, I'm fine, and even saltines cost money. There's a small wad of cash and change on my pillow.

I count it before I get into bed. "This is a lot. You got it all tonight?"

"And last Sunday," Amber says. "I forgot to get my tips then."

"I'll put it in the bank after school."

She's already in bed, her eyes closed. I stick the money in my pillowcase and switch off the lamp. Me and Amber

are the only people we know with a bank account. We used to hide our cash in different places in our room, but because we were away at school all day, that left plenty of time for Gil or Mom to search for it. After they'd "borrowed" our savings for the sixth or seventh time, we figured out how to open an account. It's actually not that hard. You just need some ID.

I'm drifting off when Amber yelps from her side of the room. Unfortunately, her bed's only about six feet away from mine, so it's like she's yelling in my ear. "Crap! Crap! Crap!"

I sit up and flick on the lamp. "Shhh, you're gonna wake Natalie."

She lowers her voice to a whisper. "I got a stupid paper due tomorrow."

Oh, God. Not again. "Let me know how that works out for you." I pull the pillow over my face to block the light.

"Crystal?" she says, her voice going all soft and sweet. "Please?"

"Forget it. I'm too tired. I did my homework already. Remember? While you were doing number puzzles before work?" She's addicted to numbers, but words mystify her.

"Pretty please?" She's now crawled onto my bed and is trying to snuggle up to me.

"Amber . . . go away."

"I'll bring you something good to eat after my shift on Friday."

She knows how to win me over. "Like what?"

"Lasagna?"

"And cheesecake?"

"Chocolate cheesecake."

I sigh. "Okay. But you're not gonna fall asleep while we do this. I'm not writing it for you."

"I know," she says. "I promise."

An hour later, we're sitting on my bed, propped up against the old garage door. Amber's dozing while I'm flipping through *The Scarlet Letter* looking for things to add to her paper. "It would've been a lot easier," I say, "if you'd actually read the book and could tell me what it's about."

"I know, I know . . . I meant to. I didn't have time."

Everyone says senior year's supposed to be a light load, but not if you have to do most of your sister's homework, too. Except for math, which is Amber's superpower, she's in all remedial classes. I'm in regular ones, which makes it hard for me to help her keep track of her homework assignments. I usually find out when she freaks out in the middle of the night. Or the day after, when it's too late.

"You're gonna have to get to school early to type this in the computer lab," I tell her. "And I'm not driving you. I'm sleeping in."

"Yeah, okay."

By the time I finish writing the paper, Amber's out cold, her head resting on my shoulder. "Gross," I say, waking her up. "You drooled on me."

"Sorry. Are we done?"

"Yeah—now get out of my bed."

In the morning, Nat wakes me up, screaming the rage of the wet and hungry. I change and feed her, but Amber sleeps right through the noise, probably because she was up to do the middle-of-the-night feeding and Nat wouldn't go back to sleep afterward. Her gums hurt from a tiny little tooth poking its way through. I never thought much about teeth before, but having them push right through the skin like that seems like a flaw in human design. Poor baby girl. No wonder she cries until she can't—she's so exhausted. Half the time I feel the same way.

I don't bother to wake Amber. If she's half as tired as I am, she needs the sleep. Before me and Nat leave the house, I set the alarm for seven thirty and put it on the pillow next to Amber's ear. That should give her enough time to make it to first period if she doesn't hit snooze too many times. I drop off Natalie at the school's daycare and head to the lab to type Amber's paper for her.

We're both going to graduate, even if it kills me.

CHAPTER 4

I'm pretty sure our school's new guidance counselor's got a college degree in perky with a minor in enthusiasm. Even her green sweater is bright and cheerful, like spring grass. Except so soft looking, I kind of want to pet it.

"So," Ms. Spellerman says. "Miss Robbins, isn't it?"

I want to say, "No, actually, it's Crystal. I'm eighteen, not thirty." But I nod instead. In the middle of our sophomore year we got a new principal, and he decided that as a matter of respect, all teachers and staff would refer to the students by their last names prefaced with Mr. or Miss. You can imagine how much more respect is flying around now. It obviously never occurred to anyone in charge that last names like Cochran and Dykster are so much easier to make fun of than Robert or Ashley. But whatever.

Ms. Spellerman holds out her hand to me. "Nice to meet

you." She's got long fingers and perfectly pink nails. When we shake, all I feel are skin-covered bones.

She shuffles through some papers for a while, the huge diamond on her engagement ring catching the fluorescent light and hypnotizing me. I wonder if we're ever going to get to the reason I'm here. I've made it through three years of high school without seeing a guidance counselor, so I can't imagine why they called me in when I'm almost done. As far as I know, I'm doing fine in my classes. I'm even doing okay in Amber's classes. Not that anyone knows about that.

I hide a yawn behind my hand—I'm super tired and missing the little nap I usually take in English. Ms. Spellerman holds up a sheet of paper and squints at it. Then she slips on a pair of square pink-framed glasses and smiles. "Don't look so worried, Miss Robbins. I just want to talk to you about your college plans."

Is she kidding me?

"Now that I've joined forces with Mr. Akerman, we're not so short on guidance counselors," she explains. "So I'm working my way through a list of those of you who haven't previously requested an advisor."

Maybe not asking was a clue that we didn't want one. I don't say anything, though. I don't think she expects me to.

"Now," she says, "you might be wondering how your name came up so early in the school year. Well, I'll tell you a little secret." She leans in across her desk and practically whispers, "I started at the end of the alphabet instead of the beginning!"

I wonder if I'm supposed to clap or something.

"So," she continues, "what are your plans for college? Where are you going to apply? What's your dream school?"

"Umm . . . I don't have one?"

"No dream school? Well, that's understandable. There are so many choices! Do you think you want to stay in Oregon, or go somewhere out of state—get away from it all, that sort of thing?"

Is this where I tell her I'm not going to college?

"You must've thought about it," she says when I sit there speechless.

"Umm . . . not really."

"Not at all?"

"I'm not going to college," I finally admit.

Her eyebrows shoot up. "What? Why not?"

I'm thinking I was wrong about her minor being enthusiasm. It must've been stupidity. Does she think she's somehow landed at a private school? Or maybe one of Portland's fancy high schools? This is Sacajawea High, and half the kids can't even spell the name of it by the time they graduate. *If* they graduate. College is not part of the plan here.

I try to keep it simple for Ms. Spellerman. "I'm gonna . . . you know . . . get a job."

"But, Miss Robbins," she says, "I'm looking at your transcripts, and you've got very respectable grades—a B average."

That's because school is easy and I have no life. At least, I didn't until Natalie took over ours. When I don't say anything, she starts asking me a million questions about my interests. I mostly answer with *I don't know* and *I guess not*. I don't really have any interests, and no, I've never considered trying to figure them out.

"With your grades, you have lots of choices."

"Really?" I ask. "Like Harvard?"

I'm screwing with her, but it goes right over her blond head.

"Well, probably not Ivy League," she admits. "I was thinking more of a state college. You might even be able to get into University of Oregon."

If I wasn't so tired, I'd laugh. Me? At U of O? Right. That's where the popular kids from other schools go. No one from here goes to U of O. I stare at the linoleum floor, which is covered with a bright orange and blue rug. It's not big enough to hide the brown prison-looking tiles around the edge of the room.

"If you could do anything at all," Ms. Spellerman asks, "what would it be?"

What she doesn't get is that I plan to do exactly what I want to do. It just doesn't involve more school. As soon as we graduate, me, Amber, and Nat are getting out of this dicey neighborhood. First we're gonna get a nice apartment, but someday we plan to buy our own house. That way we won't waste our money paying rent.

Amber's going to waitress at the Glass Slipper, and Aunt Ruby's going to teach her how to run the tavern so Amber can take it over from her someday. And I'm counting on Jimmy to give me at least forty hours a week at the gas station and garage. We know we can do it. We have it all worked out.

At least, I thought we did. Until yesterday, I'd always assumed Jimmy would be glad to have me full-time. Anger flares up when I think of his stupid nephew. Still, David won't be around forever; he's probably going to Yale or somewhere anyway. But I'm in it for the duration. Me and Amber know what we're doing, but somehow I doubt Ms. Spellerman would agree. So I don't answer.

"Miss Robbins?" She shuffles her papers some more. "You must have some dream. Something you love to do . . ."

I'm starting to think she's never going to let me go back to class if I don't come up with something, so I tell her, "I like cars."

Her smile brightens and then immediately fades. "Cars?"

I figure this answer will get me off the hook. Girls aren't supposed to like cars, so this will make her think I'm a lost cause. "You know," I say, sure she has no idea. "Working on cars. Restoring them."

"Like antiques?"

I shrug. "I wouldn't mind doing an antique car sometime. But right now I'm mostly interested in muscle cars."

Ms. Spellerman looks at me blankly.

"High-powered, two-door cars. Usually with a V8."

"Oh."

I know she has no clue and probably isn't interested, but she's got me going now and I can't stop. "I'm restoring a Mustang for me and my sister."

Her eyes light up. "You have a Mustang? My brother has one."

"Really? What year?"

She scrunches up her forehead. "I'm not sure."

"From the sixties?" I ask. "Or the seventies?"

"Oh, no, it's newer," she says. "Maybe 2014?"

Big deal. I thought she meant a cool old-school Mustang, not a cookie-cutter one. I realize I've been talking too much. When we were freshmen, I discovered the best way to get through high school was to keep quiet with my head down. I zip my lips.

Ms. Spellerman sits there, smiling, waiting for me to go on, but I don't. She tries to revive the conversation by faking interest. "What year's yours?"

I'm a sucker for any questions about my car. "'Sixty-nine fastback. It's pretty rough right now. I need to save some money to paint it. But I've overhauled the engine, and it's a smooth ride."

"You overhauled the engine?" she asks. "By yourself?"

"Well, I had help," I admit. But not the kind of "help" kids like David get. I got grease under my fingernails, and I knew what I was doing. "I work at Jimmy's Gas and Auto Repair shop. The owner helped me."

"That's very impressive."

"I can't wait until I can do the interior," I say, while my head's screaming at me, *Shut up!* My big mouth keeps going, though. "It doesn't look perfect yet, but it's never been wrecked."

"Is that important?"

"Well, yeah. If I ever want to sell it, it's worth a lot more if it's never been in an accident." Not that I would ever part with my Mustang.

"Well . . . that's . . . great." Ms. Spellerman stacks her papers and moves a file with my name on it off to one side like she's not sure what to do with me. No one's supposed to come into a guidance counselor's office and say they don't want to go to U of O because they're going to work on cars. But then she brightens. "I'm pretty sure the community colleges offer mechanic courses."

I shrug noncommittally. It seems kind of stupid to fork out money for classes when Jimmy's teaching me on the job and I'm getting paid. "I'll probably keep working at the garage."

"They'd teach you all the latest technology."

"Yeah, but I'm not interested in new cars. Only the old ones."

Ms. Spellerman looks over my head at the clock. "Right. Okay. Well . . ."

"Can I go now?"

"Sure," she says. "But, Miss Robbins, I really think you should consider a state school. It's in your range."

I wonder if somewhere my paperwork says that I'm on free lunch. Doesn't she know kids like me don't have money for college? Not to mention we have Natalie to look out for. I've already got my hand on the doorknob when someone knocks on the other side.

"My next appointment," Ms. Spellerman says.

If she's calling everyone in reverse alphabetical order, it should be Amber out there. "Are you seeing my sister next? Amber Robbins?"

She looks at her list. "Umm . . . I don't have her on here. Is she getting a B average or above?"

"She should be," I say, "but probably not." I know there are assignments she doesn't tell me about.

Ms. Spellerman shrugs. "I can't see everyone . . ."

I want to tell her that she's wasting her time calling in the kids who didn't make an appointment on their own. Here at Sacajawea High, most of us have got a better chance of doing four years to life than a four-year degree.

CHAPTER 5

If your kid's in the daycare at school, you're supposed to spend lunch period with them. Me and Amber usually alternate, because sitting in that room with a bunch of other moms licking baby food off their fingers and talking about the color of their babies' poop makes us both crazy. Today's my day, but I make Amber go in exchange for typing her paper this morning.

Last year in health class we were doing a unit on nutrition, and school lunches came up. According to some fancy study, most kids toss their lunch in the garbage. Especially the fruit. Here at Sacajawea, more than half of us get lunch for free, so there's always a long line. Sometimes it's the only meal we get all day. No one trashes the fruit unless it's moldy, which is about twenty percent of the time.

I'm in line with my friends Shenice and Han. Shenice is

a school friend—we don't really party together or hang out after hours. Han is harder to shake.

"You skip first period?" Shenice asks because I didn't show in the cafeteria for the free cinnamon rolls.

"Nope. I was typing a paper."

"For Amber?"

I shrug. For some reason it really annoys Shenice when I do Amber's homework. I don't know why—it's not like it hurts her. Luckily, I'm saved from the usual lecture when a bald guy the size of a truck growls, "Meat or bean?" from behind the glass-enclosed lunch counter. With that voice and the scar down his left cheek, he could be in a prison movie. He's one scary dude.

"Bean," I manage to say. I hear Shenice and Han laugh at the squeak in my voice.

"Good choice." The guy drops a greasy burrito onto a plate and gives me a wide smile that lights up his whole face. It changes everything about him, and he strikes me as the kind of guy who'd be good to have on your side. He winks and piles on extra Tater Tots, some limp salad, and a scarred orange, and then hands it over. I slide my tray toward the cashier and palm the meal ticket when I give it to her so no one sees it. Habit.

We take our food over to the garbage cans, dump the brown lettuce, and leave the trays behind, and then we go outside to the woods behind the school to eat, even though it's freezing.

"Woods" is a fancy name for dead grass, a couple of logs to sit on, and garbage blowing around, but there's a little bit of shelter behind some scraggly trees and, more importantly, no jocks or annoying drama freaks. We head for our usual oak. I kick a few cigarette butts out of the way and we plop down, sitting on our backpacks.

There are only a few die-hard rockers, stoners, and lunchroom losers out here with us, and while I don't put us into any of those groups, we do sort of look like them. Shenice is wearing her usual faded jeans, a long-underwear top, and a ratty plaid shirt she stole from one of her brothers. She's got her black curly hair in a low ponytail, and a stocking cap pulled down over her ears. Right now I look more like her twin than Amber's. Except I stole my flannel from Gil since I'm lucky enough not to have any brothers. Also, I don't wear glasses, and if I did, they wouldn't be blue cat-eye thrift-store ones that have a glob of glue on one side from a sketchy repair job.

Han has his usual "Death to . . ." T-shirt on and no coat, which makes him look like one of the rockers. He's got a whole collection of death shirts, and today it's the one he wears the most: "Death to Han Solo." He wants the world to know he isn't some nerdy Star Wars geek.

Han narrows his eyes, looking at me. "What's up with you? Did you have coffee? Or maybe something better?"

"Nothing's up," I say. "I'm eating, same as you."

"You've been tapping your foot the whole time," Han says. "And scoping everything out. Are you looking for someone better to eat lunch with?"

"No." I honestly don't know what he's talking about. Well, I kind of do, but I'm not going to admit it. I make myself chew and swallow, but I've got that nervous stomach thing going on.

"She's having baby withdrawals," Shenice says.

"Shut up." How'd she know?

"You and Amber are both like that, every day, man," she says. "You guys *say* you hate doing the daycare lunch, but when you don't go, you freak out."

I roll my eyes. It's weird, but it *is* hard to leave Nat all day with strangers. You'd think me and Amber would need a break from her, and we kind of do, but Amber told me she feels the same way I do. The thing is, Natalie counts on us, and even if it's a pain in the ass most of the time, we're getting used to being needed.

"You're practically dying to wipe my face," Shenice says. "Or stick your hands down Han's pants to see if he needs to be changed."

"I'm up for it if you are," Han says, and we all laugh. "Seriously." He stands up and starts unbuttoning his jeans.

"Sit down, dude," I tell him, and he does.

"Say the word and I'll drop my pants for you anytime."

We all laugh again, but this time it's a little uncomfortable. His crush is so obvious. The first two years of high school, he was in love with Amber, but she totally blew him off, and so last year his lust unfortunately moved over to me. Like he thought we were the same person, and if he couldn't get one of us, he'd have the other. He's nice, but he's definitely not my type. Tall, scrawny blonds with peach fuzz don't do it for me. Plus, I know him too well.

I figure it might help if I cut him down fast, so I say, "I met a really hot guy."

"Which class?" Shenice asks.

"He doesn't go here. He's Jimmy's nephew."

While it's true that David's pretty hot, I would never, ever in a million years be seen with him. Not that he'd want to go anywhere with me, either. But if I can make Han think there's some guy at work, and maybe he sees him when he drops by Jimmy's, things might go back to normal with us.

Han slumps against the tree while I tell Shenice about David and his car, which, honestly, I'm a lot more interested in. I don't mention that I pretty much hate the guy for stealing my job. After a while, I see how pathetic Han looks hearing about David, so I change the subject to video games, and he perks up.

After school, I'm at my locker when he comes bouncing

up to me, clearly recovered from his disappointment at lunch. "Can we go get my smokes?"

"I can't. Amber has to stay after to make up a test, and I gotta get Natalie and go to the bank."

"I'm dying for a cig," he says, following me. "I'll go with you, and then we can get them."

"Tomorrow. You'll have to bum one off your mom tonight."

Me and Amber repeated first grade because we missed so much school. Mom wasn't working then, and she should've taken care of us, but she was only in her early twenties and not that responsible. Usually all three of us slept right through the alarm. Ever since we turned eighteen last March and became legal, Han relies on us to buy his cigarettes. I hate doing it. When we found out about Nat coming, me and Amber both quit, and every time I buy them for him it reminds me how much I miss smoking. It kills me to hand them over to someone else once I've paid for them.

Han shoves money at me even though I said no, and I pocket it and tell him, "Fine. We'll get them. But you're buying me a pop."

"Deal."

Twenty minutes later, the three of us are in the Mustang heading for Safeway. I need to get the coffee and filters and some other stuff, and the cashiers there aren't as pissy to me as at the convenience store. If 7-Eleven hates selling to teen-agers so much, why open a store right by the high school?

"I'll carry Nat," Han offers when we get there.

"In the Snugli?"

"Sure."

I roll my eyes. He's so weird. "Go for it."

He can't figure out how to get it on, and I finally stop laughing long enough to help him, directing his skinny chicken arms through the straps and lifting it over his head. Then I slip Natalie into it, and she settles against his concave chest, looking up at him.

"Man," he says. "I can't believe how big she is."

"I know. Twelve pounds already."

"Hi, baby," he says in his regular voice. He always talks to her like she gets what he's saying.

She starts to whimper.

"Don't take it personally," I tell him. "She's teething."

He jiggles her around a little as we walk inside, and I ac-tually hear her laugh. Thank God. People always give me and Nat the dirtiest looks when she screams in the grocery store, like I'm torturing her on purpose.

What I *wish* I could buy requires a cart, but what I can afford will fit in a little red basket, so I grab one of those. In the baby aisle, I pick up two containers of formula and a box of cereal with a baby's face on the front. They told us at daycare to start mixing a little cereal with formula and give it to her with a spoon because she's hungry all the time now. They said she'll mostly spit it out at first, but will supposedly get the hang of it eventually. I see the gel teething rings and pick one up to check it out. I choke on the price, though, and put it back. I bet my cousin Jade has an extra one.

Jade's ex was a dealer before he was killed last year in a drive-by, and he used to give her tons of money for their kids. She used the cash to put herself through beauty school, but she also bought a shitload of baby stuff, mostly from thrift stores and garage sales. Whenever we need something, we kiss her ass, saying how cute Lapis and Onyx are, and she'll usually give us her castoffs.

"Does Nat need one of those?" Han asks me.

I shake my head. "I was just looking. You know Mei-Zhen, at the daycare? She told us it would help. You stick it in the freezer, and then the baby chews on it and her gums go numb or whatever. But Jade probably has one she'll give us."

If me and Amber ever want to get out of the dump we live in and into our own apartment, we have to save every penny we don't spend on necessities like food and diapers. Nat can live without a teething ring. I grab some bananas in produce. That's another thing they told us to feed Natalie, and if you get the brownish ones, they're cheap. Then I swing by the coffee aisle and grab the no-name filters and a small can of Folgers. The last thing I get is a case of vegetable ramen.

Luckily, it's on sale. Also, it's the one food we don't have to hide from Mom and Gil. They both hate it. Not that me and Amber love it, but it's dinner.

When I'm ready to check out, I head to the customer service counter to get the cigarettes and pay for everything together. Han looks about twelve, so I send him and Natalie outside. The cashier knows me from shopping here, but she checks my ID about fifty times before handing over the pack of Marlboros and giving me my change.

As she bags my stuff, she makes a big point out of the fact that I've got baby food and cigarettes, which pisses me off. It's not any of her business. I can't help myself—I open the smokes and flip one into my mouth to freak her out. Her face turns a little purple, and I laugh as I walk away. I wish I hadn't done it, though. Now I want to keep one and smoke it later. Han won't care, but Amber would kill me.

When I get out to the car, Han is standing there talking to Nat about a computer game he's really awesome at. I drop him off at home before going to the bank, and as he gets out of the car, he hands me a teething ring and a package of Orajel.

"For Nat," he says. "No one wants to chew on a used one."

"Thanks." I don't ask if he stole it. I don't want to know.

"See you, baby," he says to Nat, and she smiles.

If I'm lucky, he'll fall in love with her and forget all about crushing on me. But really, when am I ever lucky?

CHAPTER 6

The red Chevelle is taking up two spaces again when I get to Jimmy's on Friday night, and I have to resist the urge to key it as I walk by. I'm actually early for once because Amber had to help Aunt Ruby with the books before her shift, so I go inside and make myself some nachos, piling on the hot peppers. I give Rosa my money, and she looks the other way while I fill a plastic cup with pop from the dispenser. It's cool with Jimmy if we drink for free, but his wife's a tightwad, so we're kind of supposed to pay for it. No one does, though.

I sit on one of the stools behind the counter, next to Rosa. Most of the people who buy gas here know Jimmy from the custom car circuit. He likes to offer extra services so they'll keep coming back. We wash windshields and check the oil, and we'll even have a look at tire pressure if someone asks, so there's always at least one person outside doing customer service. Out at the pumps, Dirk, the day guy, is running around with David following behind him.

"Is he working tonight?" I ask.

"Yep. Training," Rosa says.

"Oh, joy." I try to keep the bitterness out of my voice, but it's there like an oil slick on a puddle. I lick the last of the orange goop off my fingers. My lips are burning from the jalapeños. "Jimmy in the shop?"

"Yeah."

I might as well plead my case.

When I go in, I see he's got a 1955 Chev on the lift. He's standing underneath, looking up at the rear axle.

"Hey, Jimmy."

"Crystal."

"So am I ever gonna get my hours back, or is what's-his-name squeezing me out?"

"David."

"Jimmy . . ." I'm trying not to whine, but my eyes are burning like I might do something stupid like cry. I can't break down in front of him. It won't get me anywhere.

"I only got so many shifts to fill," he says.

"Come on, man. I've busted my ass here for four years. More than that. Haven't I earned it?"

"By being late all the time?"

I kick my steel-toed boot against the concrete wall. We

both know Jimmy doesn't give a shit about me being late. He's using that as an excuse.

"He's my nephew," he says. "My balls are to the wall."

"What about next summer?"

"That's a long ways off."

"Jimmy, I'm graduating. I gotta know if I should be looking for another job or if you're gonna take me on full-time."

He finally drags his eyes off the axle, which he hasn't actually been fixing anyway, and wipes his hands on an oily red rag. "Look, I'll always have a job for you, and probably next summer it'll be full-time if you want it, but I can't guarantee work in the shop. It might only be the pumps."

The grimy clock above the workbench says five o'clock on the dot. I shake my head, my ponytail swaying. "Yeah, all right."

"Hey, Crystal?" Jimmy says as I'm on my way out.

"What?"

"I need you to train David tonight."

"Why me? Why not Raul?"

"David doesn't speak Spanish."

"I don't speak rich boy," I say, heading through the door.

Amber goes to a party on Saturday night, but I'm not even tempted. Even if Gil wasn't too wrecked to watch Nat, I'm pretty much done with parties. Me and Gil veg in front of the TV while the baby wriggles around on the couch next to me. I keep one hand on her warm soft belly so she doesn't fall off, the TV flickering in her blue eyes. Mom said they wouldn't stay that color, but so far they have, and she's almost five months old. Me and Amber think if they were going to change to brown like ours, they would've by now.

Amber could probably find a ride home tonight, but if I pick her up, then I know she won't get stuck in a car with someone who's been drinking. Gil's passed out by the time I have to go get her, so I end up trying to get Natalie into her carrier without waking her up. Unfortunately, it doesn't work. By the time I've buckled her in, she's crying, and now I'm kind of pissed that I let Amber go out at all. I get the teething ring from the freezer, and that calms Nat down a little, but she's still whiny. I wish all these damn teeth would hurry up.

Bonehead's already sleeping in the car and he's so excited to see us that I have to yank him off the baby. He wants to lick her face. He learned fast that there's usually something tasty smeared around her mouth that we missed with the washcloth. Also, he's friendly.

"Sit!" I yell at him, and surprisingly, he does. He probably thinks I'll throw him out in the yard if he doesn't, and he's right. By the time I drive the four or so miles to the party, which is at a rundown house on the other side of Lents Park, he's curled up in a ball on the seat, sound asleep again. I wish I could say the same about Nat, who's getting crankier. She's probably cold.

Amber's supposed to be waiting outside, but she's not there. I sit, the engine idling, the heater just now kicking in. I'm hoping to see someone I know so I can send them in after her, but it's pretty dark and it's raining hard. The only kids I see are fast-moving dark shadows running back and forth from the house to the cars.

Crap. I'm gonna strangle her if I have to go in.

After fifteen minutes, I kill the engine and turn on the hazard lights because I'm double parked. I wake Bonehead and tell him to watch Natalie. I doubt he understands, but he does sit up, and when I look back at the car, he's leaning over her like no one's gonna get his baby.

I dart across the yard and into a house that's almost as dilapidated as ours. For a second, I stay in the doorway, scanning the room. Most of the lights are out, and the air's heavy with cigarette and pot smoke. I can't make out anyone I know, so I go looking for Amber myself.

Peering down a hallway, I see a couple of guys who get off by harassing me all the time. Assholes. They're jealous of my car. They go to some other school, but for some reason they always seem to be at the same parties as me and Amber, which is another reason I don't want to be here. I dart out of view before they can see me. I need to find my sister and get the hell out.

I go around a corner and run into Han. He's talking to a couple of guys who are so wrecked I'm surprised they can follow the conversation. "Where's Amber?" I ask. "I thought you were gonna keep her out of trouble."

"I tried, but she got all bitchy. She's in the kitchen."

"By herself?"

Han shrugs. "She's with a guy. They wanted to be alone, but I'm standing right outside the door. I wasn't gonna let her go upstairs or anything."

"Is this your mom?" one of the guys asks, smirking.

"We're friends," Han says.

"Do you want a ride home?" I ask him. "Because we're leaving, like, right now."

"No, I'm gonna hang for a while."

"Okay."

In the kitchen, my sister's sitting on the counter, beer in hand, and making out with a guy I've never seen. "Amber!" I shout over the throbbing music. "Come on. Let's go!"

She pulls away from the guy, trying to focus on me. "Oh, hey, Crystal. Want a beer?"

"No. Come on. It's time to leave."

"Already?"

"Stay," the guy says, kissing her neck.

"Nat's in the car," I remind her.

She shakes him off. "I gotta go." She tries to get down from the counter, but he's standing between her legs and won't move.

"Come on," I say to him. "Let her down. We gotta get out of here."

He looks over at me for the first time. "Whoa! I'm seeing double."

"Yeah, you are," I tell him. "You better sleep it off."

He squints at me. "You look the same, but you're meaner than her."

"Yep. Let her down."

He stumbles back, and Amber hops off the counter, which is a relief. I don't want to get into it with a drunk. "Do you have a coat?" I ask her as we wind our way through the party.

"I don't know," she says, laughing. "Do I?"

I think back to when I dropped her off. Nope, no jacket, even though it's freezing outside. I'm so busy steadying her on the way out that I forget to keep an eye out for those jerks. We're almost to the front door when I come face-to-face with two of them. If I'd known they were here, I wouldn't have come in. Now I need to get us out. I look around for Han, but he's disappeared.

"Oh, hey, dude," the tall one says to his friend. "It's that slut and her tease sister."

"She ain't no tease, man. She's a dyke."

"Oh, yeah, I forgot."

I push past them, which probably isn't the best idea. The wide one jumps back and yells, "Oww! She touched me. I got fucking frostbite now."

"Ignore them," Amber says, as if I don't already know. I pull her out the door and we run across the yard through the rain, me holding her arm so she doesn't stumble and fall. The two guys follow us, jeering and laughing all the way.

They're just a couple of wusses who get off harassing me because I drive a cool car. Ever since that night last summer when I bitched them out for sitting on the hood of my Mustang, they've been total assholes, calling me a dyke and frigid.

By the time I get the car door unlocked and Amber in the front seat, we're soaking wet and Bonehead's barking at the guys, who're still calling me names. Natalie's shrieking at the top of her tiny lungs. Sometimes I wish I was deaf. I try to go around the back of the car to get to my door, but the stupid jerks are blocking the way. The rain's coming down in sheets now and we're all getting drenched, but they're too drunk to notice.

"Let me by, dickheads," I say.

"Oh, talk dirty to me, Ice Queen."

"Fuck off."

One of them reaches out for my arm, and I take a swing

at him with my free hand, but the other guy blocks it. And then Bonehead's between us, growling and baring his teeth. The guys let go of me quick, and I reach down to grab the dog's collar so he doesn't attack them. He pulls hard, though, and I have to plant my feet on the slick pavement. Bonehead lunges forward and my thumbnail tears on his choke chain, but I don't let go. The jerks are backing off fast, and I drag the dog around to the driver's side and shove him into the car.

Amber helps haul him in. "I'm sorry—"

"Just shut up." I fire up the engine, and as I do, there's a loud crash as something hits the back of the Mustang.

"Shit!"

"What was that?" Amber asks, craning around in her seat.

"Sit down and put on your seatbelt."

I hit the gas and we peel out. Natalie screams louder, which I didn't think was actually possible. In my mirror, I can see Bonehead standing on the back seat with his front paws in the rear window, barking his head off.

"SIT DOWN!" I yell at him, and as we turn the corner, he loses his balance and falls over. I go about three blocks at top speed, and then I find a place by the park to pull over. I kill the engine. My hands are shaking so hard, I can only keep them steady by holding on to the steering wheel.

Amber reaches over the seat, trying to get Bonehead to

sit. "Leave him," I say. "He's fine." After a few minutes he settles down.

We can't do anything for Natalie, though. She's tired and crabby and probably wet and hungry, too. Amber keeps apologizing for letting the dog out of the car.

"I thought he was gonna break the window," she says, "so I opened the door, and I was holding on to him but—"

"Forget it," I say. "It's fine. It's over."

I don't start driving again until my heart rate goes back to normal and my hands have stopped shaking. It's almost two in the morning, and all I want to do is get home to bed. We're halfway there when we get pulled over by the cops.

"Don't say a single word, Am," I tell her. "Act like you're sleeping." The last thing we need is another "minor in possession by consumption." She's already had two. They'll make her go into rehab if she gets another one.

Amber leans her head back against the headrest and closes her eyes while I roll down the window and wait for the cop to amble up to me. "Hello, ladies," he says. "We meet again."

I sigh. Our favorite officer of the law.

I think he's pulled me over about six times. He's never given me a ticket, but he's made me do the sobriety test every time. I don't know why. I'd never chance the Mustang by drinking. Or, you know . . . risk Natalie's life.

"License and insurance?"

I hand both over, and he goes to his car to run them. A few minutes later he's back. "Do you know why I pulled you over?"

"No, sir." Gil taught me to add the "sir" when talking to the police. There's a little quaver in my voice tonight—probably leftover adrenaline from fighting with those assholes at the party—but I think it works in my favor. *Please, please, please don't give me a ticket.* If he does, our insurance is going to go way the hell up.

"You've got a broken taillight," he says.

"I do?" Those goddamned guys.

"You didn't know?"

I shake my head. For half a second I consider turning them in, telling the cop where to find them, but I'm no narc. Besides, everyone at the party would get busted, and I definitely don't want to be the one responsible for that. "Someone must've hit me in a parking lot."

"Where're you headed?"

"Home."

He nods at Amber. "She been drinking again?"

"She's tired," I say.

He knows I'm evading the question, but I guess he's having a good night—he doesn't push me on it. "You been drinking?"

"Nope. Want me to blow into the thingie?"

"If you wouldn't mind."

I start to get out, and Bonehead tries to follow me. "Sit."

I palm his face, pushing him back. I get out of the car and we go through the whole routine.

"Okay," the cop says when the device proves I'm sober. "Fix that taillight tomorrow."

"I will." He knows I work on it myself.

Before he walks away, he says, "Man, I love this car."

It's probably the only reason he doesn't give me a ticket: Mustang admiration. I watch him in my rearview mirror as he gets into his cruiser and waits for me to drive off. I make sure to signal before pulling out.

"Shit. I can't believe they broke my taillight."

"Can't you fix it?" Amber asks, magically waking up.

"Yeah, of course I can. But it's gonna cost us for the part. I wanna kill those bastards."

"They're not worth it. Forget them."

I know she's right. I always let them get to me. But tonight it's not what they said. They messed with my car. If I could run them over without anyone knowing—not really kill them, maybe just break a couple of legs—I totally would. But if I did and I got caught, it would really mess with the plans me and Amber have, so except for a little fantasy on the way home—where both jerks end up in traction for about a year—I try to put the idea out of my mind.

CHAPTER 7

We spend Sunday out in the driveway, since David has my shift at the garage. It's sunny and even kind of warm for October, perfect for working on my car, but I'm pissed that I have to. Once I checked out the taillight in the daytime, I wanted to run those sonofabitches over even more. They managed to break the bulb and take a chunk out of the lens on the right side. It's probably gonna cost me more than a hundred bucks to replace it. And that's *if* I can score a deal on eBay or at a swap meet. At the parts store, I ended up getting that red plastic tape that's supposed to be temporary. Hopefully it'll be okay with the cops.

The way the engine's been surging when it idles is annoying me, so when I picked up the tape, I got some throttle valve cleaner, too. The baby's in her car seat in the driveway, and Amber's sitting in a raggedy lawn chair next to her, reading me beauty tips from a magazine she found in the bathroom at the Glass Slipper, while I work on the car. Neither of us brings up last night.

"Check this out," she says. "Revitalizing eye cream with moisturizing beads . . . only a hundred and ninety-six bucks. Gotta get me some of that."

"I'm the one who needs it. Too many late nights doing your homework."

"Don't talk about school. It's the weekend."

Unfortunately, I've got school on my mind. I can't stop wondering why Ms. Spellerman had to talk to me about college. It's not like I want to go, but now that she's brought it up, I can't seem to forget about it, either.

"Do you know the new guidance counselor?" I ask Amber. "Ms. Spellerman?"

"Nope. Why?"

"She called me to her office."

"What'd you do?"

I spray the cleaner into the valve and wipe out all the black gunk with a paper towel. I don't know if this is the problem, but it's gotta be part of it—it's really gross in there. When I'm done, I sit down on the cement next to Amber's feet to let the engine air-dry for a while.

"I didn't do anything. She thinks I should go to college."

Amber laughs.

"I know, right?" I shake my head and my hair falls out of its rubber band. My hands are filthy, so Amber scoops up my curls and redoes the ponytail for me. I lie back onto the cracked concrete, staring up at the sky. Our neighborhood doesn't look too bad if you keep your eyes up.

Bonehead whines, wanting off his chain. "Forget it," I tell him. "You can't be trusted." Yesterday morning, I was fifteen minutes late to work because he ran off when I opened the car door to let him out to pee. Amber gets up and crosses over to him, rubbing his dopey-looking head, and I snag her lawn chair. Gil won Bonehead in a poker game. He's part German shepherd, part anyone's guess, and he's got one blue eye and one brown one, which makes him look adorable and also slightly crazy. I'm hoping any idiot who might want to steal my car will think he's totally whacked.

Amber abandons Bonehead and scoops up Natalie. She raises her into the air, making faces, and Nat giggles. "What would you study in college, anyway, Crys?"

"Nothing. I'm not going." Then I tell her how Ms. Spellerman said I could learn about repairing cars, and Amber laughs again. "Yeah, I know," I say. "Because I need to pay someone to teach me stuff I can learn from Jimmy for free?"

"Totally," she agrees.

We stay up until almost midnight, watching TV and doing homework. Han hangs with us, supposedly studying for an ethics class he's taking but mostly hogging the remote. I try to grab it from him, but he holds it out of reach. "Why do you have to keep changing the channel?"

"It's a guy thing."

"Pick a show and leave it there before I have to kill you. I can't concentrate."

"Will you two shut up?" Amber asks.

She does her own math and mine while I write a persuasive essay for English class, taking the side that a Mustang fastback is superior to the original design. Han continues to flip channels while we ignore him.

On Monday during sixth period, I get called down to see Ms. Spellerman again, and some of the kids in my class say, "Ooooh . . ." like we're in the third grade and I'm busted. I grab my stuff and head to her office. Now what does she want?

"Come in, Miss Robbins," she says when I knock on her door.

Her face is really pale, and her eyes look red and kind of watery. I wonder if she has a cold. Just in case, I don't get too close. Me and Amber are germ magnets. We get everything that's going around, and then we give it to each other. It didn't used to be a big deal, but now we've got Natalie to worry about.

"I've only got a few minutes," she says, "but I have something I thought you'd be interested in."

I smile, but only because she looks like she might start crying. "Umm . . . okay."

"After our little talk last week, I did some research on the Internet and guess what I found?"

I shrug.

"A college that teaches exactly what you want to know."

I'm not following her.

"Automotive restoration!" she says. "You learn everything about restoring vintage cars."

"Really?" This *is* surprising. I'm still not going to college, but it's kind of cool to know a degree like that exists.

"It's in McPherson, Kansas."

Kansas? I can't even place the state on a map. Somewhere in the middle, maybe?

Ms. Spellerman holds out a whole pile of papers toward me. When she does, I see her left hand is bare. The engagement ring is missing. Could that be why she looks so bad? I don't really want the papers, but the idea that she and her fiancé broke up and she still took the time to do this . . . well, I'd feel a little bad not taking the stuff, so I let her give the stack to me.

"Now," she says, "there's information there on the program—how to apply, and deadlines and all that. I've made a list of the dates for the SATs and how to sign up for them, too. And that green sheet?"

I fumble around and pull it out.

"That's a step-by-step timeline for you. I know you said you don't want to go to college, but I thought maybe that's because the process is so overwhelming. This is designed to make it as easy as possible." She gives me a watery smile. "This way you don't have any excuses."

"Umm . . . thanks."

Her phone rings and she tells me she has to take it but I should come back next month to let her know how it's going. Also, she offers to write me a letter of recommendation even though we only met last week.

As soon as I'm back in the hallway and her door is shut, I drop the pile of papers into the nearest recycling can. I'm halfway to English when I turn around and go back. The bin's right outside Ms. Spellerman's door. What if she sees the papers in there? What if that was her fiancé on the phone, saying it was definitely over, and she comes out and discovers I've dumped all her hard work without even looking at it? What if she totally loses it because of me? I fish out the packet and stuff it in my backpack. It's not like I'm interested or anything—I just can't be responsible for the new guidance counselor jumping out of a third-story window.

CHAPTER 8

Two weeks later I'm falling asleep in algebra when I swallow a bug. That's what it feels like anyway, and I'm hacking for a full minute before Mr. Cartwright suggests I go get a drink of water. In the hallway, I run into Ms. Spellerman. Literally.

"Oh, sorry," I say.

"No, excuse me. I wasn't looking where I was going." Which is true. She is typing on an iPhone and has barely looked up. Must be nice to have a phone. Not that I'd have anyone to call anyway. Han swears he'll kill himself before carrying around something that will let his parents track him down whenever they want, and none of my other friends can afford one.

I slip away before she recognizes me—one of the advantages of going to a school with four thousand kids—and I get my drink of water. Back in the classroom, Cartwright drones on and on, and I fumble through my ratty backpack for a stick of gum. Instead, I find the papers Ms. Spellerman gave me, which I haven't looked at, at all.

I spend the rest of the period reading them over, and when I'm done, I know five things.

1. McPherson College is in McPherson, Kansas, which looks like one of those small towns from the 1950s, where the girls wear poodle skirts, the guys grease their hair, and everyone goes to the prom sober.
2. Taking the SATs costs a small fortune.
3. They take only fifty people into the restoration program at any one time, but you can enroll in the college, take all your other classes, and apply again if you don't get in on the first try.
4. That comedian who used to be on TV and loves cars gives away a full-ride scholarship every year.
5. Last year, the students restored a 1949 Hudson Hornet, and it looks amazing.

For about half a second I get butterflies of excitement in my stomach. I could do that program. I could have helped with that Hornet. But then reality sinks in. There's no way I could ever talk Amber into moving to Kansas. She's too locked into being around our family. She needs everyone a lot more than I do. When we all get together, our aunts and uncles, cousins, and all the kids, I'm overwhelmed, but Amber's in her element. She won't leave that. Plus there's the whole thing with Aunt Ruby and the Glass Slipper. None of Ruby's kids are interested in the tavern, and she's basically promised to leave it to Amber if my sister keeps working there. That's Amber's dream and part of the plan I've agreed to. I shove the papers in my backpack and try to forget about them.

That night, I'm sitting at the kitchen table with Mom. We're both eating coffee cake and doing crossword puzzles. I try not to eat the crap she brings home from the bakery. No offense, but I don't want to balloon out like her and be a whale. Unfortunately, there isn't anything else to eat in the house. Hopefully Amber will bring me a veggie burger from work.

About once a week, one of the cooks, Brad, sends Amber home with some free food because I give him rides sometimes. If I don't end up with something tonight, I'll get a box of mac and cheese at the corner store.

Normally I'd be at work right now, but most of my shifts this week have gone to David again, and I'm trying not to think about it. "Five letters, starts with *e*," Mom says, holding out her crossword to me. "It's an automotive misfortune."

"Edsel."

"That's my girl."

The phone rings. Neither of us moves. Gil is closer. A minute later, he yells, "Crystal! It's for you."

I go into the living room, where the phone is plugged into the wall. We had a cordless one for a while, but the battery wore out. Amber found this one in the basement of the Glass Slipper, and Aunt Ruby said we could have it.

"Hello?"

"It's Rosa. Can you come in?"

"Now?"

"Raul's got the flu or something."

"What about David?"

"He's got some school thing. I really need you, Crystal."

"Yeah, okay. Give me twenty minutes."

"Make it fifteen. Raul is barfing between customers."

It's not until I hang up that I remember I've got Natalie. Normally she goes to the Glass Slipper with Amber, but there was no point tonight, since I was home. But it sounds like Raul's in a bad way, and Rosa can't pump gas, so I don't really have time to drop off the baby at the tavern, either.

"Can you watch Nat?" I ask Mom.

"No can do, sweetie-pie. I'm on my way out."

She's still sitting at the table like she's never going to move, but I saw her counting her change earlier, so Aunt Pearl's probably coming to get her to go to bingo before their shift. In the living room, I take one look at Gil, who is prostrate on the couch, and decide Natalie will have to come with me. As long as Jimmy doesn't find out, it shouldn't be a problem. Besides, I'm doing him a favor.

"You brought the baby?" Rosa says when I come through the door, the bell jingling behind me.

"No choice. I'll stick her in Jimmy's office. Yell if she starts crying."

It's a slow night, so I'm inside with Rosa more than I'm outside pumping gas, which is fine with me because it's pretty damn cold, even for the first week in November. And the stinging rain is coming down slantwise, making it hard to stay dry.

At midnight, I lock the door from the inside and turn out all the lights except the ones over the register. Rosa counts out her till, and I get Nat from the back and set her on the floor behind the counter. I've already swept and cleaned the glass doors, and I start restocking the cigarettes at lightning speed so we can blow the second Rosa's done.

We're talking about nothing important when we both hear the bathroom door at the back of the store open. Me and Rosa give each other frightened looks as a man with greasy hair and wearing an overcoat comes out and staggers his way toward us.

I look at Rosa again, and her eyes go wide. In an instant, my heart's beating so fast, it's like there isn't even any space between the beats. This is it. Mom always told me I shouldn't work here because it's too dangerous, and now she's gonna be right.

Behind the counter is a hole in the floor where Rosa drops the money into the safe all night long so there's nothing much in the register. There're signs posted all over saying we never have more than thirty-five bucks in cash and we don't have the combination to the safe, but druggies aren't usually big readers.

The guy stops on the other side of the counter facing us. His eyes are bloodshot, and he has to hold on to the edge to keep from falling. Maybe we could take him? We keep a bat behind the counter . . . Slowly I move my hand toward it, but then I remember Natalie's here.

Oh, God. Please don't cry, Nat. Please, please, please.

"What d'you want?" Rosa says in a tough voice, and then her eyes roll back in her head and she passes out at my feet. It's the fake faint that she's been telling me she's gonna do if we're ever robbed, and now she's finally got her chance.

The guy blinks twice and shakes his head like he's not sure what he saw. Then he says, "Give me some Marlboros."

That's when I clue in to what's going on. Since gas stations don't keep money in the registers anymore, most of the robberies around here are about beer and smokes. So far, I don't see a weapon, but I grab four cartons of Marlboros and slide them across the counter without hesitating.

He stuffs his hand into one of the deep pockets of his coat, rummaging around forever. Every muscle in my body tightens until I feel like I will shatter if I try to move. I just know he's going to pull out a gun. I live in a crappy neighborhood, but I've never actually seen one in person. There's this weird little part of me, like the ghost of Crystal, that sort of floats above my head and *wants* to see a gun. *What the hell is wrong with me?*

On the ground where the guy can't see her, Rosa is wide awake. She's already hit the silent alarm and is sending texts on her phone, probably to her kids to say she loves them. I see Natalie shift in her carrier. *Please. Please. Please don't cry.* My hand is shaking as I reach for more cigarettes and start piling them in front of the guy. There's a nice little wall of red and white cartons between us now.

"Dude." He laughs. "I mean, dudette. I only want two packs, man." He lays a twenty on the counter.

"What?"

"Two packs," he repeats.

"Two packs?" I say like I'm a stupid friggin' parrot.

"Yeah, man. I'm not made of money."

I stare at him, and he stares back at me, making his eyes bug out, and then he laughs like we're sharing some joke, his nose crinkling up, a gap showing between his back molars.

And then I get it.

We're *not* being robbed.

The guy just wants to *buy* cigarettes.

The breath I've been holding whooshes out of me and I start laughing in relief, which makes him laugh more. I laugh so hard tears stream down my face, and he slaps his hand on the counter like he can't believe how funny we both are. On the floor, Rosa's looking at me, horrified. I guess because she's been so busy texting, and everything's kinda surreal anyway, she still hasn't figured out we're not being robbed. Now she thinks I'm losing it, which is not that far from the truth. My whole body is shaking, like I'm in an earthquake or something.

Finally, when I don't stop laughing, the guy gets quiet and narrows his eyes at me. "You're some weird chick. Can I have my change or not?"

"We're closed," I tell him, sobering up.

The guy looks around at the store and says, "I thought it was kinda dark in here."

This cracks me up all over again. I'm so relieved that I'm not about to die, that Natalie's not going to be murdered or kidnapped, that I grab a whole carton of Marlboros and hand it to him. "Take it," I say.

He smiles a big, crooked slow grin and nods. "Really? Cool. I like you. You're all right."

"I'll let you out." I go around the counter, wiping tears off my face, and turn the lock with a shaky hand. As I open the door and let the guy through, I hear the distant wail of sirens.

Oh, shit.

When I finally get Natalie loaded into the back seat and we hit the road, it's almost two o'clock in the morning. The police weren't thrilled about the false alarm. They still had to do a full investigation in case there was a guy hiding somewhere and threatening us, making us lie to get the cops to go away. The officers even checked our cars.

And then Jimmy and his wife, Betty, showed up, and we had to go over the whole thing again. If that wasn't bad enough, Betty was pissed I'd given the guy the cigarettes. I didn't even mean to admit that part—it just came out. She told Jimmy to dock my pay, but he glared at her and handed me a lit smoke to calm my nerves.

Natalie was an angel the whole time, but I got a talking-to by a police officer and another lecture from Jimmy about bringing her to work. That won't be happening again. Not that I'd be that stupid after tonight. Hell, I don't even want to come back.

When I pull up to the house, Bonehead goes crazy, barking and tugging on his chain. Probably no one remembered to feed him. The front door opens and light spills out into the yard, and Amber and Gil come running out. Well, she's running, he's weaving, but he's on his feet.

Mr. Hendricks screams at Bonehead from across the street, and Amber's yelling at me, wanting to know where we've been, and then Nat totally loses it and starts crying at decibels that could shatter windows.

"Shut the hell up!" another neighbor yells. "Or I'm gonna call the cops!"

I hand Natalie to Amber and drag Bonehead up onto the porch, not unhooking him until I can shove him through the door into the front room. Mom doesn't want him in the house, but he's so excited by now that it's the only way to shut him up. She's not home anyway. He dances around in pure jubilation, his claws scratching the plywood floor even worse than it was.

"Have you been smoking?" Amber demands, sniffing me.

"Take care of Natalie—she's wet. Let me feed the dog, and then I'll tell you what happened."

Gil's already passed out on the couch again, thank God. A minute later, Bonehead is slurping down his food in the kitchen, and I drag my ass into the bedroom, where Amber is cooing to Natalie and putting baby powder on her butt. I collapse onto my bed.

"Where the hell were you?" she whisper-yells. "You were supposed to pick me up. I called here and no one answered, so Aunt Ruby had to drive me."

"I was at work."

"How come you didn't tell Gil? He was freaking out too."

"He was passed out when I left. Mom knew."

"I couldn't get her on the phone."

"Sorry. I—"

"What were you doing at work until two o'clock in the morning?"

"We got robbed," I say, finally shutting her up. She's so shocked, she lets go of Nat, who almost wiggles right off the Rubbermaid container we've set up as a changing table. Amber grabs her before she falls, and Nat squeals in pain. I hope Amber's fingers don't leave a mark on the baby's arm. That's the sort of thing they check for at the school daycare. In the rich part of town, a mom can probably save her kid from falling, but around here, the authorities don't believe in accidents.

"Are you okay?" Amber asks, sitting on my bed and holding Natalie so tightly the baby whimpers.

"I'm fine," I lie. "But Nat's probably hungry."

"Okay. I'll get a bottle. But don't fall asleep before you tell me what happened."

Now that all the adrenaline has left my system, the tension's completely gone and I'm a wet rag. I lie there in that weird eerie light from the halogen floor lamp and close my eyes. When Amber comes back, I ask her about Bonehead.

"He's curled up on the couch next to Gil. Do you want me to put him in your car?"

"Leave him." I'm too tired to care. And then I explain the whole night to Amber without even opening my eyes. And what does she zero in on? The smoking.

"We agreed no more cigarettes," she says. "Especially around Nat."

"You know what, Am?" I say, sitting up. "When you get robbed, or think you're getting robbed, you can have a cigarette too. You can have a whole fucking pack, for all I care."

"Yeah . . . okay. Sorry."

We sit there in silence as she finishes feeding the baby. By the time Amber's burped her, I'm under the covers and almost out again.

"I'm glad you're okay," she says, keeping her voice low. "I hate this city."

Me and Amber both know Portland has lots of great areas—we just don't happen to live in any of them. Tonight, I hate it too. We didn't even get robbed, but I'm not sure I could've been any more scared even if we had been. I turn on my side and look over at my sister. She's wearing an old white T-shirt that's gray from being washed with our jeans, and her long red hair tumbles around her shoulders. She's shivering from the cold, and she looks small and fragile as she reaches for the lamp. I wonder how I can protect her and Natalie if I can't even protect myself?

Once Amber has turned off the light and we're wrapped

in the familiar darkness, I say, "Hey, Am? What do you know about Kansas?"

"There's no place like home," she mumbles.

Exactly. That's why I'm thinking maybe we should leave. Small-town America suddenly sounds pretty appealing.

CHAPTER 9

I wake up to Natalie's whimpers. Lately she's been doing this in the morning instead of full-on wailing. It's like she's figured out she'll get more sympathy and attention if she sounds resigned to her fate. Amber's dragged herself out of bed and is picking her up. I so want to roll over and go back to sleep, but we're doing those lame-ass statewide fitness tests in PE, so I have to go. I'm the only senior in our class, which makes it even more pathetic — most students fulfill the PE requirement in the first two years of high school, but me and Amber had bronchitis for three weeks when we were freshmen and had to sit around in the library, missing PE class. She made it up junior year, but I put it off until the last minute.

I don't mention Kansas while we're getting ready. In the light of day, it seems like a stupid idea. Even if I got into college, how could I go? Amber would totally freak if I backed out on our plan now. The only reason she's even stayed in school this long is because I've promised to help take care of Natalie while she learns the ropes at the Glass Slipper. If she thought I was going to screw her over by making her move to Kansas, she'd quit high school right now just to get back at me.

That's what I tell myself, anyway. But honestly, every time I think about going to work at Jimmy's again, my hands start to shake and my heart revs up like the Mustang's motor. McPherson, Kansas, population 13,322, is sounding better all the time. Also, I can't stop thinking about how cool it would be to actually learn all the stuff I want to know, not just what Jimmy can teach me in his small shop. People who restore cars make a lot of money. A lot . . . even during recessions. Rich people don't worry about the shit everyone else does. If I took this course, someday the three of us could live anywhere we wanted. We wouldn't have to buy a fixer-upper, either. We could get one of those big new houses in West Linn or a cool condo with underground parking in Northwest Portland. We could live in style. I'd be making real money. I think if it weren't for leaving our family—and the Glass Slipper—for four years, Amber would be cool about moving because she'd understand it would help us in the long run. But Kansas is too far away.

I spend lunch with Natalie at daycare, going over the papers Ms. Spellerman gave me. By the end of the period, I almost have the info memorized. The bell rings, and I lift

Nat up off the rug where she's been rolling around and put her back in her crib. As I lean over to kiss her, she grabs two fistfuls of my hair, and her grip's so strong, it takes help from Mei-Zhen to get me free. For some reason, this makes my heart swell up and I don't want to leave her. Mei-Zhen has to shoo me off to class, but a part of me lingers with Natalie. Sometimes I'm so amazed she's ours.

On the way to algebra I decide there's no point in arguing with Amber over McPherson now. I'll get the stuff together and then *maybe* I'll apply. And then *maybe* if I get in I'll tell her. And *maybe* she'll be excited and want to go. I doubt they'll take me anyway.

I'm not too bad at schoolwork, but Amber usually fills out any forms either of us need, so I'd be on my own there. But still, I can probably handle the application. And last year in English, we practiced writing college essays, which was the biggest joke ever. Only something like ten percent of the kids from this school even go to college, and most of them enroll in the two-year ones, not universities. None of us need to know how to write an essay. Except, maybe now I do.

If I really want to go ahead with this plan, my biggest problem is all the fees. Not just to apply to the college, either. According to Ms. Spellerman's paperwork, I have to take the SATs, and that costs a bunch of money. I'm not sure how I can siphon it out of our bank account without Amber noticing. I won't have to pay for the test until I sign up to take it in

January, so if I really do apply—and I'm not saying I'm going to; I'm thinking about it for now—I'll figure something out then. Maybe I have a couple of extra car parts Han can sell for me on eBay.

There's also an SAT study course, which Ms. Spellerman has highlighted and said I really need to take. It's on Tuesday nights, and she's included a form I can fill out to get them to waive the tuition, but I'd still have to buy two workbooks for twenty bucks each. Also, what will I tell Amber when I go to class at night?

This is a stupid idea.

I almost give up right then, but I keep thinking about how scared I was at the gas station and how much I like working on cars but hate pumping gas. I could tell Amber I need a hundred bucks for parts. She'll freak out a little, but as long as it sounds legitimate, I know she'll give in.

That night, I tell the first of what I know will be a lot of lies, even though I'm still not sure I'm actually going to apply. "The car's gonna need a new battery."

"Seriously?" Amber spoons applesauce into Nat's open mouth. "How much's that gonna cost?"

"Probably a hundred bucks."

"I thought we bought one last August."

Damn. I was hoping she wouldn't remember. "Yeah," I say, "but it was a rebuilt one. They don't really last."

"Why'd we buy it, then?"

"Because they're a lot cheaper. I should've bought a new one."

She sighs. "Well, I guess you gotta do what you gotta do."

"I'll take care of it this week."

Now I have the okay to get the money out of our account, which is good, but I also have to pray the battery I bought last summer makes it through the winter. Or else I'm busted. And I guess I maybe have to apply now.

On Thursday night, I offer to take Natalie to Forward Momentum. It's a parenting class for moms that we're forced to take if we want to keep Natalie in the school daycare program. Me and Amber got the okay to alternate going every Thursday because we're raising the baby together and sometimes one of us has to work. If we both have to, then we're excused, but only if we show Mei-Zhen and Jocelyn our schedules.

"Why?" Amber asks. "You went last week. It's my turn."

"I know, but I'm not working until Saturday and I thought you might want to chill."

Lie. Lie. Lie.

She fills in a few numbers on the puzzle she's doing. "You hate it there."

"Not really."

Lie. Lie. Lie.

Amber loves going to Forward Momentum, and she knows I don't. I have to be careful now so she doesn't get suspicious. "You look really, really tired," I say. "And I'd have to drive you anyway."

She sighs. "Yeah, all right—if you want to go, that'd be cool."

The only reason I'm volunteering is because I need to see if Jocelyn, the lady who runs the show, will write me a letter of recommendation. According to my to-do list, I need three references. Ms. Spellerman's writing me one, and Jocelyn's the only other adult I can think of to hit up besides Jimmy.

"What's the topic for tonight?" Amber asks me, since I went last week.

I search my brain. I hadn't really been paying attention. "Umm . . ." And then I remember. "Dealing with authority."

"What's that mean?"

What did Jocelyn tell us? Oh, yeah. "How to act when you get pulled over by the cops."

"You already know that."

"And getting your utilities turned back on. Stuff like that."

"Huh," Amber says, not looking up from her puzzle. "Maybe you should send Mom to that one."

"Yeah, seriously."

Our phone gets shut off about four times a year. And last winter, our electricity was out for two weeks before she won enough at bingo to get it turned back on. The house was so fucking cold. I shiver now just thinking about it.

"If you really don't mind going," Amber says, "I'm beat."

"I know. It's cool."

"But don't dig through the free stuff until you get home."

"I won't. I promise."

At Forward Momentum they always give us a bunch of freebies for the baby, and at the first meeting of the month, the moms get a bag too. Natalie's sack has boring but totally necessary stuff, like diapers, formula, zwieback, and sometimes a toy. But the bags for the moms are all fancy because they're donated by rich ladies. In September, we got Godiva chocolates, nail polish, a set of towels, and a gift card to Safeway. In October there was an MP3 player. We had Han sell ours on eBay for fifty bucks.

Tonight's meeting isn't too bad at first. Jocelyn's brought her tall, lanky nephew to act like the bad guy. Before we start, she makes each of us draw a slip of paper with a problem on it. Travis is supposed to be the guy in power, and he sits behind a table like it's a counter and we have to go up to him with our issue.

My slip of paper says "Trouble with the landlord," which makes me laugh. Isn't that my life already? Mom and Gil are so far behind on the rent that we'd all be out on our asses if the place wasn't such a hellhole. But no one else in their right mind would rent it, so I'm sure the landlord figures a few hundred bucks whenever Mom wins at bingo is better than nothing.

The first girl who volunteers is one of the Haileys (there are three here tonight) and she really gets into it. Too into it, in fact.

"My electric's out," she says to Travis.

"Do you know your account number?" He's smiling at her and nodding his head, making his dreadlocks swing.

Hailey looks at Jocelyn but gets no help there. "Uh . . . I guess not."

"What's your name?"

She tells him, and he pretends to type it into a computer. "Your account's a hundred and twenty days past due," he says. "It shows here that we issued a final notice for payment on the thirtieth of October."

She crosses her arms. "I didn't get it."

"There's a note in my computer that says you called and promised to pay it in full the next day."

"I never got nothing."

"But—"

"Are you calling me a liar?" Hailey demands.

We all look around at one another, and a bunch of us are

trying not to laugh. One of the other Haileys says, "Look out, Mr. Electricity." And then we do crack up.

"No, ma'am, I'm not calling you anything." Travis's smile wavers. "I just—"

"I got a baby. And it's freezing in my house. What're you gonna do about it?" Hailey asks, her voice getting louder.

Now some of us are full-on laughing. Travis is leaning back in his seat, out of face-slapping range, which might be smart.

He tries again. "I'm sorry, but I can't—"

"This is bullshit!" Hailey yells. "I have a baby. Do you understand what that means, you sorry suck?"

"Okay, okay, okay." Jocelyn steps forward. "Let's back up here a minute. How many of you think Hailey's going to get what she wants if this is how she acts?"

Two girls and Hailey raise their hands, but the rest of us shake our heads.

"Let's talk about how she might handle it differently," Jocelyn says.

After that, the class gets kind of boring. By the time it's over, Travis looks a little shell-shocked and I'm ready to grab my free stuff and go home. I manage to pull Jocelyn into a corner and ask her for a recommendation first, though.

"I'd be happy to write you a letter," she says. "I think it's great you want to continue your education."

"Thanks."

"But," Jocelyn says, "I want something in return."

Great.

"What?" I ask.

"I want you or Amber to come to Forward Momentum *every* week from now on."

"Sometimes we both have to work," I tell her. "You said it was okay to miss if—"

"It's time the two of you start making parenting Natalie a priority."

As if our lives don't revolve around the baby already?

"Think of this class as part of school," Jocelyn says. "In other words, it's not optional anymore. Either you or your sister need to be here for every class."

I sigh.

She holds out her hand to shake. "Do we have a deal?"

I'm pretty sure I can get off work even if Amber can't, because David keeps stealing my shifts. And I really need this letter. "Yeah, okay." I start to leave but remember one important detail I forgot to mention. "Hey, Jocelyn? Don't tell Amber I'm applying to college, okay?"

"Why not?" she asks.

Because she'll kill me? Because she'll think I'm ruining our lives and going back on my word? Because she'll know I lied to her about the money to fix the car?

Because I might not actually apply.

"I don't want to get her hopes up."

Jocelyn nods. I can't tell if she believes me or not, but I grab the freebie bags with one hand, balance Natalie on my hip, and get the hell out of there before she can ask any more questions. Two recommendations down, one to go. I'm not looking forward to asking Jimmy. Getting him to say yes is one thing; him actually making time to do it is another thing entirely. He hates paperwork even more than Amber hates school.

CHAPTER 10

Saturday morning is my first shift back at work after the whatever-you-want-to-call-it on Tuesday . . . the not-getting-robbed-but-feeling-like-we-were situation. I thought I'd be nervous, but it's a bright, cold morning, and in the light of day, the station looks exactly like it always does. People are hanging out by their cars, talking while their tanks fill, there's a line of hopeful losers at the lottery counter, and some kids are choosing—or probably stealing—Jolly Ranchers in the candy aisle. When I go to punch in, Jimmy's waiting for me.

"I need you in the garage. Raul's got the pumps."

"Excellent," I say.

He pats me on the shoulder and goes back into his office to grab his coffee and smokes.

"He told me he misses working with you," Rosa says, which makes me stand a little straighter. "Apparently that

David kid never shuts up. Asks about a thousand questions an hour."

I'm like Jimmy—a silent hard worker who only asks when I really need help. Otherwise, I figure it out on my own. Sometimes when I'm doing a tricky repair, I sneak inside the store and Rosa lets me use her cell phone to look things up on YouTube so Jimmy doesn't know I'm not following what he showed me.

He comes out and we head across the parking lot to the garage. Jimmy would love to have a full-time shop and ditch the gas station, but there's not a lot of restoration work for such a small outfit. He could fix new cars after they've been wrecked, but he refuses to do it. "Anything with a computer in it is bullshit," he says. Mostly, we do small repairs on vintage cars that have already been restored, and mechanical stuff like changing brakes and shocks.

"Today, we got something special," Jimmy tells me. He unlocks the garage and puts in his alarm code. The lights flicker to life, illuminating the shop. In the third bay is a Studebaker Hawk, stripped all the way down to the metal.

"'Sixty-two?" I ask.

"Good girl," he says.

We cross over to it, and I run my hand along the smooth hood. "What's up?"

He leads me around to the back and shows me a dent in

the right rear fender. "They trailered it into Custom Designs to have it sprayed and some idiot lost control and backed into something. I don't know what."

"Couldn't they fix it there?"

"Sure," Jimmy says, "but the customer was royally pissed off, so he brought her to me instead. They're taking her to Frank's for the paint job after that fuck-up."

I nod.

"She's all yours," he says. "I gotta get the timing belt on that Camaro done before the guy gets here. I was supposed to do it last night."

"Cool."

If there's one thing I know how to do, it's pull out dents and make the body look so perfect that once it's painted you'd never know I'd been there. The Mustang was full of dings and dents when me and Amber bought it off Jimmy three years ago, and I fixed every one of them.

I'm mixing up the Bondo when David comes in around nine thirty. He hovers over me, asking questions, but I "mm-hmm" and "uh-huh" him until he goes off to bug Jimmy. In the few weeks he's worked here, we almost never cross paths, and when we do, I'm like a brick wall. The asshole stole my job.

When Jimmy finishes the Camaro, he comes over to check on my progress. Not that he needs to or anything.

David's following him like a looming shadow. "Looks good," Jimmy says.

David nods like he's an expert too.

"Thanks." I stand up and stretch. I might as well get a cup of coffee while I wait for the Bondo to dry.

The dent isn't very big, but it's in a tough spot, right on a curve, so it's detailed work. It takes me until lunchtime to get it right. Jimmy sends David out for subs, telling him to get me one too, and he even pays.

"You could do this for a living," Jimmy says.

I throw my rag on the floor. "That was the plan before David showed up."

"I know, I know . . . Come outside with me?"

I follow him to the parking lot and he lights up a cigarette. I stand close, inhaling deeply.

"The deal is," he says, "the kid wants to go to some fancy school where they teach you how to restore old cars, but my sister and her husband, the dickwad, want him to go to Stanford or some bullshit school like that to be a doctor. They think if he spends some time with me and sees what it's really like to work in a repair shop, he'll give up on the idea."

I wonder if Jimmy is talking about McPherson College in Kansas? Probably. I mean, how many schools could there be that teach people how to restore cars? I know this is my opening to ask Jimmy for a letter of recommendation, but it seems like once I do, then I really will have to commit to applying. He'll ride my ass for wasting his time if he writes it and then I don't use it. So I chicken out.

I nod. "Yeah, okay. I know it's not your fault he's here." I consider bumming a smoke, but I had two after the pseudo-robbery, and if I have another one so soon, I'll never be able to stop and Amber will kill me. "How much longer is he gonna be around?"

Jimmy shrugs. We hear the engine on the Chevelle half a block away, and by the time David shows up in the break room with the sandwiches, I've filled my plastic cup with pop and I'm kicking back, waiting.

He hands me my three-cheese-and-sautéed-peppers special, and he and Jimmy sit down across the tiny table. I can't tell what David's eating, but at least it has some lettuce poking out. Jimmy's sandwich is a meatball sub oozing tomato sauce. It smells a lot like Bonehead's dog food, and I try not to gag.

"So this school you're gonna go to," I say. "Is it the one in Kansas?"

David nods, his mouth full. Once he swallows, he says, "McPherson. Yeah."

I try not to think about how weird it is that a few weeks ago I had never heard of this program and now I've met someone who actually wants to go there. I mean, it's not really that much of a coincidence, considering where I work, right? It's not like the gods are telling me something. (That's one of Mom's favorite sayings when she lays down a bet . . . *The gods are telling me to bet on seven.*) It's just a fluke, right?

Jimmy has wolfed down his sandwich before we're even halfway through ours, and he goes back outside to smoke and probably call his wife. She likes to grill him about what he eats for lunch. He'll tell her he had a salad, and then she won't bug him when he wants a steak and a couple of beers for dinner because it's Saturday night.

Except for that first time I saw David in Jimmy's office, I haven't ever really looked at him. But now he's sitting three feet away and I can't help it. The only other thing in my line of vision is a girlie calendar. He's not bad-looking—not as hot as his car, but he does have thick blond hair and blue eyes. He took off his coveralls before he went to get the sandwiches, and he's wearing a white polo again, which makes me want to smear grease on it, just on principle.

"My parents don't want me to go to McPherson," he says.

"Yeah, I heard."

I remind myself he's the enemy and stop looking at the way his hair curls around his left ear. The only real reason I got to do the fender job today is because Jimmy's pulled a million and one dents, and after seeing my stellar work on the Mustang, he swore he'd never do another one if I was around. If it had been anything else, I'd be pumping gas and he would've been showing Stanford Boy the ropes.

I crumple up my sandwich wrapper without saying anything else and toss it in the trash can. On my way out, David asks me if I'm going to college, but I pretend like I don't hear him and keep walking. I've almost decided to apply, but the idea of actually going is not really something I think will happen. People like me work at gas stations their whole lives, go to cruise-ins with their cars, and join softball leagues for fun. If I had to lay a bet on our futures, that'd be mine, and David would be wearing a Stanford sweatshirt next fall and studying pre-med.

Raul wants to go home because he's still feeling sick from the flu or whatever he has, so I'm stuck outside pumping gas for the rest of my shift while David hangs out in the garage with Jimmy. I'm kinda bitter, but I hide it well. Years of practice.

Han comes by in his dad's plumbing van for a fill-up. He stands next to the driver's door while I wash his windshield. "What're you guys doing tonight?"

I shrug. "Nothing. Amber's working."

"I could come by and hang out with you and Nat."

"If you want to."

"Sure. I'll see you later."

He pays at the pump and drives off with a wave. I think it's kind of pathetic he doesn't have anything better to do on a Saturday night than sit around with me and Natalie, but it's not like I've got big plans of my own. Maybe he'll bring Chinese food. Anything besides pizza would be awesome.

Right before it's time to call it quits, I'm inside with Rosa and she's telling me how she thinks this job's too dangerous because of the late hours, so she's looking for a new one where she can work only day shifts. David comes in and starts checking out the gum display.

"Hey, Crystal," he says. "Rosa."

"Hey," we both say back.

He leans on the counter, trying to act cool but knocking over an old Halloween display of half-price mini chocolate pumpkins. I go around to help him pick them up because they're rolling all over the store.

"Sorry," he says.

I grab two before they can disappear under the beef jerky fixture.

"I was wondering, Crystal . . . You going to the swap meet in Bremerton next Saturday?"

"Doubtful."

"How come?"

What an idiot. Does he think I have money to blow driving all the way up to Seattle to look at car parts I want but can't afford? "I probably have to work."

"Oh, yeah . . ."

I look at Rosa, and she rolls her eyes and tries not to

laugh. All day she's been telling me he's hot for me and I should let her matchmake, but she's crazy. I am so not interested in Stanford Boy. When I do hook up with a guy, he'll be able to work on his own car. Besides, like I told her, there is no way a rich guy who drives that Chevelle and looks like him doesn't already have a girlfriend.

"What about Sunday?" he asks.

"No," I say. "Even if I get the day off, I've got things to do."

He nods. "Yeah, okay. I only asked 'cause I know a guy up there with a 'sixty-six Mustang, and I thought you might like to meet him."

Rosa smirks. "You fixing her up?"

He shrugs and his phone rings. He looks at the display and then answers it. "Hey, babe."

I give Rosa a told-you-so look, and she raises her hands in defeat.

He wanders off to take his call, but after he hangs up he comes back. "Well," he says, "I'm going to Bremerton, so if there's anything you need, let me know and I'll look out for it."

I could really use a right taillight, but I'm not asking him for shit. "I'm good," I say. I'm not gonna be his friend after he stole my job.

He nods like he gets it and punches out for the day, leaving Rosa to speculate on who "babe" is and me to eat nachos.

On my way to the Mustang after my shift, I find Jimmy in the shop leaning over a '49 Ford.

"Can I ask you a question?"

He doesn't look up. "As long as it don't got nothing to do with my feelings."

"You have feelings?"

He shakes his head. "Last night, Betty kept going on about how I feel about her. Do I like my cars better than her and all that shit."

"You didn't tell her the truth, did you?"

"Hell, no. How stupid do you think I am? Of course I said I love her more than my cars."

I laugh and he grins. I hand him a clean rag before he can even ask for it and watch while he wipes away an almost invisible smudge on the fender. "So you were saying?" he asks.

"Do you know anyone who actually went to that program at McPherson?"

"Why? You going there too?"

I shrug.

"You should," he said. "You'd come out ahead."

"You think?"

"What the hell you gonna do around here if you don't? Wait for me to croak and then buy the business off Betty?"

I shrug again, not willing to admit that that was pretty much my plan. Not that I'm hoping he'll drop dead anytime soon or anything.

"Go to college," he tells me. "Open your own place. The old-car guys'll flock to a woman mechanic as long as you know your shit." I smile. He's probably right. He lowers the hood on the Ford and wipes his hands on his coveralls. "You're the real deal, Crystal. Hell, you'll probably put me outta business."

I feel a little embarrassed by his praise, so I say, "You're not trying to get rid of me, are you?"

"If I was, I'd just fire your ass for being late all the time."

"Yeah, yeah. I'm only late so you got something to complain about besides your love life."

"Yank my chain harder, honey. I like it," he says. Then he slaps his hand over his mouth in fake shock. "Sorry. I forgot about all that sexual harassment bullshit. You're not gonna sue me, are you?"

"Not if you write me a letter of recommendation for McPherson."

"Aw, shit," he says. "You know I would, but I hate paperwork. Can't I call them?"

As predicted. But I'm feeling pretty smart because I've come up with a solution. "I need a real letter," I say. "But how about if I write it and you sign it?"

He nods. "Perfect."

Before I leave, he gives me a drag on his cigarette and a piece of gum. Now that I've got my recommendations lined up, it's time to have a look at the application. All the way home I try to think of some way to ditch Amber tomorrow. I want to go to the library and check out McPherson's website without her looking over my shoulder.

The next day I tell Amber I'm taking the Mustang to a cruise-in at Mikey's Diner. After all these years, she should know there aren't any in November because most people have garaged their cars for the winter, but she totally buys it, and I'm stabbed with guilt as I drive away, leaving her and Natalie in front of the television with Gil.

CHAPTER 11

I get a surprise when I check out the application online on Sunday afternoon. I don't need any letters of reference. Why the hell did Ms. Spellerman have them on my to-do list? When I stop by her office on Monday to point this out, she doesn't remember who I am at first, and then once I remind her, she tells me I might want the recommendations to apply for scholarships or to help me get a job in Kansas and that I should go ahead and get them anyway. I've already talked with Jocelyn and asked Jimmy, so I figure why not?

On Tuesday night I have the SAT prep course I've signed up for. David couldn't work for me, but Raul said he'd swap for Wednesday, so that was good. When it's time to go, Amber's huddled under a raggedy quilt on the couch with Natalie to keep warm. There's a space heater in the corner, but it's one of those old-fashioned ones that glows red and might burst into flames at any second, so none of us get too close to it. Amber's trying to do her calculus homework, which she has spread out on the coffee table, but it's obviously hard with frozen hands and Nat in her lap.

"Where're you going?" she asks when she sees I've got my coat on.

I've got my lie ready. "Library."

"Why?"

"Paper for English." I scoot toward the door.

"I'll come with you," she says. "It's got to be warmer there."

Luckily, my class is at the local college, so I have an out. "I'm going to PCC. You know they don't like it when we bring Nat." I head for the kitchen. Unfortunately, it's only through the archway and Amber's voice follows me.

"Mom can watch her."

"Yeah, sure," Mom says, not looking up from her crossword puzzle. "She can hang out with Grandma. As long as you're back by eleven."

Crap. I wasn't counting on this. And the clock is ticking. "Yeah, okay. But let's go."

Amber hands me Nat, and I automatically check her diaper. She needs to be changed and I know Mom'll never get around to it, so while Amber finds her shoes, I do the dirty deed.

"Poor little baby," I say to her when the cold air hits her naked butt. "You're a summer baby, aren't you? You don't like this cold air, do you?"

She wrinkles up her face like she might cry, and I rush through my job and get her wrapped back up quickly. Now I really am going to be late. And I still don't know how I'm going to get away from Amber once we're on campus. I guess we'll go to the library together, and then I'll try to ditch her.

"What're you gonna do?" I ask her when we get inside the library.

"I don't know," she says. "My calculus. Maybe go online."

"Great. I'll meet you back here when I'm done."

"How long?"

"Not sure," I say, rushing off before she can stop me.

I hover by the front door until I see her logging onto a computer, and then I slip outside and run through the breezeway, hoping I'm not too late. I'm looking all over for room 207, and I can't find it anywhere. Finally, I ask a hipster with a bushy beard and a ferret wrapped around his neck.

"It's down there," he says, pointing at a little hallway by a bathroom.

I have my hand on the knob when I hear a click, and then I pull and the door won't open. I knock. There's a second where nothing happens, and then the door opens and a guy about a mile tall stands over me, looking down his nose.

"You're late."

"I couldn't find the room."

He waves me in and then proceeds to tell everyone that once the door is locked, no one gets in, so we should all be early from now on. My face is burning, and I wish my hair wasn't up in a ponytail so I could hide under it. I keep my eyes on my desk.

For the next two hours he drills us. He gives us tips and tricks and practice tests, and I feel like someone's pounding little nails into my head. I'm also distracted by the idea that Amber might get bored and go looking for me. Another problem is that the SATs are full of trick questions. I guess that's why we have to take the course, so we can figure out the game they're playing with us.

As soon as the instructor says we're done for tonight, I stuff my workbooks into my backpack and head for the hallway. I'm almost through the door when I hear my name.

"Hey, Crystal!"

I turn and see Stanford Boy. "Oh, hey." So this is why he couldn't cover my shift.

"How's it going? Man, my brain feels like mush."

"Yeah, mine too."

"You want to get a coffee?" he asks.

I'm totally surprised. I mean, he's always been polite to me, but I haven't exactly been friendly to him. "Uh, no, I can't. I have to meet my sister at the library."

He nods. Everyone else is heading for the parking lot, and I peel off, hoping to lose him, but he follows me. "I was thinking," he says. "If you change your mind and want to go to Bremerton on Sunday, you could ride with me."

For about half a second, I consider it. Who wouldn't want to ride in the Chevelle? But then I snap to. Even if he drove, I'd have to offer gas money, pay to get in, buy lunch, maybe even dinner.

"What would your girlfriend say?" I ask.

He smiles. "It was her idea. She keeps telling me to get some car friends because she's not interested."

"I know the feeling. My sister never wants to hear about my car."

By now we're standing in the lobby of the library and, like she knows we're talking about her, Amber materializes.

"Whoa," David says. "I'm seeing double all of a sudden."

We laugh politely like we've never heard it before, and I introduce them. The whole time they're talking, I'm praying he doesn't mention the SAT prep course. Amber looks a little pissed off, but I can tell she's trying to hide it in front of David.

I really want to get out of here. "We should probably go."

Amber's totally silent until we're in the car, but before I can start the engine, she says, "You lied to me."

Crap. How did she find out?

I try to sound innocent. "What do you mean?"

"Did you really have a paper to write?"

"Yeah, I did." I'm relieved because technically I did. I always seem to have a paper to write.

"You weren't meeting that guy?"

"No. God, no. I don't even like him. He stole my job, remember?"

"Why were you standing in the lobby?"

"I was looking for you."

She nods like she believes me, but when I pull into the driveway, she says, "I was at the same computer all night, Crys. If you want to meet a guy, go ahead. But don't bullshit me."

If Amber's pissed off about this, just think what she'd say if she knew where I'd really been. Next week, I'm going to have to come up with a better plan.

CHAPTER 12

It's a good thing I decided to blow off David and the swap meet. By the weekend I'm so sick I can barely drag myself to work, forget a road trip. On Saturday I stumble around the gas station until Rosa sends me home at three o'clock, and when I get there, Amber's already in the bathroom throwing up. Unable to wait, I race into the scraggly excuse for a backyard and empty my gut out there.

When I stagger back inside, Amber's curled up in a little ball on her bed. I check on Nat, who's in the living room in her playpen. She smiles up at me and promptly puts a foot into her mouth. I'm not sure what to do about her. She looks fine. But for how long? If we take care of her, won't we make her sick too?

I lie down on the couch where I can see her without breathing on her. Mom goes into the kitchen and I call to her, but I'm not sure any sound comes out. She steps back into the living room and looks at me.

"Why does it smell like someone died in the bathroom?"

"We're sick," I manage to get out before clamping my hand over my mouth to keep from heaving.

Mom reaches down and touches Natalie's forehead. "She seems okay."

"Me and Amber. What do we do about Nat?"

"Leave her to me," she says. "If she doesn't have it already, it'll be a friggin' miracle, though."

I watch her pick up the baby, but then my eyes close, and I have these crazy dreams about someone chasing me with a giant toilet plunger. They go on from there, too many and too whacked to remember. Then someone's smashing snow in my face, and I struggle to get away.

"Shhh . . . baby . . . shhh . . . it's okay. Let me put this cloth on you." I open my eyes and Mom's looming over me with a damp rag.

The next time I wake up I'm in my bed. Someone's taken off most of my clothes, and I have no idea how I got here. It's pitch-dark and my throat's on fire. "Am?" I think I say. I hear a little moan across the room, and then I'm out again.

I'm in my bed and Natalie's on the floor, reaching toward me, her little arms plump and her hands opening and closing.

I try to get up. She shouldn't be on the ice-cold floor, but my body's heavy and I can't lift my head.

"Pick me up," Nat says, and I'm only a little surprised she's talking. "Pick me up!" she says again; this time her voice is shrill and high. "Pick me up! Pick me up! Pick me up!"

"I'm trying, I'm trying," I say, but my voice is crushed by the pain in my throat, and then I'm on my side and Natalie's standing in the middle of the room in one of Amber's lacy T-shirts. She's got long red hair, all the way to the ground, and she's a little girl now.

"Don't leave me!" she cries out, her arms still reaching for me. I toss around on the bed, but something invisible's holding me down.

"I'm coming," I say. "I'm coming."

And then she's not Natalie anymore, she's Amber. She's naked, and she's holding her arms tightly around herself, shivering. "I'm going now, Crys."

"No! No! Don't leave me!" I try to say, but I can only hear the words in my head.

"I have to go," she says. "I'm so cold. You'll be fine without me."

"Please, Amber?" I plead. "Please, stay." I know if I can just get up, I can grab her and keep her warm. Keep her here. But the blankets feel heavy, like when Bonehead lies across my lap and I can't shift him no matter how hard I try. I thrash around, but I can't get out from under the covers.

"What about Nat?" I ask Amber as she starts to fade away. "Stay for Natalie."

"She has you," Amber says. Her voice is faint, and I can barely see her now.

"She needs us both. We made a pact to take care of her." And then someone's crying. It might be me, but it sounds like Natalie. "No, Amber! No!" I shout.

Someone is shaking me. I'm still under a heavy layer of something thick and dark, like warm water, and I want to sink back into the comfort of it. The person keeps shaking me, though, and I try to get my arm free, but whoever has it won't let go.

"What? What d'you want?" I ask. There's a light in the room now, and my eyes are starting to focus a little.

"Wake up, Crys," Gil says. He's still shaking my shoulder, and then he tosses a glass of cold water in my face, soaking me and the pillow, and I sit right up.

"I'm sick. Leave me alone."

"I know," he says. "But Amber don't look right. I think she needs a doctor."

In the other room I hear Natalie crying and a voice I can't place trying to soothe her. I'm surfacing now and my head's pounding, but I'm already getting up. And it's such a relief to be able to move. My bare feet hit the cold cement floor, which wakes me up even more. In her bed, Amber's flushed and tossing around, but her eyes are closed. Her hair's damp with sweat, and when I touch her, she moans. My dream was so real that seeing Amber still alive sends a flood of relief through me. But she's not okay. She won't wake up.

"How long's she been like this?" I ask Gil.

"Well, she's been worse than you. She threw up all day Saturday and then more on Sunday. You mostly slept."

"What day is it?"

"Tuesday."

I've been asleep for almost three days? I try to figure out what to do. I don't know if we can move her to the car. She's not that big, but neither am I, and Gil's not usually very steady.

"Where's Mom?"

"Sleeping."

Natalie's still shrieking in the other room, and I wonder if she's sick too.

"Maybe we should call an ambulance."

"The phone's out again," Gil tells me. "Can you drive?"

"I don't know . . . I guess." He lost his license years ago for drunk driving, and Mom's never bothered to get one. It's gonna have to be me. I pull on some jeans and a sweater over my uniform shirt, which I'm still wearing from Saturday. "But how're we gonna get her to the car?"

"Your friend's here," he says.

"My friend?"

"That skinny guy with the death T-shirts?"

"Han? What's he doing here?"

"He stopped by 'cause you weren't in school."

Han helps us half carry, half drag Amber to the car. By the time we get her in the front seat, I'm doubled over with dizziness, and we have to wait until things stop spinning.

"Maybe I should drive?" Han suggests.

"You know how?"

He looks at me funny. "I drive the van all the time."

I'd totally forgotten he works with his father doing plumbing jobs. I'm not really thinking clearly. Besides, the world's spinning again. "I guess you better," I say, which proves how sick I am. No one's allowed to drive the Mustang except me.

Han takes us to the walk-in clinic, but when he goes in and asks for someone to help carry Amber inside, they send us to the emergency room at the hospital. On the way there, I remember Natalie.

"Where is she?"

"Gil's watching her."

"Is she sick?"

"She's okay, so far. That's why I was hanging out at your house. I knew you guys couldn't take care of her."

"You were babysitting?"

He shrugs. "I guess."

Han leaves me in the car in the emergency turnaround and goes inside. Pain is beating in my head like a heartbeat. The next thing I know, they've got Amber on a stretcher and

I hear the whoosh of the doors and she disappears. A minute later, someone comes out with a wheelchair for me.

I shake my head, immediately regretting it as my brains slosh around painfully. "I'm okay."

"The guy said you're both sick."

"I'm not. I mean, I am, but—" I try to stand, and then the ground's coming up to meet me fast, but someone catches me and sits me down in the wheelchair. The next bit is a blur. Eventually I'm lying in a bed with bright lights shining down from the ceiling, and a doctor is standing over me asking what kind of drugs me and Amber have been doing.

"We have the flu," I say. "Or something. A guy at work had it . . ."

A while later, I'm hooked up to a drip, and I'm actually starting to feel a bit better. "Your brother's here to see you," a nurse says, and Han steps into my little curtained-off area.

He's already visited Amber and tells me she's going to be okay, but she's super dehydrated from throwing up so much. "That's what's wrong with me, too," I say.

"I know."

He stays with me for a while and then goes to see Amber again. Later, they tell me I can go home, but to drink lots of fluids and only eat soup until my stomach calms down. They're keeping Amber overnight. I don't want to leave her, but they tell me I have to. Finally, I agree to go if I can see her first. They've moved her to a shared room, and they let Han wheel me there.

"Two minutes," the nurse reminds me.

Amber looks pale, which is better than flushed. She smiles, tells me it sucks that she has to stay and I get to go, and asks me to thank Han, who's waiting in the hallway. "Is Nat okay?"

"I think so. She's at home with Gil, but Han says she doesn't seem sick."

"Thank God." I sit there in my wheelchair, holding Amber's hand. "I thought I was gonna die," she says.

"Me too." I don't tell her about the dreams. If she had the same ones, it'd be too freaky. I'm still shaky at the idea of losing my sister. My insides seem to leak out of me at the thought. I'm like a bag of skin but no bones, no organs, no nothing, my body slumped in the wheelchair. Not only would half of me die with Amber, but I know I could never raise Natalie on my own.

"What would happen to her?" Amber asks.

I shake my head. What *would* happen to her if we both died? We have no plan at all. We've never even bothered to have her baptized, so she doesn't have any godparents. I'm sure Mom would raise Nat, but is that the kind of life we want for our baby?

"We're gonna be fine," I say.

"This time. But—"

"Stop it, Am."

"There's Aunt Ruby . . ."

"Amber? Please? Just stop." I can't think about Natalie being on her own. It makes my heart hurt, sharp and deep like someone's crushing it in a vise. We might not be the best mothers—hell, most of the time we're winging it—but we do love her. And we're all Natalie has. I'm going to do everything in my power to be there for her. And I know Amber will too.

"We're gonna be fine," I say again, more to reassure myself.

Amber squeezes my hand. "You should go home and go to bed. You look like shit."

"Yeah, okay."

As I wheel myself out, I remember to tell her the phone's been cut off again. "But don't worry. Someone will come and get you tomorrow. I promise."

"Love you."

"Love you back."

Han drives me home, helps me into my room, and goes out to feed Bonehead while I get undressed. A few minutes later, Han brings me a bowl of chicken noodle soup.

Me and Amber have been vegetarians since we were five and Jade told us meat was animals. "I don't eat chicken," I remind him.

"It's not real. It's Campbell's."

"Very funny."

"I'm serious," he says. "I read it on the Internet. It's soy protein or something."

We both know he's lying, but I'm too sick to argue, and I eat the soup to make him happy.

Sorry, Chicken Little.

Han leaves after I finish, and I lie there in my cold bed. Thank God for Mom's health insurance from her job. As long as me and Amber are still in school, we're covered. But once we graduate, I'm not really sure what happens. Health insurance is another reason for me to go to college. I wonder if free healthcare will still be around next year for Amber? I drift off to sleep, trying not to worry about how much stuff we didn't consider when we made our plan to get out of here and be on our own.

CHAPTER 13

Four days after Amber comes home from the hospital, Gil's tossing his cookies nonstop in the bathroom. The smell's so bad that Mom threatens to move out until we're all better, but she doesn't because someone has to make sure Gil doesn't die. "I need his paycheck from Big Apple if we're gonna eat," she says, like she's only half kidding. We know she'd be lost without him, though.

We miss a week of school, and when we go back, Mei-Zhen tells us she thinks Nat never got sick because she goes to daycare and is constantly bombarded by germs. Whatever the reason, we're all super relieved to get over the worst of it. Me and Amber walk around like coughing zombies for weeks, though. Gil recovers faster. Maybe we should've tried beer for our "lots of fluids."

Jimmy schedules me to work mostly in the shop or at the lottery counter so I'm not stuck outside in the cold. I guess that's how come me and David end up kind of being friends. More like car buddies. We eat lunch together on Saturdays, and twice we go out for coffee after the SAT review. There's nothing romantic between us. It's all cars. Sometimes he tells me about his girlfriend, Olivia, but I think it's his way of making sure I don't fall for him. Believe me, that's so not going to happen. I could never see myself with someone who carries titanium chopsticks in his glove compartment so he doesn't have to eat sushi with wooden ones at restaurants.

Now that David's not hovering all the time, it's easier to tolerate him being around. Jimmy's got him doing easy repair jobs, and I even show him how to change his brakes one afternoon. His car is so beautiful, it's a joy to work on it. When it's up on the lift and I'm standing under it looking at the immaculate undercarriage, I have to ask him, "How the hell do you keep it so clean?"

"I don't drive it in the rain."

I shouldn't be surprised. That's how most car guys treat their babies, but I guess I never noticed David driving anything else. "How do you get around eight months of the year?"

"That Mini Cooper in the lot's mine," he says. "Well, my mom's."

"Oh, right. I should have known. I've seen it taking up two spots too."

He laughs. "My mom'll kill me if I ding it."

"It's, like, the size of a shoebox," I say. "You could park it sideways and still only use one spot."

He laughs again. "Yeah, okay. Point taken."

The Sunday before Christmas, me and David are cleaning up the break room because we're having our holiday party in there later in the day. Usually, Jimmy takes us all out for Mexican food, but his wife's laid down the law this year, saying it's too expensive, so we're having a potluck at work. Me and David are talking about McPherson, and he's totally jealous I'm applying. His parents have flat-out refused to pay for school if he goes there.

"They say on their website that there's a lot of financial aid," I tell him.

"Yeah, well . . ."

He lets his words hang there until I realize what he means: they don't give financial aid to rich boys. I resist the urge to tell him that if it was me, I'd rather borrow the money than go to Stanford and study something I know I'll hate. But I don't want advice from him on how to run *my* life, so I keep my mouth shut.

"I can work on cars on the side," he says.

"I guess."

Suggesting that David get financial aid reminds me that Natalie's not the only thing keeping me awake at night. There're all those forms. I know I could go ask Ms. Spellerman for help filling them out, but she never remembers who I am and . . . I don't know. I guess I don't want her to think I'm totally stupid.

"You know my sister, Amber?" I ask David, proving just how stupid I am. Of course he knows her. He met her at the library.

"Yeah?"

"Well, I'm really good at fixing cars . . ." My face is heating up, not because I'm bragging but because I hate asking for help. I open the microwave and start scrubbing all the gunk off the insides so I don't have to look at David. "And Amber . . . well, she's really good at forms and stuff."

"Right . . ." Out of the corner of my eye I can see he's stopped sweeping and is staring at me.

"And I'm . . . not. I mean, I can do it if I have to, but the application for McPherson? And all the financial aid stuff? I don't want to screw it up, you know?" My face is really hot now, and I practically stick my head in the oven to hide my blushing, like it's a matter of life or death.

"Amber won't help you?" he asks.

"I told you at the SAT class—she doesn't know I'm applying."

"I guess I thought you would've told her by now."

"Not yet."

"How come?"

I sigh. "It's a long story."

I'm already feeling guilty enough about the lies I'm telling Amber; I don't want David to know about them too. I force myself to look at him. Okay, maybe not at him, but at a spot near him. "But I was thinking if you could, you know, look over my application and my essay and stuff, before I send them in, that would be really good." I spit this last part out all in one breath.

He shrugs. "Sure. No problem."

"I could trade you something. Show you some car stuff, or—"

"It's not a big deal. Whenever you've got it ready, I'll have a look." He says this with an easy smile, and I realize he's not so bad after all. Actually, I've known that for a while, or I wouldn't have asked him.

"I've got the essay in my car," I say.

"Great. I can help with the financial aid too, if you want."

"Really?"

"Sure."

Some of the pressure that's been squeezing my shoulder muscles loosens. "Thanks."

He can see I'm embarrassed and makes a show of looking around the room. "Okay, that's all the cobwebs. Now, what do we do with this?" He holds up a dead spider by one leg. If he thinks he's going to make me squeal like a girl, he obviously doesn't know me very well.

"Put it on the top of the Christmas tree," I say. "It'll be the angel."

He laughs and tosses the spider in the trash.

The more people I ask to do favors for me, the more balls I have to keep in the air. It's one thing to juggle the SAT review class, the applications, financial aid forms, and letters of reference; it's a whole other thing to keep Amber from noticing my new secret life. But so far, so good. She's insisted on coming to this Christmas party, so at three thirty, I head over to the Glass Slipper to pick up her and Nat.

Amber's inside helping Aunt Ruby decorate the tavern for the holidays, which is really not my thing, so I decide to wait in the car. For once I'm actually early, and I take the opportunity to study my SAT workbook. I missed one class when we were sick and I need to work harder if I'm going to figure this shit out.

It's just now getting warm inside the car and I can't bear to turn the engine off, so I leave it idling and settle into my seat. The book is open on my lap, and I start going over some vocab questions. I'm doing a half-assed job, though, because I don't have anything to write with, and between the warmth from the heater and being up all night with Natalie, who wouldn't stop crying for no apparent reason, the words start to swim in front of me. I try to keep my eyes open, but they blink heavily, threatening to close. It reminds me of that episode of *The Flintstones* (Gil loves that show when he's stoned) where Fred's really sleepy and so he props his eyes open with toothpicks. Only he's so tired that they snap, breaking in half, and Fred falls asleep anyway.

The next thing I know, the passenger door's opening and cold air swoops in. I start, looking around. "What? Oh, Amber, hey."

"Hi, Crys." She pushes the seat forward and loads Nat into the back, and then she climbs in front. I'm still blinking, trying to shake off the drowsiness when Amber plucks the SAT review book out of my lap. "What's this?"

"Huh?"

She flips through it. "The SATs? What do you have this for?"

I'm not usually good at lying to my sister, even when I'm on my game. I mean, we know everything about each other, but lately I've been getting so much practice that a lie flies out of my mouth without me really thinking.

"It's David's. He left it in my car."

She glances over, giving me a skeptical look, but then she buckles her seatbelt and settles into her seat. "What was he doing in your car?"

"I was quizzing him. On a break at work."

That has to be the lamest lie ever, because why would we sit in my car instead of using the break room?

Instead of calling me on it, Amber smiles and raises her eyebrows. "Tell me the truth. What's going on with you two?"

"Nothing."

She's grinning. "Yeah . . . I don't believe it."

And then it occurs to me, *Why not let her think something's going on?* She's gotten there on her own, so it's not like another lie. Still, it seems pretty dangerous because it's not like I can ask him to pretend—what about his girlfriend? Maybe I can let her think I'm interested and that's it . . .

Instead of answering right away, I shift into reverse, back out of the parking spot, and head to Jimmy's. "It's nothing," I say again. "But we did go out for coffee a couple of times."

"On Tuesdays, right?" she asks. She's still smiling, so I go with it.

"Yeah."

"I knew it! You could've told me. Is that, like, the only night you two both have off from work?"

If I say yes, then this gives me a free pass to keep going to SAT review. "Yeah, we both have Tuesdays off. But, Amber, it's mostly just a car thing. Nothing's happened."

". . .Yet."

I feel my face turn red even though I don't like David that way. "Just don't say anything at the party, okay?" I ask.

"Mum's the word," she says. "You know me. I can totally keep a secret."

"Yeah, I know. You're the best that way."

God, I suck.

When we get to the gas station, I unload Natalie, who's sleeping in her carrier. As we go in, we pass David on his way to help a customer. Amber gives me an exaggerated wink, and I know I've asked for trouble now, but it's too late to do anything about it.

Friends and family were invited to the potluck, but I'm the only one who brings anyone. Dirk shows up long enough to get his bonus and then leaves. Rosa has to cover the counter and keeps popping in and out for the egg rolls David picked up and the cupcakes Amber made. Raul loads up a plate and eats in a corner by himself. The rest of us sit around the table, talking and stuffing ourselves. Amber maneuvers herself so I'm next to David and gives me another look, which I pretend not to see.

Natalie gets to try a bite of frosting, which she really likes, and whines when we won't give her more. We try distracting her with some refried beans Amber squeezes out of one of the quesadillas Rosa brought, and the baby loves those, too.

"You're asking for it," Jimmy says. "They're volatile."

"Yeah. Give her something else, Am, or you're on diaper duty all night."

Amber hands Natalie a piece of a tortilla to gnaw on, keeping an eye on her so she doesn't choke. The baby gets her hands into everything these days, and it's a battle to keep her from grabbing stuff off the table. We have to pass her around so me and Amber can take turns eating.

Raul gives Rosa a break, and she comes in and scoops up Natalie out of Amber's arms. Nat smiles and gurgles as Rosa lifts her into the air, clucking at her and saying something in Spanish in a squeaky voice. I think I hear the words for "baby" and "beautiful," but even after a year and a half of studying it in school, it's still a foreign language to me.

"You look exactly like your mama, don't you?" Rosa says in English. She lifts Nat up high again. "Except your eyes. You must have your daddy's eyes."

I see Amber tense, and my stomach clenches too. We have a rule to never talk about Natalie's dad. The thing is . . . we don't know who he is. It sounds kind of slutty, and I guess in a way it is, but it's one of those things—a drunken party at Jade's house to celebrate Labor Day. We try to think of it as a good thing, though. It means we never have to share Natalie with some guy we barely know.

"You should grab some food," I say, taking Natalie from Rosa.

"Yeah, okay."

The tension in Amber releases and she slumps back in

her chair. I roll my shoulders to ease the strain in them, and a second later we're all talking about Christmas plans. Crisis averted.

We head home around six o'clock, and David walks out with us. At the car, I remember the McPherson essay, but I hesitate because of Amber. David knows it's a secret, but she's gonna think it's weird if I give him something, and haven't I already acted suspiciously enough today? I really need to get his opinion, though, so I grab it out of the glove box.

"Here's that paper," I say, giving him a look that I hope reminds him to keep his mouth shut about why he's reading it for me. Amber's busy buckling in Nat and doesn't look up.

He nods. "Thanks. I'll give it back to you on Tues—"

"Whenever's good," I say.

Amber apparently *is* paying attention—I can see her grin at the mention of Tuesday.

"Night, Crystal," he says. "See you, Amber."

"Bye," we say.

"What was that you gave him?" Amber asks as I climb into the driver's seat. "A love letter?"

"Shut up," I say, laughing. "It's a paper I wrote on Mustangs. He wanted to read it."

She nods. I lost her at "Mustangs," so I'm safe for the moment. But the fact that she doesn't press me actually makes me feel even more guilty. There's a little knot in my stomach, and it's growing bigger with every lie I tell my sister.

We drive home, and we're unloading Natalie when a rattling car comes around the corner and backfires, making us all jump. Bonehead starts barking as the car slows in front of our house. "Shit," I say. "Take Nat and go inside. I'll deal with him."

"Are you sure?" Amber asks.

"Just go."

As Amber passes our landlord, who is now striding across the frosty grass toward the driveway, he tries to stop her, but she keeps walking, so he heads for me.

"You got the rent?" he demands.

CHAPTER 14

I lean against the side of the Mustang, trying to be cool
and unconcerned. I'm usually the one who has to deal with
the landlord, but it still makes my heart pound. It's not like I
think he'll kick us out, but there's no way we could find somewhere else this cheap to live, so it stresses me anyway.

"Your car sounds like shit," I tell him.

"Yeah, I know. If I had the rent money I might be able to
get it fixed."

"You should let me take a look at it."

"Nice try."

The only light out here is from the neighbor's porch—the
streetlight burned out a couple of weeks ago. My stomach's
tight because I can't read his expression. "I'll get you some
money on Friday."

"I've heard that before."

"Yeah, I know, but school's out for Christmas. I'll take

Gil in to work to get his paycheck and make him sign it over to you. And then I'll drive it over to your house myself."

"How much?"

"Four hundred."

"That doesn't even cover September. What about the rest?"

I shrug. "I'll fix your car. Bring it by tomorrow."

"My old lady's gonna kill me if I don't get more than that out of you."

He knows me and Amber have jobs and money of our own, but we took a vow never to pay our parents' bills or we'd be broke. We buy most of our own food, gas, and insurance— and pay for everything for Nat as it is. We'll never escape if we give in and take over Mom and Gil's debts. The least they can do is pay the fucking rent.

"I'll hit Mom up too," I say. "Maybe she's got something saved for Christmas presents."

If I think this will earn me any sympathy, I'm sadly mistaken. Not that it should, really. I mean, the place is a dump, but this guy is owed his rent. He lights a cigarette and blows out the smoke. I inhale deeply. It's not the same as actually smoking, but I'll take what I can get.

"What time should I bring the car over?" he asks.

"Eleven?" That'll give me enough time to go and get some filters and fuel injector cleaner for his car, which should stop it from backfiring. If it's the plugs or wires, he's on his own.

I'll change those for him, if I have to, but they're too expensive for me to shell out for.

"I'll be here," he says over his shoulder.

Before falling into bed, I manage to talk Mom out of seventy-five bucks, which she says is for presents but I know is gambling money. In the morning, I use some of it to buy parts and give the rest to the landlord when he drops off his car. I spend two hours freezing my ass off in the driveway tuning up his piece of shit while Amber and Nat are inside, buried under blankets, watching TV and trying to stay warm.

Me and Amber decide to skip holiday presents so we can buy Natalie something really special, since it's her first Christmas ever. Amber wants to get Nat's ears pierced, so that's what we do. It seems mean to me, and Natalie really hollers. I'm sure it hurts like hell. It kind of pains my heart to hear her wail like that for no good reason, but Amber's thrilled with the results, and after the baby gets over our betrayal, she looks pretty cute. We end up buying Amber a pair of matching studs, but I don't want any. I never wear earrings.

The day before Christmas it's slow at the gas station and I get off early. I come home and find Amber at the kitchen table surrounded by wrapping paper, gift tags, and about thirty little boxes of chocolate truffles from the dollar store. She jumps up when she sees me, her face turning pink.

"Don't be mad."

I sigh. I know what she's up to. I think it's a waste, but she can't help herself. "Why would I be mad?"

"I spent thirty bucks."

"Jeez, Am, I'm not Scrooge. If you want to give everyone in the family a box of candy, do it. It's not gonna break us."

She smiles. "Oh, good. Thanks. Want to help me?"

"Yeah, okay."

The two of us wrap and tag each box. There's one for each of the aunts and uncles, our grandma, all the cousins, Mom, Gil, and me. Even the babies get their own boxes. I make a mental note to pick up something for Amber so she's not the only one at Aunt Ruby's without a gift tomorrow.

Mom and all my aunts have addictions—gambling, booze, food, or some combo. Except for Aunt Ruby. She loves money too much to waste it. She owns a tavern, but she never drinks, or plays poker in the back room, or eats the fried food. She just counts the takings. She's the one who gives me and Amber hope. She lives in a nice house that she paid for herself by working hard. And also, she's taken Amber under her wing.

She's generous, too, and closes the bar every Christmas Day, inviting the whole family over to eat like pigs and get drunk on free beer and wine. It's a madhouse of staggering aunts and uncles, competing cousins, wrapping paper, and crying babies.

We've been at the tavern for hours, and Natalie's crashed

out in the playpen with her cousin, Rocky. I'm not drinking because I'm driving, and after the hangover from the last party Amber went to, she hasn't wanted to partake. Tonight she's allowed herself one hot chocolate with peppermint schnapps as a Christmas treat, and she's nursing it to make it last.

Me, Jade, and Amber are playing darts, and Jade's kicking our asses.

"Thirty," Amber says, laughing, as she pulls her darts out of the board. "Man, I'm no good at this anymore."

Jade throws two bull's-eyes and an eighty without even setting her drink down. She tosses her freshly dyed candy-apple-red hair over her shoulder like, *Take that!* Ever since beauty school, she can't leave her hair alone. She might as well wear a sign that says, "I'm a hairdresser!" I'm surprised she didn't add green streaks for the holidays. "You're no good at darts, Am," she says, "because you never have any fun anymore. You spend too much time at school."

"Don't tell her that," I beg.

Jade ignores me. "Did you hear? Mom had to fire one of her waitresses yesterday. Rita, I think."

"Are you serious?" Amber asks. "Why?"

"I don't know. Stealing booze, I'm pretty sure. You could get your GED and work here full-time. Forget about washing dishes anymore."

I throw a dart at Jade, and she yelps when it hits her bare arm. "Hey! That hurt."

"Don't be a baby." I throw another one, and it hits her in the thigh. The darts are soft-tipped, so they barely leave a mark.

"Jeez, Crystal. Chill." Jade throws one back at me as hard as she can, but I catch it.

"Amber's graduating in June," I say. "Stop screwing with her."

"I'm not," Jade says. "But you could be earning real money, Am, six months earlier if you start now—"

"I know. That's what I keep telling Crystal."

I let out a sigh that sounds more like a growl. It's Christmas, and I've been pretty relaxed today, but Jade's starting to piss me off. "Six months isn't going to—"

"Ask my mom." Jade grabs Aunt Ruby's arm as she walks by.

"Ask me what?"

"You're a businesswoman," Amber says. "Tell Crystal I should get my GED and work for you now, since you have an opening."

Ruby looks us over, sizing up the situation. She puts an arm around Amber's shoulder. "Finish school, sweetheart. You've got all kinds of time."

"But—"

"Amber, honey, you and me already have a deal for after graduation. You made a plan with your sister. Stick with it. The worst thing you can do in life is to give up your goals before you reach them. You'll never accomplish anything that way."

Amber sighs. "Yeah, okay. I guess you're right. I'll stick to our plan."

"There's a good girl." Aunt Ruby smiles at me like, *Problem solved,* and I try to smile back, but I can't help wondering what she'd say if I told her I'm the one who's totally messing with our plan for the future.

I'm hit with a wave of nausea. I rush to the bathroom and throw up the two slices of pecan pie I ate. I don't think my stomach can take all this lying. As I walk by the bar after rinsing out my mouth, I see my uncle Liam chipping away at a giant candy cane with an ice pick. Maybe I should borrow the pick when he's done. I could stab Amber in the back right now and get it over with.

When it's time to leave, it takes Amber almost an hour to go around hugging everyone and telling them Merry Christmas. I watch her give each and every one of our relatives her full attention, smiling and laughing, and I know that while I love them all too, I can definitely live without them. Amber's like Mom—she wants her family around her. I don't think me and Natalie would be enough for her in Kansas. She'd be lonely and that would kill me.

． ． ．

Han comes over the next day with a present for Natalie—
the most gaudy, girly dress ever made. It's red velvet with a
big plaid bow, and there's one of those stretchy headbands to
match. I try not to laugh because he's so proud of it. He got
it at an after-Christmas sale for eleven bucks.

"Maybe she can wear it for New Year's?" he asks.

"Yeah," I say. "She's got big plans that night. Pooping.
Eating. Sleeping. More pooping." I'm joking around, but Han
looks crushed, and Amber smacks me in the shoulder.

"I think it's great," she says.

"Me too. I was just kidding," I say.

Neither of us tells him that redheads don't wear red. Instead, Amber tries the dress on Natalie. It clashes with her
hair, but she still looks beautiful, and we all *ooh* and *aah* over
her. Han takes a couple of pictures with a digital camera he
found on the bus. The display's busted, so we won't know if
the pictures will turn out until he downloads them, but it's
better than nothing.

"I'll print you some," he says.

I try to make up for my sucky manners. "Cool . . . thanks."

We don't actually have very many pictures of Natalie
because we don't have a camera or phone, so this'll be
good. Sometimes Han is so nice, I don't mind having him
around.

• • •

Two miracles happen in January within minutes of each other, and while the second one is awesome, the first one changes our lives for good. And it's about frickin' time.

Natalie sleeps through the night.

Instead of waking to whimpers or crying at three in the morning because she's hungry, I open my eyes and am shocked to see the clock says 7:18. And the baby's not even screaming. She's sitting in her crib, babbling away.

There's got to be some sort of mistake. "Amber?"

She rolls over. "Huh?"

"Did you get up with Natalie last night?"

She burrows down in her blanket. "No. Didn't you?"

"No! Do you know what this means?" Amber's eyes open wide. "They said this would happen, but I never believed it!" I jump out of bed and throw myself at my sister, hugging her.

"Cue the friggin' angels," she says, quoting Mom.

"She slept through the night! She slept through the night!" we sing together.

We jump out of bed and pick up Natalie, swinging her around.

"You slept through the night, you sweet, sweet, beautiful baby," I say.

We're still twirling around when we hear Mom yelling

from the other room. "I won the lottery! I won the god-damned lottery! Where is everybody?"

Amber and I stop dancing and stare at each other. This can't be happening—good things like this don't happen to us. But then Mom comes thumping through the house whooping and hollering. It must be true! We almost crash into her as she comes lumbering into our room, arms wide, face pink, eyes sparkling.

It turns out that while it's not millions, the jackpot *is* five grand.

"Five thousand buckaroos!" Mom yells.

"Woohoo!" Amber says, and we all hug.

I spin Natalie around some more until Amber points out that she looks like she might get sick if I don't stop. Gil wanders in then and sees us jumping up and down. "Something happen?" he asks, rubbing his eyes.

Mom squeezes him against her huge chest. "You're a kept man, now, baby!"

He grins up at her. "My one and only goal in life."

Mom's had a couple of big wins like this before, and we have a system so it doesn't all disappear. Once we have the check, she signs it over to me and Amber. We take half of it and pay back rent and also rent as far into the future as it'll stretch. Then the five of us pack into my car and hit the grocery store.

We spend over three hours wandering up and down the grocery aisles with two shopping carts, filling them with all the stuff we can never usually afford. Gil gets a steak, which he promises to cook when we're not home, and a box of instant mashed potatoes to go with it. I throw some sour cream into the cart.

"Live large," I tell him.

He pumps his fist in the air. "Hell, yeah!"

Then we get cheese, real butter, pickles, fresh bread, that fake vegetarian lunchmeat that tastes really good but is super expensive, yogurt, and two gallons of milk. Amber wants a whole case of Chunky vegetable soup, so we pile that onto the bottom of the cart, and then we get about ten boxes of mac and cheese, some instant rice, and ramen noodles.

Mom picks out tomatoes, olives, and canned mushrooms. She's gonna make her special spaghetti sauce on her night off. We all agree on hot chocolate mix, crackers, chips, a pound of fancy coffee—which takes forever for me and Amber to figure out how to grind in the machine—and fifty pounds of kibble for Bonehead, plus some rawhide treats.

Finally we hit the baby aisle and spend a ton on Natalie—cereal, cases of baby food, formula, diapers, a new bottle, a three-pack of bibs, and Desitin . . . the real stuff, not the generic brand. After we unload our loot at home, we get dressed up and go to the Olive Garden for bottomless soup, salad, and pasta. Amber puts Nat in the red dress, and I try not to laugh at the stupid headband because I know my sister likes it.

I don't have anything dressy, and I refuse Amber's offer to loan me something. Instead, I find a not-too-ratty sweater I don't usually wear because it's itchy, and my good jeans. There's a tiny hole in the right knee, but you can barely see it.

Dinner is so good, and we totally stuff ourselves. Mom wants us all to order one more round of everything except the soup so she can fill the Ziploc baggies she carries in her purse, but we remind her the fridge is already overflowing, and she gives in. To top it all off, we each order a different dessert and share them. Natalie has a couple of bites, but then she falls asleep in her highchair, exhausted from the excitement of the day.

By the time we get home, we're all fat and happy and totally beat, but me and Amber have one more job to do. We get Nat to bed, and after Mom and Gil disappear into their room, we hide the rest of the money all over the house like we're the Easter Bunny. At the bank, we got a bunch of fives, tens, and twenties, and three fifties. We stick them under cushions and in the sugar bowl that no one uses, behind the fridge, in the back of the silverware drawer, places like that. For some reason, Mom gets a real kick out of finding money. This way she won't blow it all at once, too.

As we finally sink into our freezing-cold beds, the one thing I've been refusing to think about all day creeps around the edges of my mind. Tomorrow, when Amber thinks I'm at work, I'll actually be at the community college taking the SATs. The bottomless pasta turns over in my stomach, and I swallow hard to keep it down.

CHAPTER 15

Because I started studying for the SATs so late, I've put off taking the test until the last minute. Applications to McPherson are due by February first, and I'll get my test scores back in about three weeks, so I should just make it.

It never occurs to me to set the alarm, because Natalie's been our wake-up call for the last six months. Of course, now she's sleeping through the night, which I wasn't counting on. It's only when Mom comes home from her graveyard shift that I manage to shake off some crazy dream and realize I've got twenty minutes to get to the college.

Natalie and Amber are already up, and I get dressed fast. I run a brush through my hair while I take a pee, then wash my face and hands. I kiss Natalie goodbye and I'm almost out the door when Amber looks up from the puzzle she's doing at the kitchen table and says, "I thought you were going to work."

"I am," I say automatically.

"How come you're not wearing your uniform?"

Crap. "Oh, yeah. I guess I . . . I was late and I wasn't thinking."

She smiles. "I ironed it for you so you could sleep in."

I have no choice but to thank her and change into the shirt and pants. When I get to the college, I'm red-faced from running through the parking lot, and I'm wearing a gas station attendant uniform and clunky steel-toed boots. All the other kids are in sweats or jeans, with one or two in pajamas, and they all look at me like I'm from Mars.

"Well, at least the name on your shirt matches your ID," says the guy who's checking me in.

I look down at my uniform. "Yeah."

Whatever.

As soon as I finish, I know I blew it. I try to tell myself everyone feels that way, but I'm more bummed about it than I expected. What the hell was I thinking? I've wasted a bunch of our money on something stupid that's never gonna happen. The only good thing is that I didn't tell Amber about the new plan.

I want to give up, but David won't let me. For the next three weeks, my schedule is packed with work, school, Natalie, and lies. Me and David continue to meet every Tuesday night to go over application stuff—including writing a letter of recommendation in Jimmy's name; I figure if he's willing to sign it, I might as well have it in my file—and I let Amber think it's something romantic, proving once again what a lousy person I am.

One night I come home cross-eyed after two hours of rewriting my essay with David. I'd gotten a B from my English teacher and I'd thought that was pretty good, but David ripped my paper to pieces and helped me put it back together. Now it's stellar, thanks to him.

"So?" Amber says, smirking when I walk in. "Your back seat or his?"

I force myself to smile and whack her on the shoulder. "Shut up."

"Seriously, what's going on? I want details."

"I told you it's not really like that . . ."

"But you like him?"

Oh, God. I sigh. This is one lie I can't keep up anymore. "Amber, we're just car buddies. He's way out of my league."

She puts her hands on my shoulders and looks me right in the eyes. "Don't ever say that, Crystal. No one's out of your league. Especially some stuck-up rich boy."

"Sorry."

She thinks I mean I'm sorry because I don't believe in myself, but it's more than that. I'm sorry for going behind her back, for spending our money, for the hours she's taking care of Natalie and I'm not doing my share. And I'm also sorry because the idea that I'm doing this for our future might be the biggest lie of all. Yeah, it would help us, but honestly, I'm applying to the college because I can't imagine not doing it anymore. And thanks to David and all his encouragement and help, I can see myself at McPherson. Part of me thinks I'll crack in two if I don't get in, but I also think even if I do get accepted, I won't be able to go, so I'm wasting my time. Plus, by then I'll probably have an ulcer from all the lying. My stomach hurts every day, and I've lost about five pounds.

And yet I'm still meeting David at the Coffee Klatch every week. It's this fancy place in northeast Portland where most of the drinks are about five bucks each. David has paid every time, and I'm such a loser, I let him. I offered to buy them once, but he waved me off, knowing I can't drop ten bucks every time we meet.

Tonight David shuts his laptop and looks across the table, giving me a big smile. "You know," he says, "you're really lucky. You should get a great financial aid package."

"You mean because I'm so poor?"

His face turns pink. "Uh . . . I didn't mean—"

"I'm teasing you. It's okay. I know I'm broke."

"I meant because your sister's done you a big favor on your taxes. It should pay off."

Amber loves forms almost as much as she loves numbers. She fills out surveys that come in the mail, questionnaires on the bus, and takes every quiz she can find in magazines. The year we turned sixteen, Jimmy gave me a real job instead of the under-the-table work I'd been doing for him in the shop, and Amber's been filing my taxes for me ever since. She's freakishly excited about that kind of stuff.

She does Mom and Gil's return every year too, which, according to David, is why I'm probably going to get a bunch of money for school. Since Amber took over, she hasn't let them claim the two of us as dependents because they don't pay for shit for us. I know Amber didn't help me on purpose, but now when the financial aid people look at my income, they're going to see a very poor, independent adult instead of a teenager depending on her parents for everything. I could kiss Amber! Except I can't tell her what a favor she's done for me. At least not yet.

David stands up and stretches. "So until we get your SAT scores, that's about all we can do." His shirt lifts a little, and I see that blond trail of hair going down into the waist of his pants. I would never, ever try to hook up with someone like him, but I can't help checking him out when he does shit like that. And I'm not the only one. A couple of girls on a couch by the fake fireplace are eyeing him over their lattes too.

"My scores should be online tomorrow," I tell him. I grab Natalie's carrier from under the table where I stashed her. She's been asleep the whole time, which is surprising, since it's so noisy in here. God, she's beautiful when she's asleep. Her little red curls and feathery eyelashes make my heart surge with affection. Moments like these help me remember I'm not just being selfish—I'm doing this whole Kansas thing for us, for the three of us. And if I have to tell a few lies to make it happen, well, that's how it is.

"Do you work tomorrow night?" David asks as we walk out to our cars.

"Yep."

"Okay. See you then. And you better have gotten a perfect score," he says.

"Yeah, right."

He waits while I buckle in Natalie, and then he gives me a hug. I'm totally thrown for a second, but I try not to show it. "Good night, ladies," he says.

"Night."

The next morning, I tell myself there's no chance of getting decent enough scores to get into McPherson, but the past few weeks have still made me hopeful. I leave Amber sleeping and take Natalie to daycare as soon as the school is open, and then I hit the computer lab. I sign in to the account I've created, and there are my SAT scores. At first I think it's a huge mistake, because I didn't do that bad. I got 510 on math, 502 on reading, and 498 on writing. That gives me a cumulative score of 1510. Completely average. Well, that's a relief. I mean, these scores should be high enough to get me into McPherson. I'm still not sure how I did so well, though. I definitely felt like shit after I took the test.

But my name is there, right above the scores. And I guess, in a way, it doesn't really matter what I thought before. If that's what the computer says, then that's what I got, right? By the time I get to Ms. Spellerman's office, I'm already worried I should've done better on the math. But if I'm honest, I'm probably lucky I did that well, since Amber usually does my math homework. The guidance office secretary's not around, so I knock on Ms. Spellerman's door. She calls out for me to come in, and I tell her my news.

"Good job," she says.

I can tell she has no idea who I am, but I don't care. I'm here for a specific reason. "I was wondering," I say. "When I send in my application to McPherson, can I use the school's address instead of my own?"

Ms. Spellerman looks puzzled for a second, and then she nods and smiles. "I don't see why not. Are you moving?"

"Maybe." I'm not going to tell her the truth. I don't want Mom or Amber to see the admissions letter before I do. "Should I put your name on it too?"

"Probably. 'In care of J. Spellerman' should do the job. I'll call you into my office when it comes."

"Great—thanks."

"Oh, and Miss . . ."

I knew it.

"Robbins," I prompt.

"Right. Miss Robbins. You are aware McPherson's a private school, right? I mean, you could stay in state and pay a lot less. Have you thought about that?"

She obviously doesn't remember that McPherson was her idea. "I don't want to go anywhere else. It's the car thing," I remind her.

"Car?"

"Antique automotive restoration?"

Something clicks into place. "Oh, of course. Okay, well, good luck."

"Thanks."

As I head to my first class I can't help feeling kind of shiny and proud. Too bad there isn't anyone to tell except David. If I have time, I'll email him at lunch.

After school, Mei-Zhen is waiting for me and Amber next to Nat's crib. She gets right to the point. "Your baby needs a winter coat."

"Yeah," I say. "We know . . . She grew out of the one we have."

Mei-Zhen crosses her arms. "You have to replace it."

"We were gonna do that today, right, Crys?" Amber says.

We'd actually planned to go home and take naps before

work, but if there's one thing having a baby has taught us, it's that she always comes first.

"Yeah," I say. "We're going to Walmart right now."

"I expect to see her wearing a coat tomorrow," Mei-Zhen says.

"You will," Amber tells her.

Mei-Zhen stands over us, watching while we struggle to layer the three sweaters on top of Natalie's overalls, which we've been doing for the past two weeks. The baby wiggles and whines while we yank and pull, and it takes both of us to get it done. A coat would definitely be easier. We had one from Jade, but Nat grew out of it. She's growing so fast, it's like she's on steroids.

Amber buttons up the top sweater, and Nat's arms stick out to the sides. "You see," Mei-Zhen says. "Even if she's warm enough, she's not comfortable."

I want to point out that Nat's smiling at us, so she can't be that miserable, but Amber can tell I'm about to give Mei-Zhen an earful and she drags me off to the parking lot.

"We're not really going to Walmart, are we?" Amber asks once we're in the car.

"Nope. Goodwill." It's sad to think that even Walmart's out of our budget, but Natalie grows so fast that it's true.

Twenty minutes later we've got her in a cart and we're wheeling it through the baby aisle. There isn't much to choose from in her size, though. "Maybe we should get it big?" Amber holds up a pink and purple leopard-print parka.

I laugh because it's for a two-year-old. "She'd have room to grow, that's for sure."

Amber hangs it back up. "Mei-Zhen would probably report us for trying to suffocate her."

"No doubt."

We find an ugly boy's coat in the right size for six bucks.

"Seriously?" Amber says.

"I don't see anything else." We take off Natalie's extra sweaters and try it on her. "It fits. What do you think?"

"Yeah, okay."

We're both bummed that our baby can't have the best of everything, or even something decent, but Nat's still grinning and bubbly—she doesn't care. And the coat does have fake fur around the hood, so it's probably extra warm. Because we deposit almost every bit of money we get into the bank in order to keep it safe, I'm counting out some change from the bottom of my backpack when Amber tells me Shenice quit school.

"Really? I was wondering where she was." Thinking back, I haven't seen her at lunch for at least a week. I'm only there every other day because of Natalie, though, and Shenice always misses a lot of school, so her absence hadn't even registered. "What's she gonna do?"

"They promoted her from cleaner to full-time stocker at the grocery store. Her mom's making her get her GED, but she's golden. Paid holidays, vacation, and you wouldn't believe her hourly wage."

I can see where this is going, and I hand over the coins to the cashier before she's even rung up the coat. I want to get out of here before me and Amber have another fight about dropping out of high school.

"Here," I say, lifting up Nat and giving her to Amber along with the keys. "Take her out to the car and I'll put the cart away."

By the time I get outside, Amber's got Natalie in her car seat, but she's standing next to the Mustang like she's waiting for me. Crap. I was hoping we were done talking about Shenice.

"You know, Crys," she says, "if Shenice had dropped out a couple of months ago, I would've wanted to quit school too."

I wait a beat before saying, "But you don't now?"

She smiles at me, and it's funny—I see so much of Natalie in her. "No. I'm not gonna drop out. And do you know why?"

"Why?"

"Because you and Aunt Ruby are right. We've made a plan, and we've got to stick to it. Exactly like we said we would. It's crazy, but when I heard Shenice quit, instead of wanting to do it too, I got kind of . . . I don't know . . ."

She wipes at her eyes almost like she's crying. The wind is whipping around us, though, so I'm not sure. "This is stupid. Maybe it's my period making me all . . ."

"All what?" I ask.

"Emotional, I guess. It's just that instead of wishing I could quit too, I feel so grateful to you."

She's freaking me out a little, acting all sensitive like this, and I'm getting uncomfortably hot in my denim jacket even though it's freezing out here. "Me? Why?"

"You're always looking out for me and Natalie. You work so hard at your job, you help me with my homework, and you made this great plan for us. I love you, Crystal. Thank you so much for keeping me on track. I never could've gotten this far without you." And then she does something we don't really do in our family—she throws her arms around me and hugs as hard as she can.

I am the worst human being on the face of the planet.

When I get to the garage that night, David's grinning. He whistles when I walk in. "Look at you! You're the one who should be going to Stanford."

I know he's humoring me, but I let it ride. "How'd you do?"

"Not as good as the last time I took them."

"Were your parents pissed?"

"Not at all."

"Really?"

He reaches into his pocket, pulls out a creamy piece of heavy stationery, and shows me his acceptance letter from Stanford.

"Hey, congratulations!"

I give him an awkward hug. Jeez, I'm becoming a hugger. First him last night, then Amber this afternoon, and now him again. What's wrong with me? I take two steps back real quick while he explains that he'd applied for early admission, but his parents were afraid his scores weren't good enough and he'd be put on the waiting list, which is why he took the test again.

"All that wasted time," I say. "You could have been working on that weird-ass clunking sound your car makes when you shift."

"My car purrs, baby," he says. "Must be thinking of yours."

"The Mustang's a sound piece of machinery. You wish you could have something so awesome."

Jimmy comes in then and gives us an earful because we're standing around while we're on the clock, and so we get to work. The whole night, I'm grinning to myself. My scores are only average, but according to the McPherson site, that's all I really need. After work, David and I go to the Coffee Klatch with his laptop and finish up my application.

"You ready?" he asks.

I take a deep breath. "Go for it."

"Don't you want to hit 'submit' yourself?"

"Just do it, already. You're making me nervous."

He laughs and taps his finger on the touchpad, sending my information off into cyberspace. "Good luck," he says.

"I'll need it." And I'm not only thinking about getting accepted to college.

CHAPTER 16

The website says McPherson mails you a letter three to five days after you apply. I figure I've got to include time for it to get to the school, so I give it eight, and then go to Ms. Spellerman's office every afternoon. On day eleven, I can't wait and go by in the morning, but no one's around. Later, when I'm on lunch duty with Natalie, my stomach's so anxious that I can't eat. I end up sneaking out a couple of minutes early. If I hurry, I can get to the guidance office without being late for fifth period.

I come around the corner near the main entrance of the school and Ms. Spellerman's standing in the hallway with Amber. Shit. My sister's holding up a single sheet of paper in one hand, and in the other is an open envelope. I freeze. I watch her scan the contents, her expression changing from confusion to anger so fast—exactly like Natalie's face when we take something away from her that she's determined to stick in her mouth.

Before I can say or do anything, Ms. Spellerman looks up and sees me. "Oh!"

As I step forward, Amber whirls on me. "You're a fucking traitor."

She says it so low, it's scarier than if she'd screamed. She crumples up the letter and throws it at me. It bounces off my forehead.

"I . . . I . . . thought she was you," Ms. Spellerman says.

"We're twins," I tell her, stating the obvious.

Amber runs down the hallway and I go after her, catching her arm as she pushes through the front doors of the school, and drag her back inside. "Wait!"

"Don't touch me!"

"I want to explain. I was gonna tell you. Will you give me two fucking minutes?"

"No. I won't! Let me go, Crystal, or I'll scream."

She tries to shake me off, but I'm holding on tight. A security guard stands up from his stool. "Ladies? Is there a problem?"

"Yes," Amber says. "She's harassing me."

"No, I'm not. I'm her sister."

Amber wrenches her arm free and shoves her way through the double doors.

"Come here," the guard says to me.

I ignore him and run after her. The bell rings and all the kids who left campus for lunch hurry up the outside stairs, laughing and pushing against us. Amber weaves through them and I try to keep up, but a bunch of jocks are between us like a solid wall of muscle, and I can't get through. "Amber!" I yell. "Wait. Let me explain!" I duck between two guys, but I've lost sight of her. And then I see her crossing the street against the light. A couple of drivers honk at her, and she leaps out of the way of a Ford Escort. Great. She's gonna get killed and it'll be my fault.

I can't get across the street without being flattened, so I have to wait. By the time the light turns, Amber's gone. I scan the streets in every direction, but it's like she's vanished. I sit on a bus bench, my face in my hands. *I won't cry. I won't cry. I won't cry.*

After a few minutes, I realize I'm still holding the crumpled letter I picked up after Amber threw it at me and I smooth it out on my knee. The stationery's not as fancy as the one David got from Stanford, but the message is the same.

Congratulations! We're happy to inform you . . .

Like it fucking matters now. It might as well say: *We're happy to inform you that you're a liar and a traitor and you're getting exactly what you deserve.* Why didn't I ask Amber about college way back in October? Why was I so stupid? Why do I always mess up our lives?

• • •

I want to go home and crawl into bed. After my fight with Amber, my stomach hurts so bad that I'm practically doubled over for the rest of the day, but I can't just hide. I have to work four hours at the gas station, and then I have to take Nat to Forward Momentum because Amber is scheduled to work at the Glass Slipper. I sweet-talked David into covering the second half of my shift so I could leave work early.

I head straight to Jimmy's as soon as the last bell rings. David will be in to relieve me at seven. It's freezing cold outside, and the rain looks thick, like it wants to snow or maybe sleet. We're busy, and I blow on my hands between customers. I only have one glove because Bonehead found them in the car and chewed one to shreds, so my right hand's like a chunk of ice. Around five thirty, Rosa yells over the loudspeaker that I have a phone call. I finish up with a customer and jog inside.

I'm hoping it's Amber and she's calmed down. "Hello?"

"Crystal Robbins?" a voice asks.

"Yeah?" I say, my heart sinking into my shoes at the serious tone of the caller.

"This is Mei-Zhen Clark at daycare."

Oh, shit. "What's happened? Is Natalie okay?"

"She's fine, but no one came to pick her up today, and we'd all like to go home."

"Oh, God. I'm so sorry. I thought Amber was getting her. I'll be right there."

"You can't leave," Rosa says as I toss down the receiver.

"I have to get Natalie."

"Who's gonna pump gas?"

"Dirk's still here."

"Only for seventeen more minutes."

"Ask him to stay late," I say. "It's an emergency. I'll be back as soon as I can."

"You know he won't," she yells after me, but I keep going out the door, the bell tinkling behind me.

I dodge an incoming car and head around back to where the Mustang's parked. It'll take at least fifteen minutes to get to the high school at this time of night. The daycare closed at five, so we're gonna get fined, and maybe even put on probation. What the hell's Amber playing at?

I rev the engine and take off before it's really got a chance to warm up. Hopefully it won't die at the first stoplight. When I see Amber, she's gonna wish I didn't. I don't think for a minute anything's happened to her. She's trying to piss me off and screw up my day. What really makes me mad is that she didn't even give me a chance to explain about McPherson. I wasn't going to move to Kansas without her and Nat. What kind of a person does she think I am?

I seem to hit every red light, and in my head I hear the little *ka-ching* of our fine going up for every minute I'm late.

When I finally get to school, I slide into a spot in the teachers' parking lot. It's closest to the daycare, and I pray I don't get towed. I race through an empty hallway to get to the group of classrooms that have been turned into the children's enrichment block.

"I'm so, so, so sorry," I say as I burst into the dark room, breathless and sweaty. Mei-Zhen's already turned out the lights and has her purse over one shoulder. She's even put Nat in her hat and coat, and probably because the baby is so warm, her cheeks are pink and she's half asleep. While I scoop up our sleepy girl and all her stuff, Mei-Zhen's pen scratches on the citation she's filling out for me.

"This is your first violation," she says, handing me my copy of the paper. "So I'm only giving you a warning, not putting you on probation. But I still have to fine you."

I check it out. Fifty-eight dollars. One dollar for every minute we were late picking her up. "I'm sorry," I say again.

"Let's go."

Mei-Zhen's usually pretty nice, but it's her job to be a hard-ass at the daycare, and she takes it seriously. It's supposed to teach us responsibility. As we walk out, she says, "If you can't pay your fine in thirty days, one of you can work it off cleaning after school."

"Thanks. I'll let you know."

I'll probably just pay it. I make more per hour at Jimmy's than she'd give me credit for. Or maybe Amber will feel guilty enough about it to do the cleaning. When we get outside, Mei-Zhen raises her eyebrows at both my parking job (two spots) and the fact that I'm in a staff lot, but she doesn't say anything. I don't really care what she thinks anyway—my mind's already moved on to other things. What the hell am I gonna do with Natalie? I can't take her back to work with me, but David won't be there until seven to cover. If Dirk left at six, there isn't anyone there to pump gas, and if Jimmy finds out, he'll have to fire me.

It's not until I unlock the Mustang that I realize I don't have Nat's car seat. Shit. Amber walked her to school this morning because last night Natalie spit up all over the carrier. I cleaned it up in the tub, but the fabric was still wet when we had to leave for school.

I throw all the baby stuff in the trunk and start walking, carrying Natalie in my arms. I have to admit that for about ten seconds I considered wrapping her in a blanket and putting her down on the floorboards behind my seat. I mean, it's only seven blocks to our house. But what if something happened to her? Amber would never forgive me, and she already hates me as it is.

When we get home, my sister's on the couch with Gil watching *The Flintstones*. From the stench in the air and their red eyes, they've obviously been toking up. "What the hell?" I say. "I thought you must be dead."

She doesn't answer.

"I'm supposed to be at work, remember?" Gil giggles at the TV. "It was your turn to pick up Natalie at daycare!"

Amber's eyes stay glued to the screen, but I can tell she's listening. I yank open the window.

"Hey, man," Gil says. "It's freezing in here."

"Do you want to get the baby high?"

"Oh, right. Sorry."

"So what happened, Amber?" When she doesn't answer, I get right in her face and yell, "Hello? Anyone home?"

A door bangs and Mom comes lumbering down the hall, shouting, "What the hell's going on out here? I'm trying to sleep!"

Natalie bursts into tears in my arms. "Amber was supposed to pick up Nat at daycare because I had to work, but instead she's sitting here getting stoned with Gil! And now we've got a fifty-eight-dollar fine!" So far, Amber's face has been totally passive, but she flinches when I say how much we owe because of her stupid sulking. "Yeah, that's right. Fifty-eight bucks. And who's gonna pay it, Am? You?"

She still doesn't look at me.

"Because last time I checked, we pool our money, so even if you pay it, it still comes out of *our* savings. But you go ahead," I say. "Sit there like you didn't do anything wrong. Don't worry about the fact that I'm supposed to be at work right now, which means I'm probably gonna get fired! Does that make you happy, Amber? Is this what you wanted? To get back at me by getting me fired? Because if Jimmy finds out—"

"For fuck's sake, Crys," Mom says, grabbing my arm and making Natalie cry harder. "Will you calm down? Put the baby in the playpen and get out of here already."

"*You* have to watch her," I say. "They're too wrecked."

"Yeah, yeah, just go and stop yelling. You're killing my head."

"I mean it," I tell Mom. "And don't let them shut that window until the smoke clears out of here." I set Natalie in the playpen, and she blinks at me but stops crying. I kiss her cheek and head for the door. "I'll be back at seven fifteen to take her to Forward Momentum."

"Fine," Mom says. "Whatever."

I run all the way back to the school parking lot, and luckily my car's still there and I don't have a ticket. That's the last thing I need right now. It's already 6:40 when I get back to the gas station, and as predicted, Dirk is long gone. Rosa has taped up signs on all the pumps saying they're temporarily out of order, and I can tell from the steam coming out of her ears that I better stay far away from her. I spend the next twenty minutes shivering outside. As soon as David shows up, I'm gone, heading for home.

When I get there, Mom's doing a crossword and my sister's passed out on the couch asleep.

"Amber's supposed to be at work," I tell Mom.

"I think she called in sick."

"Oh, well, I'm so glad I gave up the rest of my shift so I can go to Forward Momentum."

"Have a good time," Mom says, not looking up from her puzzle.

I should know by now that sarcasm's lost on Mom. I go to pick up Nat, who is a whimpering mess, and she stretches her arms up to me. She's got tear streaks down her cheeks and she totally stinks.

"Did you feed her?" I ask Mom.

"Was I supposed to?"

"Jesus Christ," I mutter. "We'd all fucking starve to death if we relied on you for common sense."

"Funny," she says, not looking up from her crossword. "I thought I was doing you and your sister a favor."

I bite back my response. I don't trust myself not to start yelling again, and I don't really have time for that shit. In the bedroom, I change Nat, promising her food as soon as she's dressed again. I yank off my work shirt and pull on a flannel I find on the floor. Good enough. When we go out to the kitchen, Mom's made a bottle.

"Thanks," I say. I grab a jar of carrots and lentils to feed her at Forward Momentum. I have to come back in for her car seat, which is still in the tub, but eventually I get Nat settled in the back seat and she holds her bottle between her palms, sucking greedily.

"I'm sorry, baby," I tell her.

Once I'm buckled in, I make myself take five calming breaths before I back out. Jocelyn would be so proud. Maybe I *am* learning something at all these classes. We're fifteen minutes late, but at least we're there and I won't get fined or anything. We have a speaker on nutrition and everything goes okay until the very end. I'm so tired and stressed that I pack up Nat but forget to get my free baby stuff. As I'm strapping her into the car seat, Jocelyn comes out to the parking lot with the bag of freebies.

"I thought you might want this," she says.

"Yeah, thanks."

Jocelyn watches me for a second and then says, "Honey? How old is that seat?"

"What?"

"Where'd you get that car seat? How old is it?"

"Umm . . . I don't know. My cousin gave it to me, but I think she got it used."

"Did you know car seats expire?"

"Like milk?" I say, trying to make a joke.

She smiles. "Exactly like milk. Lift her out of there and I'll show you."

The last thing I want to do is take Nat out of the car seat, but Jocelyn's waiting. I don't have any choice. I bounce Nat in my arms while Jocelyn unbuckles the straps and pulls out the entire seat. She turns it over and shows me the base.

"Just like I thought. This one expired in 2010."

It doesn't take a genius to know how she spotted that I had an old car seat . . . the plastic is grubby from Jade's kids, and the fabric's worn through in places. "It seems okay to me."

"You're going to have to get something else," Jocelyn says. "It's not safe."

Great.

"But—"

"It's the law."

"Yeah, okay."

I am so, so, so, so, so, so tired. Why do I have to be in charge of everything? Why is everyone looking to me to solve all their problems? Mom with the rent, Gil with . . . well, everything, Amber's screw-ups? And especially Nat. I want to collapse onto the asphalt and sink down into it and disappear. But I can't show any weakness because then Jocelyn will call child services and say we can't take care of our baby. I force myself to straighten up.

I sigh. "I'll check into it."

"I'm serious," Jocelyn says. "I can't let you drive her around in that."

It hits me that she actually means right now. "But how am I supposed to get her home?"

Now it's her turn to sigh. "All right, well, it's probably better than nothing for tonight. But promise me you won't use it again."

I promise and she finally lets me go.

Fan-fucking-tabulous.

First a fifty-eight-dollar fine and now I'm supposed to pull a new car seat out of my butt. And to think that I thought the day I got into McPherson would be one I'd want to remember forever.

CHAPTER 17

By the time me and Nat get home from Forward Momentum, my head is pounding, my stomach's knotted up with sharp pains, and the baby's caught my mood. She's whiny and irritable as I lift her out of the car, kicking at me with her little feet. All I want to do is hand her off to Amber and crawl into bed and pull the covers over my head. What should've been my secret to enjoy until I was ready to share it was stolen from me by the inept Ms. Spellerman.

I have no doubt how it went down. Ms. Spellerman was probably coming back from the front office after emptying her inbox and saw Amber. Because I've been bugging her, she remembered who I was and said, "Oh, Miss Robbins, I have your letter for you."

Amber must've known she'd mixed us up but figured it would be easier to take whatever the woman had for me and hand it over later. But then Ms. Spellerman probably encouraged her to open it right there, thinking she could congratulate me or console me, however it worked out. And so Amber, always curious and thinking it really wouldn't matter because we don't have any secrets, opened my letter.

And that's when I came around the corner.

I shake off the memory and do the usual routine: unload Nat and leave her in the kitchen, feed Bonehead, clean up his turds, and put him in the car for the night. My life seems to revolve around cleaning up shit these days.

There's no one around in the house, so my dreams of pawning off Nat on my family dissolve. My stomach hurts so much, I swear there's something eating me from the inside. In the kitchen, I have to hold on to the back of the chair and take long, slow, deep breaths until the pain eases. The television's off and I assume Amber's gone out because it's only nine o'clock and she never goes to bed this early. Anger pulses through me. It's almost cold enough in the house to see my breath, but I'm flushed and hot from the waves of pain. All day I've felt guilty, but right now my sister's being such a bitch that I could shake her. No matter how bad she's screwed up in the past, I've always listened to her, given her a chance to explain. She's actually lucky she's not around, because I want to throw something at her.

I take Natalie into the bedroom, which has been

pitch-black ever since the night-light burned out. I flip on the floor lamp and stop and stare. Amber's divided the room in half by hanging a blanket from the rafters—a couple of blankets, actually, and an old stained sheet I think belongs to Bonehead. She's clearly trying to block off her bed so she doesn't have to look at me. Since the room's only the size of a single-car garage, it's now shrunk considerably and feels even more claustrophobic than usual. My breathing goes all weird and shallow, and I have to set Natalie's carrier down fast because I'm woozy. I sink onto my bed. Maybe I have the flu again. No—it's a combo of being pissed and feeling guilty that's making me so shaky.

"What the hell's all this?" I ask. I know Amber's behind the curtain, probably just lying there, but she doesn't answer, so I yank one of the blankets down.

Sure enough, she jumps off her bed and grabs it from the floor. "Stop it. Go away." I watch her struggle to hang it back up, and all the fight goes out of me. If she wants to be like this, I don't even care.

"Whatever," I say. "Let me know if you decide to grow up."

She loses her balance and almost falls off her bed, but I don't even reach out to steady her. I'm too tired to fix this now. I haven't stopped moving since the minute I got up this morning, and the last thing I had to eat was my free lunch and a couple of bites of strained carrots when I was trying to convince Natalie how delicious they were by eating them myself.

"Watch the baby," I say. Or maybe snarl. Either way, Amber doesn't answer.

I go out into the kitchen and dig around for something to eat. All the stuff we bought back in January with Mom's winnings is long gone, but I have hope the rest of my family isn't as smart as me when it comes to hunting and gathering. Behind the pots and pans in the drawer under the oven, I find a hidden box of mac and cheese.

While the macaroni's cooking, I get the last of the margarine and scrape off all the breadcrumbs and throw that bit in the garbage. We don't have any milk, so I use water. Not the first time.

When the food's ready, I take the pot and a fork out into the living room and plop my ass down on the floor in front of the space heater to eat my gourmet dinner. I haven't heard a peep out of Amber and Natalie's not crying or anything, so I pretend like I live here alone. It's almost peaceful, and my stomach unclenches a little. I scarf the whole thing by myself, resting the pot in my lap for warmth.

Later, after I've brushed my teeth with water so cold that I swear there are little ice crystals in it, I go back to our room. Amber's got the blankets hanging up again. Natalie's asleep in her expired car seat and I lift her out, praying I don't wake her. I put her in my bed between me and the wall so she won't fall out, and I turn off the light. We're afraid Nat will freeze to death in her crib, so lately we've been taking turns sleeping with her.

I know I should let it go for tonight, but I can't. "Are we ever going to talk about it?"

Silence.

"You didn't even let me explain." Nat wiggles next to me, her body warm against my chest. "I only applied to see if I could get in. I wasn't going to take off or anything. I want you to come with me."

"To Kansas?" she finally asks, like I've suggested a trip to Iraq. "Why the hell would I want to go there?"

"I don't know . . . I just . . . It's a really good opportunity for me, and in four years—"

"What kind of an opportunity?"

That's when I realize she doesn't know about the automotive restoration course, that she thought I'd just randomly picked Kansas. Like anyone would do that. For the next ten minutes I tell her all about the program. The bedroom is dark and cold and she doesn't say a word, but I can hear the excitement building in my voice and for the first time since I saw Amber with that letter, my stomach relaxes. I tell her how much I'll learn, how I'll never have to worry about a job or money again, how I could take care of us all. I give her the hard sell, and then I wait to see what she thinks.

"What about me?" she asks.

"What do you mean? I just said—"

"Yeah," she says. "I heard you. I . . . I . . . I . . . But what about Aunt Ruby and the Glass Slipper? What about our apartment? What about our plans to buy a house together?" My stomach tightens again as I try to explain. "Aunt Ruby isn't even forty yet. She's not gonna retire anytime soon. You could go with me, and in four years—"

"What? I'm supposed to go along to be the babysitter?"

"I thought you could maybe get a job. Or you could go to college too."

"Yeah, right. I hate high school, so sign me up for four more years."

"It's not the same thing—"

"Forget it."

"Come on, Am—"

"No," she says. I hear a scuffling noise, and then the light comes on and she's standing over me and I'm blinking up at her. Natalie squirms and whimpers next to me.

"Amber—"

"You lied to me. I know you took the SATs. I went back and asked Ms. Spellerman. She said you even took a class on Tuesday nights. All those times you said you were seeing David you were lying to me. And I was happy for you, excited you'd finally met a nice guy. But now, after that, I can't trust you, Crys. I'm not leaving my family and moving to the middle of nowhere with you. If you won't stick to our plan, then forget it. You're on your own."

"But—"

"Leave me alone. I'm going to sleep."

I struggle to get up, but Natalie's body is pressed against me, and she's finally fallen asleep again—I really don't want to wake her. Amber switches off the light and I decide to let her have the last word for tonight. But then I can't help myself. "We'll talk about it tomorrow."

"No, we won't."

This time I keep my mouth shut. I lie there in the dark, telling myself I can fix this. Somehow I'll make Amber realize I'm doing this for us. I cuddle our sweet baby close and something magical happens, like it always does when she's in my arms. My body relaxes, the worries I carry all day melt a little, and this basic need to take care of Natalie and protect her wells up inside of me, like soothing warm water and some sort of longing combined. My mind shuts down and I sleep until she wakes me at five in the morning by tugging on my hair.

"Stop that." I pry her little fingers out of my curls and drift off again. I know she's awake next to me, but I'm so tired I can't shake off sleep. Maybe she'll lie there quietly for a while. "Go back to sleep. Please?"

At first she's happy it's a new day, and she lies there

babbling, but after a while, because she's a baby and she doesn't care if I'm about to drop dead from exhaustion, she decides it's time to get up. She wiggles around, squirming and kicking. Then she grabs my arm, digging her sharp little nails into the skin.

"Ouch!"

She's probably hungry and undoubtedly wet, and I know I have to get up, but I just want five more minutes. When I don't respond, she starts to whimper and kick me harder. It's so cold in the room, I can't face the day yet. I try again to cuddle her. But I know it's a lost cause when she starts to scream.

"Okay, fine. I'm getting up." I drag myself out from under the covers into the icy air.

There's noise from Amber's side of the room and then she bumps into me in the dark. "Where is she?" she asks. "I'll take her."

"Really?"

"I'm awake anyway."

She lifts Natalie out of my bed and they go into the living room. As I settle back in for a couple more hours of sleep, I feel a huge sense of relief. Amber didn't sound angry at all. She must've forgiven me.

Amber and Natalie are gone when I finally wake up. I've missed PE again. God, I hope I don't flunk that course. How pathetic not to graduate because I failed sit-ups and running a mile in the rain. I don't see Amber all day, but I figure she's cooling off and thinking about everything, so I don't try to find her. After school I zip over to Jimmy's to get my paycheck so I can deposit it. Amber usually picks up Natalie on Fridays, but just in case, I plan to swing back by the daycare afterward and make sure.

There's a huge line at the bank—it's payday—and I have to wait for over half an hour. I don't know if it's all the tension in my life or what, but my feet hurt and my lower back aches. It's like I'm a little old lady. Finally I get up to the counter and hand over my check, telling the woman how much cash I need back.

I have to fill the Mustang's tank, pay our daycare fine, and buy some food. I asked Han at lunch to help me find a car seat. He's the thrift store king, and he promised to score something ASAP, so I'll need a little money for that, also. I made sure he knew to check for an expiration date.

When the teller hands me my receipt, I glance at the balance out of habit. I like to see our account growing. Except . . . it's not. My insides plunge like I'm on one of those scary rides at Oaks Park. I've already taken a step away from the counter, but I stop and go back. "Excuse me?" I say. "Is this right?"

The teller looks at her computer and my slip and nods. "Yeah. Is there a problem?"

"I should have almost twice that much."

I know what's happened before she tilts the monitor toward me so I can see the screen, and all the pains in my body ratchet up. "There was a withdrawal this morning," she explains. "And then you made a deposit just now." I swear, my heart stops for what seems like forever. Amber's removed half of our savings. It's pretty clear she's bailed on me the way she thinks I've bailed on her. Nothing could've prepared me for how much this would feel like being run over by a garbage truck. I grab the edge of the counter until the wooziness passes. What have I done to us?

CHAPTER 18

At the daycare, Mei-Zhen is surprised to see me. Not only did Amber pick up Nat an hour ago, but she paid the fine, too. I duck back out into the pouring rain. It's only four thirty and the days are finally getting a little longer, but the sky's so gray that it's almost dark. When I pull into the driveway, Amber's coming out the front door. She's got Natalie strapped into the Snugli, and she's pulling a pink rain poncho over them both. I hope Nat can breathe under there.

I slop through the mud that Bonehead's churned up, making a wide arc to avoid him and his filthy paws. As always, he's thrilled to see me. He probably thinks I'm gonna let him in the car. On the tiny porch, Amber's struggling to open an old polka-dot umbrella of Mom's.

"Where're you going?" I yell over the pounding of the rain.

"Work."

"Let me change and I'll give you a ride."

"No, thanks." She steps around me.

"Amber, don't be stupid. You'll both get soaked and you'll get sick again."

"Germs make you sick," she says, "not bad weather."

"Well, you can still get a chill."

She ignores me, heading for the sidewalk. I go after her, but then Bonehead gives his chain a desperate yank and pulls the stake right out of the soft ground. By the time I've caught him, unhooked the chain, and shoved him into the back seat, Amber's a block and a half away. I catch up to her, slowing the car and rolling down the passenger side window.

"Get in," I say. "You've made your point."

She keeps walking, the wind tugging on the umbrella until it turns it inside out. Bonehead leans over the seat and sticks his head out the window, barking at her. I hear a wail come from under the poncho.

"Amber! Goddammit. Just get in the car!"

She's at the bus stop now, and she steps into the shelter, throwing the useless umbrella on the ground. I'm in the no-parking zone, but I don't give a damn. I'm about to get out and force her ass into the car when the bus comes barreling up behind me and the driver lays on his horn. I don't have any choice but to step on the gas, and as I drive away, I glance in my rearview mirror and see my stupid, stubborn, soaking wet sister get on the bus. Fine. Whatever.

After work, I stop by the Glass Slipper, but Aunt Ruby says Amber and Natalie caught a ride with Jade. "I didn't even know she had a car," I say.

"New boyfriend," Aunt Ruby says by way of explanation. "He's even got a job."

I hope he's had a vasectomy, too. Otherwise, with Jade's record, he'll be a father in nine months.

When I get home, Gil's cuddling Nat on the couch. "Where's Amber?"

"Out with Jade."

It's never good news when Amber hangs out with our cousin. I watch TV with Gil, but the whole time I'm listening for a car. At one in the morning I give up, change Nat, and take her to bed with me again. It's Amber's turn, and the fact that she's not here because of what I've done penetrates every tired, aching muscle with a sadness that follows me into my dreams.

I have the early shift on Saturday, which works out great because now Amber won't have to take Nat to the Glass Slipper tonight. Bringing the baby is fine with Aunt Ruby, but neither of us really likes it. Natalie shouldn't be hanging out in a tavern, even if she is too little to really know where she is. But we do what we gotta do.

By the time the Chevelle comes roaring into the lot at

five minutes to three, I'm half frozen and more than ready to go home. "I'm out the door, Rosa."

She nods, never taking her eyes off the cash register. "See you, Crys."

David's climbing out of his car when I get to mine. "Hey, College Girl. Congratulations."

"Thanks, Stanford Boy." I haven't seen him since I got my letter, but I was dying to tell someone who'd be happy for me, so yesterday I emailed him from the computer lab at school.

"Anything exciting happen today?" he asks.

Yesterday's storm has blown out, leaving the weather sunny and breezy, and I lean against the Mustang, feeling the cold metal through my thin jacket. "Mmm . . . nothing much here at work. Amber's still pissed, though."

"She'll get over it," he says. "Once she figures out you're doing it for all three of you."

I told him in the email about Amber and Ms. Speller-man, too. Now I kind of regret being such a blabbermouth, but it's nice to have someone on my side. "We'll see," I say. "You better get your ass inside before Rosa has a coronary. It's another big lottery night."

"Okay. Let's do coffee. Soon."

"Yeah, all right," I say. But I laugh as I get into the car because seriously, who says "Let's do coffee"?

At home, Han's in the living room drinking a beer with Gil while Natalie naps in her playpen. She looks so sweet when she sleeps that I can almost forgive her for all those midnight feedings. Strewn around the living room are half a dozen Nordstrom shopping bags.

"What's all this?" I ask.

"Sit down. You are about to be amazed." Han's grinning at me. He leads me over to the couch and hands me one of the bags. "Go ahead. Dig in."

I lift out the cutest pair of green overalls in exactly Nat's size. There's a white turtleneck—sprinkled with pink and green flowers—to go with them. They look brand-new. "Wow. These are—"

"Keep going." Han is hovering over me, holding another bag and practically dancing. Gil's watching, his eyes sparkling in the light from the TV.

I set the overalls aside and pull out three more pairs—red, navy, and yellow. All of them have matching turtlenecks, too. "Han, this is incredible. Are they for Natalie? Where'd you get them?"

"There was an ad online for a bunch of baby stuff, and I called the lady about ten seconds after she posted it. She said she'd give it all to me as long as I picked it up today."

"She *gave* you all this? For free?"

"Yep. She'd been saving it for her next baby, but then she had twin boys."

"Wow."

All the clothes are folded really nice, like they've come straight from the store, and in the bottom of the first bag, I find a white fur coat with a shiny purple lining. There's even a matching hat and tiny mittens "Oh my God." It's all so beautiful. I get that tingly feeling in my nose, like I might cry, and I blink hard.

"Check this out," Gil says, reaching into the bag at his feet. "Blankets!" He pulls them out, one after another, like Kleenex out of a dispenser. They're all pinks and creams and lavenders—some of them look handmade, too.

"But why would she give me blankets if she had twins?"

"Duh," Han says. "Those are too girly for boys."

I press a yellow blankie to my face and surreptitiously wipe away a few tears. Han and Gil pretend not to notice. "Look at this, Nat," I say, getting up and taking it over to the playpen. She's awake now and looks up at me with her baby blues as I lift off the stained quilt Jade gave us and drape this new one over her. She immediately grabs it with her tiny fists and sticks a corner in her mouth. "She likes it."

"You haven't even looked at all the stuff," Han says. "Her kid's, like, four now, so these other bags have bigger clothes in them."

Now I do cry. I want to hide it because I feel silly, but there's no point. I wish Amber was here to see it all. At least then we'd both be crying together. "I'm sorry," I say, wiping my eyes with the tail of my work shirt. "It's just so . . . so nice. I can't believe it."

"Oh, you haven't even seen the best parts yet," Han says. "Close your eyes."

I do, and a minute later he tells me I can open them. Sitting in the middle of the living room is one of those totally deluxe baby strollers. It's got big thick tires, a sun shade over the top, pockets everywhere, and a padded seat that's adjustable so you can lay it down if your baby gets tired. It looks brand-new, too. It's so much better than the chintzy canvas one we've been using that I don't even care who sees me crying now.

"This is so . . . I don't understand. Why didn't she keep the stroller?" I ask, the tears running freely and my smile about to break my face.

"She got a double one," Han says. He reaches behind the couch. "And get this . . ." He lifts up a hot pink and bright yellow car seat that's about a hundred—no, a thousand—times better than the piece of expired crap we have.

"She *gave* you that?" I say, rubbing my hands over the soft fabric. "For free? I can't believe it."

"She didn't want it because she thought her twins should have matching ones."

"Did you and Amber have matching car seats?" Gil asks, laughing.

"Yeah, right." I say. "That's just stupid. But I'm glad she's so stupid. And nice."

"That's rich people," Gil tells us, like he knows a lot of them.

"Thank you, Han. Thank you so much." I actually hug him, and he pats me lightly on the back like he's afraid of breaking me. It's hard to talk over the lump in my throat. "It's like Christmas in the movies. You're awesome, Han. You're totally awesome. I needed this so much right now."

He turns a little pink and then says, "The lady told me the car seat's a convertible one. When Nat gets bigger, you make a few adjustments and it becomes a forward-facing seat. Whatever that means."

I laugh. I'm not sure either, but if it means we don't have to get another one anytime soon, I'm extra grateful. I sift through all the amazing stuff while the guys watch basketball on TV. Every once in a while I catch Han looking at me, his eyes bright, proud of himself. He should be.

There're tights and shirts and dresses, pajamas, and about a dozen of those elastic headbands Amber loves so much. There are even four pairs of shoes: two everyday ones and two patent-leather pairs. Some of the stuff still has the tags attached. I can't wait to throw out every old, stained, crappy thing of Nat's.

After a while I lean back on the couch, all the stuff piled

around me and across my lap. I'm buried in treasure. "Where's Amber? Did she see this?"

"Not yet. She went to work early," Gil says. "I volunteered to watch Nat until you got home. It's easy, since all she ever does is sleep."

"I wish," I say.

All these nice things . . . this is what I want for Natalie. And for me and Amber, too. If I can graduate from McPherson, I'll make the kind of money that lets me be the one who gives away hand-me-downs to young moms. I wish I could make Amber see that somehow. That I would be doing the program for all three of us, and I'm not trying to mess up her life.

After a while, Gil's asleep, and me and Han are so cold that we dress up Natalie in a new turtleneck and overalls and go to Chuck E. Cheese's. Pizza is the last thing I want, since Gil brings it home all the time, but Chuck E. Cheese's is one place that welcomes babies and the food's pretty cheap. It's so warm in there that it's almost hot, and I shed my jacket for the first time all day. Han buys himself a pizza and me the unlimited salad bar, which we secretly share. I tell him all about McPherson and the automotive restoration program.

"That sounds fantastic," he says.

I shrug. "Yeah, well . . . I doubt I'll really get to go."

"I think you should. Don't give up too easy."

"Are you trying to get rid of me?"

"God, no. I'd miss you all a lot."

This is kind of sweet to hear, but also a little embarrassing for us both, and I jump up to get more salad. When I come back, we don't talk about anything important. After a couple of hours, Nat's sound asleep and I'm dead tired myself, so we get ready to head out. I know Amber's still mad, but when I button up Natalie's soft new coat, I can't help thinking that all in all, it's been a pretty good night.

CHAPTER 19

W hen me and Nat get home from Chuck E. Cheese's, we find Amber in the kitchen and she's trashed. She hasn't been this bad in more than a year. I want to blame Jade—I know Amber was over at her house—but it's my fault. I let her down. I lied to her. I went behind her back.

She's stumbling around the kitchen trying to make herself a grilled cheese sandwich on some flattened white bread Mom brought home from the bakery, using cheese she's peeled off a slice of old pizza.

"You don't really want to eat that, do you?" I ask, setting Nat down. Her new car seat's so deluxe that it's too big for the table, so I have to put her on the floor.

"Hi, Cattie Battie Pattie Mattie Nattie!" Amber says, leaning over the baby and grabbing her toes.

"Stop it," I say. "She's asleep."

"Oh, well, excuuuuuse me!" Amber backs off, holding her hands in the air until she stumbles and has to catch herself on the kitchen counter. "I wouldn't want to mess up your plans for her life like you did mine."

"Sit down and I'll make us some sandwiches."

I've hidden some Velveeta behind Nat's cereal in the top cupboard, and I climb on a chair to get it down. While I'm making the food, Amber stalks off, but she's back a minute later carrying an armload of the new baby clothes.

"Did your boyfriend give us all this?"

"Han's not my boyfriend." I know she's winding me up because he used to like her and now he crushes on me.

"Whatever!" She throws everything up in the air and laughs as little shirts and dresses fall down around her, some landing on Natalie.

"Would you stop it?" I pick up the clothes and take them back to the living room. "Sit down. Here's your sandwich."

She grabs it, and I'm left holding the plate. She tears the bread into pieces and stuffs them into her mouth like a lunatic. I clench my hands to keep from slapping some sense into her. I know it won't help.

"I'm not moving to Kansas," she says, spraying crumbs all over her shirt.

"I kinda figured that out already."

"Just because you're so smart you think you can tell me

what to do all the time. But you can't. We might be twins, but you don't own me."

I sigh. I'm holding my sandwich, but I don't really want it anymore.

"You gonna eat that?" Amber asks.

I hand it over and she stuffs it into her mouth, hardly chewing. I wait until she swallows in case she chokes, and then I take Nat into our room to get ready for bed.

Later, I offer to hold Amber's hair while she pukes, but she tells me to get lost. Instead, I stand outside the bathroom door listening to her retch, and when she's done, I try to help her down the hall, but she shakes me off again. She wants to take Nat to bed with her, but I won't let her, and she yells at me that I'm a lousy sister and that it's her turn to sleep with the baby.

"It was your turn last night," I say. "You weren't here."

This seems to confuse her enough to sound reasonable, and she ducks behind the wall of blankets and falls onto the bed, giggling. When I can tell by her breathing that she's asleep, I turn her on her side just like old times. In the morning I bring Amber a glass of water and a couple of generic painkillers while she's still in bed.

"Tell me one thing," I say. "Did you take your half out of our savings?"

"Yep. And I could've taken more," she says, implying she's kicked in more than I have.

It's probably true, but we've always called it even. "Take it all," I say, hurt she's been keeping track.

"I'm looking out for myself. Just like you."

"Whatever. But please tell me you didn't hide it in our room."

"What do you think I am? Stupid? I opened an account of my own."

That's one good thing, I guess.

Weeks go by and Amber has pretty much stopped talking to me entirely. But every Sunday she leaves her schedule on my bed so I can figure out who will pick up and watch Nat when. I drop the baby off at daycare every morning now, since Amber won't ride in the car with me anymore. We pass Natalie back and forth with a minimum of words, each doing our share according to the schedule I make, and Amber basically ignores me the rest of the time.

Not having my sister talk to me is like I've cut off my arm or ripped out one of my vital organs. My heart is missing. There's no one to bitch to, or laugh with, or ride in the car with me. Sure, Natalie's around, but it's not the same as having Amber. My sister's been next to me for my whole life. Without her, part of me is gone, and it leaves me with an ache so deep that I can't shake it. My only consolation is that maybe she's feeling it too. If she is, she hides it better than me.

By the third week of Amber ignoring me, it's time to send in the deposit to McPherson if I want to go. That's when I decide to forget all about Kansas. Maybe if I do, me and Amber can make up. And at this point, that's all I care about. I can't go on like this, on my own.

At least, that's what I tell myself. But part of me obviously wants someone to talk me into paying the money, which is probably why I bring it up with David while we're changing the oil in a '39 Dodge. It's a one-person job, but business is slow and Jimmy's in a good mood because his wife's gone to visit her sister for a couple of weeks, so he doesn't care if we slack off.

David's under the car and I'm leaning against the fender with the hood up. "I guess I'm not going to Kansas."

"Why not?"

"Amber's not gonna change her mind. Besides, I never paid the deposit."

"You should send it in. You can always get it back," he says. "You don't want to give up your spot, in case she comes around."

"It was due today, and it's too late to send a money order now."

David rolls out from under the car on a creeper. "Pay with a credit card."

I laugh. "Yeah, right. Let me see . . . should I use my gold card or my air miles one?" I drop a rag on his chest and he wipes his hands.

"Oh, right. Yeah, sorry. Well, use mine. You can pay me cash."

My heart speeds up a little with excitement. If I pay online today, I won't lose my place. "Really?"

"Yeah. No problem," he says as he dumps the dirty oil in the recycling barrel. "Do you want my platinum or my black American Express?"

"Whichever one you'll let me keep."

We laugh and head for the break room, where we use his phone to get online and pay up. "I'll bring you the money on Monday," I promise.

"Whenever."

Nice to be him.

The sense of dread I've been carrying around about giving up so soon on college lifts a little, and on the drive home I can't help thinking that while it sucks Amber's so mad, maybe David offering his credit card is a sign she'll come around.

That night, Mom finally notices me and Amber are fighting. Or not so much fighting as not really speaking. I'm sure she must've figured out something was wrong sooner, but she only likes to act hasty when she's gambling. The rest of the time, she's on her own slow schedule.

"So why aren't you talking to your sister?" she asks me while I'm making a bottle for Nat.

"Correction," I say. "She's not speaking to me."

"Tell me it's not over a guy and I don't need to know any more."

"I applied to college and got in."

"College, huh? Good for you, Crys."

She says this without even looking up from her crossword. Seriously? I get into college and that's all the enthusiasm she can muster? It's not like school's that important in our family. I get that. But you'd think college would be a bigger deal. I don't know why I'm surprised at her lack of interest. This *is* Mom we're talking about. Once we turned eighteen, she was done with us. If not long before.

I test the temp of the baby formula like they showed us in prenatal class. It's fine and Natalie grabs it from me. I can't believe how big she's getting. It's crazy. In a week, she'll be nine months old. How did that happen so fast? She can sit up on her own now, and she's a lot . . . I don't know . . . it's like her personality is blooming more and more every day. I wish I could talk to Amber about it.

And not only is Natalie growing up fast, but *I'm* getting really old too. Next week, me and Amber will be nineteen. God. We're ancient. I sit down at the table, exhausted by the thought.

"Okay," Mom says, "I'll bite. Why's Amber mad about you going to college?"

"Because it's in Kansas."

This finally makes her look up. She even sets her pen down. "Kansas? What the hell's in Kansas?"

I tell her.

She nods, picking up her pen again. "Seems like your kinda place."

"I know. And once I graduate, I'll be able to get a really good job. Maybe even open my own shop."

"So what's the problem?" Mom asks.

"Well, you know . . . we had a plan."

"Oh, right, to leave this place and never darken our doorstep again."

"Not exactly. We just want to move out. And I did say I'd work full-time while Amber learned the business from Aunt Ruby. If I go to college, that won't really be possible. I want Amber to come along, but she doesn't think the Glass Slipper can wait."

"Maybe she doesn't want to sit around putting her life on hold for four years."

I sigh. "I know, I know. It's a lot to ask, but this is for our future."

"I hate to point out the obvious," Mom says, "but the last time I checked, you two girls weren't actually *Siamese* twins."

I stare at her, startled by the idea.

"You mean go to Kansas without her?"

She shrugs.

Oh, hell.

Could I really do that?

CHAPTER 20

On our nineteenth birthday, Amber's gone when I wake up. Before I go to work, I leave a bouquet of daffodils and a new book of number puzzles on her bed. She gives me exactly nothing. I try not to take it personally, but it's kind of hard.

For about five minutes, I consider what Mom said about me going to McPherson without Amber, but I know I can't do it. We made a deal. I might've lied to my sister, and spent our money on things she didn't know about, and kept secrets from her, but we agreed to raise Natalie together, and if she won't go to Kansas, then I can't go without her.

Not only did we promise each other, but what would be the point? It's not like I could take Nat with me and still go to college. And if she stays here, then how's Amber going to train to be the manager at the Glass Slipper? It's one thing to take a baby with her to work now, but when she's a tod-dler? Not gonna happen. Amber might not be speaking to me, but we're still in this together until Natalie's grown up and doesn't need us anymore.

In early April, David catches me at the pumps and asks me to go to the swap meet with him on the weekend.

"I've got to work," I say.

"It opens Thursday. How about then?"

"Don't you have school?"

"Senioritis," he says. "Let's skip."

"Yeah, okay, but I have to go to first period."

"You have a test?"

"Uh, yeah," I say, not willing to admit I'm taking PE for the second time, even if I did flunk it before because I had bronchitis. Somehow the excuse seems lame.

"Your ride or mine?" he asks.

"You know you want to go in the Mustang."

He grins. "You drive, I'll pay for parking."

"Deal."

David loves my car way more than he likes his slick piece of machinery. There's nothing to do to his Chevelle except change the oil every once in a while. I think he can totally imagine himself working on my car, though.

Before PE, I find Han. "Can you do me a favor?"

"Sure."

I love how he doesn't ask what it is before he agrees. I

wish Amber was that easy. "Can you go to daycare at lunch? It's my day, but I need you to cover for me."

"Amber can't do it?"

"I'm skipping to go to the swap meet. I don't want her to know."

"Is it cool? I mean, with the daycare?" Han asks.

"I don't know. Maybe tell Mei-Zhen I've got a make-up test I forgot about? She knows you from coming in with us. She might not let you stay, but at least if you show up, I don't look totally irresponsible."

"Yeah, okay," he says. "Me and Nat are buds. We'll hang together."

"Thanks. I owe you."

"No problem."

I pick up David at Jimmy's around ten o'clock and we head out to the Expo Center. It's insanely busy, and we have to take a shuttle to get from the lot to the exhibits because we've parked so far away.

"I'm looking for a right taillight lens," I tell David. "If you see one, point it out, but stay cool."

He laughs. "Yes, boss."

Now that me and Amber keep our money separate, I can spend mine on anything I want, and if I can find a lens, I'm getting it. We walk up and down the aisles for hours. There are tons of grandpas pushing babies in strollers, and for a minute I think I should've sprung Nat, since it's such a nice day out, but honestly, I'm really glad to be somewhere without her that isn't work or school.

We've checked out all the cars for sale, both running and not, and picked out our favorites. Then we decide it's time to eat. We find a hippie selling veggie hot dogs—it is Portland after all—and load them up with mustard and onions, then walk while we eat.

I've just taken a huge messy bite when David starts laughing. I think I've got food on my face, but then I see he's pointing off in the distance at a man walking toward us. The guy's probably in his sixties or so, has a gray beard, and is wearing one of those old-fashioned hats. I forget what you call them. He's got on jeans, cowboy boots, and a yellow tank-top, but what David's obviously laughing at is the sandwich board he's wearing.

It says: 1934 STUDEBAKER PARTS WANTED.

Underneath that, there's a phone number and email address.

"Hey," I say to David, instantly recognizing the guy. "Don't laugh at him."

"Sorry. It just seems funny. A walking want ad."

"Do you know who that guy is?"

"Should I?"

"He's only the most awesome metal guy in Portland. Probably on the West Coast." For all I know, maybe in the whole country. "He can build anything from nothing. Jimmy told me he's making one Studebaker out of two or three bodies he cut into pieces, kinda like his own version of a kit car."

"Cool."

"I know, right?" I say. "Legend has it he needed a trunk lid and there're only, like, three in the whole country for a 'thirty-four. So he talked a guy into shipping him his and then he cast a mold from it and made himself one, and then sent the original back. You can't even tell the difference between the two, though. He's a car god."

We're walking by him at that moment and David makes a show out of bowing down to him. The guy breaks into a big grin, holds his hands together, bows back, and says, "Bless you." We all laugh and he keeps going. He doesn't know what the joke is, but obviously he doesn't care. I'm too shy to actually talk to him today, but Jimmy said he'd introduce us sometime.

"To him, restoration's a real art. That's why I want to go to McPherson," I say. "But even if I don't get to study there, I'm gonna be just like him."

"Except without the beard."

I laugh. "Hopefully."

I make it back to daycare in time to pick up Natalie, and when we get home, Amber's in the kitchen doing a puzzle and eating pizza. She ignores me when I say hello, but as I walk by, she holds out a thick envelope.

"What's that?"

"Your friend Ms. Spellerman asked me to give you that," Amber says. "She couldn't find you. I guess you were skipping?"

I look at the return address. My chest instantly tightens and my breathing gets shallow. It's my financial aid. Natalie's wiggling around in her carrier, whining to get out, so I lay the envelope on the table, almost like it's too hot to touch. In a way, it is, and I'm scared. I put Nat in the playpen, and I can feel Amber's interest so intensely that it's almost like she's staring at me, but when I look over, her eyes are on the puzzle book.

I want to tear open the envelope, but I can't bring myself to do it yet. If it's good news, I might be able to convince Amber to go to Kansas, but if it's just middle of the road—a lot of loans or not a big enough package—then I'm sunk.

"Well? Aren't you going to open it?" she asks.

"Uh, yeah. Okay." I pick up the envelope and slide my finger under the flap, promptly cutting myself. A little line of blood appears, bright red, and I lick it off. My heart's racing like the Mustang's engine. Okay. This is it. I unfold all the papers and have a look.

This can't be right.

Can it?

It has to be some sort of mistake.

But maybe it's not . . .

"So?" Amber asks.

"I'm . . . I'm not sure . . . but I think I got a full-ride scholarship . . ."

The hostility Amber's been carrying around for so long vanishes right in front of my face. For a second she looks proud of me, and hope flares in my heart. "Really?"

"I think so." I scan the next couple of pages. "And work-study, whatever that is. And it looks like some grants."

I'm so close to asking Amber to look at the packet, to make sure I'm reading it right, when the familiar wall around her goes back up. "Well, that's great," she says. "I hope you'll be very happy there. Send me a postcard."

"Amber, I can't go without you."

"Well, you're gonna have to. Because I'm not going anywhere."

"Don't you get it?" I ask. "This is like *real money*. It's a gift. We don't have to pay it back!"

"So what? We never planned to borrow money in the first place. We planned to get an apartment and save money for a house of our own. Remember?"

"But this will make going to college so easy. It's not only my tuition and books. There's money to live on. We can keep our savings."

Amber sets down her pen and takes a deep breath, letting it out super slow. "I'm not trying to be a bitch, Crys. But we had a plan, and it's a good one. I get that you could maybe earn more if you go to college, but someday Jimmy's gonna retire, and he's probably gonna leave you the garage. Or at least by then you'll be able to get a loan and buy it. I know you don't think going to Kansas is any big deal, but I don't want to be away from my family."

"You'd have me and Nat."

"I know that's enough for you, but it's not enough for me."

"It's only for four years."

Amber throws her puzzle book across the room in frustration. "Yeah, well, that's what you told me about high school, and it feels like about four *hundred* years."

"This would be totally different. Please, Amber? Say you'll think about it?"

My heart's beating faster than normal and my hands are so damp they've left marks on the papers. I can almost see her wavering. But then Amber crosses her arms and my hope disappears.

"I'm sorry, Crystal. It's too much to ask. I don't want to leave Portland. I would be so lonely there. I know I would. And it doesn't matter to you because you'd have your classes to go to and cars to work on, but I can't do it." She looks at me for the first time in weeks, meeting my eyes. "We'll be fine here. Really. Our plan's a good one. Please stop asking me to go to Kansas."

CHAPTER 21

The next couple of weeks are weird. In a way, things get better between me and Amber, but only on the surface. I don't mention college, and she starts talking to me a little bit. Nothing important, but she's not stonewalling me anymore.

David has a look at my financial aid stuff, and it's even better news than I thought. Work-study means I can get a job on campus, up to twenty hours a week, and it pays way better than a regular job. Also, the grants give me money toward my living expenses.

"Essentially," he explains, "they're paying you to go there."

"If I get to go," I say.

"You better or I'll never forgive you."

He thinks I should go without Amber, but I still don't see it as an option. It would screw up all three of our lives instead of making them better. I've decided that she's right and I will probably own Jimmy's shop someday, so if she doesn't change her mind, then I'm going to suck it up and forget I ever heard of McPherson. I send in my acceptance paperwork, though. Just in case.

The other weird thing about these past couple of weeks is that Han has disappeared at lunch. Ever since Shenice quit school, it's been the two of us on the days I'm not with Natalie, but now I'm stuck eating on my own because I can never find him. The days are warmer, so sometimes I take a nap in the Mustang. I'm even more exhausted than usual. David's so busy with all his fancy high school awards banquets and his tennis team that he doesn't want to work much, and I've picked up his shifts at the garage. I'm now working almost every night except the Thursdays when I have to go to Forward Momentum.

Between work and school, I almost never see Han or Amber anymore, and although Natalie's growing and getting her own little personality, I'm kind of bored with only her for company. That's why one Saturday night, I invite Han over to play video games. Not my favorite activity in the world, but he likes it.

"Will there be pizza?" he asks.

"Seriously?"

"I love Big Apple pizza."

"You're such a loser," I say, and he laughs. "Yeah, okay. I'll get some."

Han comes by about nine o'clock. Amber's at the Glass Slipper and Gil and Mom are playing cards at Aunt Pearl's, so it's the three of us. Nat's happily swatting at a mobile and rolling around in her playpen while we play games on Han's computer.

"So where've you been?" I ask after a while.

"When?"

"At lunch."

"Oh . . . around."

He's totally hiding something. "Do you have a girlfriend?"

He blushes.

"You do! Who is it?"

"I don't have a girlfriend."

"A boyfriend?" I never pegged Han for the type.

He turns even redder. "No boyfriend."

"So what's up? You haven't joined the chess team or computer club or something geeky like that, have you?"

"No."

"Oh, God. Don't tell me you tried out for the spring musical."

He laughs. "Yeah, right."

"So? What, then? What's the big secret?"

He takes a deep breath. "Don't be mad at me."

"Why would I be mad?"

"I was trying to help."

My insides tighten at his defensiveness. "What the hell's going on?"

"Nothing, really."

"Han?"

"Okay . . . I've been hanging out with Natalie."

"Natalie who?"

He looks at me like I'm stupid and points at the playpen. "That Natalie."

"You mean with Amber? When she goes to daycare at lunch?"

Is he dating my sister and they didn't want to tell me?

"Not exactly."

And then something snaps into place. On Thursday, I'd had the weirdest conversation with Mei-Zhen. She told me that we couldn't keep sending Han in to hang out with Natalie at lunchtime because she's our responsibility. At the time, I thought she meant that day I skipped to go to the swap meet, but now I get it.

"You mean you've been going instead of Amber?" I ask.

"Why?" Han's staring at me with those huge blue eyes, and he looks scared. "What's going on? Why hasn't Amber been going to daycare at lunch?"

"Uh . . ."

"Spit it out."

"Maybe I shouldn't be the one to tell you this."

Panic surges through me. I already know where this is going, but I have to hear it. "Say it!"

"Amber dropped out." He scoots away like I might hit him. Or maybe he's afraid of the streams of fire shooting out of my eyes.

"That stupid bitch," I say. "I'm gonna kill her." I start packing up Natalie's stuff so I can take her with me to the Glass Slipper. There's no way I'm waiting for Amber to finish work before I yell at her.

But Han stops me. "I'll watch Nat," he offers.

"I don't know when I'll be back."

He shrugs. "Doesn't matter."

He's looking at me kind of funny and I say, "What?"

"Nothing . . . Just drive safe, okay?"

It occurs to me as I head out to the car that he's offered to watch the baby in case I drive too fast. Like I would ever do that with her in the car. Still, I am pretty fucking mad, and once I get my hands on Amber, she's gonna be toast. Since I don't have Nat with me, I do end up speeding, daring my stupid friendly neighborhood cop to pull me over.

It's darts night at the Glass Slipper, and the parking lot's packed. I squeeze the Mustang in between two big-ass trucks. Hopefully I'll leave before the drunks come out and bash in my doors with theirs. The last thing I have time for is more body work on my car.

The kitchen door is open to let in the late-April air, and I take the crumbling steps two at a time, the screen door banging behind me.

"Hey, Crystal," Brad says from his place over the deep fryer. "Put your hair up if you're gonna be in my kitchen."

The guy serves the greasiest, most questionable food in Portland, but he's a freak about hair. I grab a net from the box on the counter and pull it over my ponytail. "Better?"

He nods and I go into the hot, damp room where Amber's loading the industrial dishwasher with her back to me. "You dropped out of school?" I yell over the hiss of the sprayer she's using to clean off bits of stuck-on food.

She jumps about a mile and then slides the plastic crate of dishes into the washer without even looking at me, slamming down the lid like it's a guillotine and she wishes my head was under it. There's a second of silence before the machine kicks in with a *whoosh* of water.

"So?" I ask.

"Last time I checked," she says, keeping her back to me, "you weren't my mom."

"We had a deal."

"I didn't think deals mattered to you anymore."

This is crazy. For the last two weeks she's been talking to me like normal and I thought maybe we were getting somewhere. "You promised!"

"Huh," she says, all sarcastic like. "I guess I lied. Now you know how it feels."

One of the cocktail waitresses shoves a bin full of glasses through the little window and sticks her head in. "Ruby needs these ASAP."

"Yeah, okay." Amber loads them upside down on a blue plastic rack. The dishwasher finishes its cycle with a *thunk*, and she pops the doors open, engulfing us both in a cloud of hot steam that smells a lot like Bonehead's farts. Once she's got the glasses in, she turns and faces me, her expression blank.

"I'm busy here," she says. "You can go."

"Amber? Come on—"

"Forget it. It's too late."

It can't be. I know for a fact she was still going to school a few weeks ago. "What happened? Did you do this to get back at me for applying to McPherson?" Her face hardens for a second and I think she's going to yell, but instead she bursts into tears. Instantly my heart melts.

"Hey, Am—"

"Where's the damn glasses?" Aunt Ruby yells through the window. She sticks her head inside and sees us both. "Come on, Amber, less talking and more washing!" Amber's got her back to Ruby so our aunt doesn't see she's crying. I step around my sister and pull the hot glasses out of the dishwasher, then slide the whole tray to Ruby.

"Thanks, babe!" she says. I can't help but be impressed when she grabs the burning tray with her hands of steel and walks off, yelling at some customer to "get off the goddamned table!" My palms are red just from touching the plastic for one second.

I expect Amber to pull herself together, but when I look over at her, she's crumpled onto the floor, sobbing into a striped dishtowel. The waitress shoves more glasses through the window, and I grab a plastic apron off a hook by the door and get to work. I've helped Amber tons of times, mostly before Natalie was born. I'd come in and we'd work together double time so we could get out of here and go party. I fall into the routine easily enough, and the next time Ruby yells for glasses, they're ready.

"Thanks, Ambie Pambie," she says to me, not even realizing we've traded places.

Eventually, Amber stops crying. I may look like a cold-hearted bitch for leaving her on the floor like that, but neither one of us likes to be comforted. It's too embarrassing. Me doing the dishes is cool, though. She sees I've got it under control and goes out, probably to wash the mascara off her face.

A few minutes later, Amber comes back with an order of onion rings and two root beers. I've kept up pretty well with the dishes, and the kitchen's closed now, so there'll be a lull for a little bit before we have to do all the end-of-night glasses and stuff.

We stand there with the plastic basket of onion rings between us on the stainless-steel counter, eating but not talking. After a while, Amber goes to refill our pop glasses, and when she sets them down again, she's ready to tell me what happened.

"I didn't mean to drop out," she says. "I just . . . without you riding my ass all the time and checking my homework, I got behind."

I nod.

"And I missed a couple of tests . . . I slept in two days in a row. It was like I was in this stupid hole and I didn't know how to get out."

I pick at an onion ring, not looking at her so she'll keep talking.

"I tried to make a chart like you always do for me," she says, "but . . . oh, screw it. I'm a loser and we both know it. I never would've gotten this far without you."

"That's totally not true," I say. It kind of is, but only the part about me helping her get organized. She's not good at that. Also, unless it's numbers or something physical, like this job or taking care of Nat, she can't make herself care very much. I can see tears glistening in her eyes again, so I look away and rush on. "How long ago did you drop out?"

"Two weeks, I guess. It was right after you got your financial aid. But that's not why. I was way behind already, and I couldn't take it anymore, the looks from my teachers and stuff."

"Did you officially quit, like go into the office and sign the papers, or did you just stop going to class?"

Amber looks up at me, surprise in her wet eyes. "You mean you have to sign papers to drop out?"

"I think so. Otherwise they just think you're skipping."

She shakes her head, a tiny smile tugging at her mouth. "God. I'm such a fuck-up. I can't even drop out of high school right." And then she starts laughing. Her shoulders are shaking, and it's totally contagious and I crack up too. We laugh until we're gasping for breath, tears streaming down our faces.

We're standing there still shaking with laughter when Brad comes in with a pile of baking sheets and pots for Amber to wash. "Okay, you two. Break it up, you slackers." He's smiling at us, though.

"Bite me," Amber says, laughing harder, and he shakes his hair-netted head and goes back to the kitchen.

We spend the next hour and a half working side by side like the old days. Instead of talking about our future and the apartment we're going to get together, we plan a way for Amber to graduate. I'm going to go with her to talk to her teachers, and if that doesn't work, we'll get Ms. Spellerman on our side.

"We still have three weeks until finals," I say. "You can do it."

"Maybe if you help me."

I squeeze her shoulder. "Promise."

I know Amber thinks I've let her down by wanting to change our plans, but I've got her back this time. When I get my diploma, she's gonna be right there beside me. And who knows what will happen after that?

CHAPTER 22

Aman in a suit ducks between us. "Sorry," he says, stepping out of the way.

Mom holds up the digital camera she borrowed from Aunt Pearl. "Now one with the baby."

Nat seems less like a baby every day. Tomorrow's her first birthday, but today's our day, and Gil hands her to Amber. I adjust my sister's graduation gown when it rides up under Natalie's diapered butt, and then I put one arm around Amber and we lean our heads together, our caps meeting in the middle. Right when Mom snaps the picture, Nat grabs my tassel and yanks, and we all laugh as the cap flies off. I hope Mom got that shot.

I had the cap bobby-pinned on during the ceremony, but I pulled it loose right afterward so me and Amber could pretend to throw them in the air for pictures. There was no way we'd really toss them, though. It's against school rules and they're frickin' Nazis about it. Apparently they're afraid someone will get their eye poked out and there'll be a lawsuit. They told us if we throw them, they're holding our diplomas, which I don't really think they can do, but at this point we aren't taking any chances.

I rescue my cap from Natalie's grip of steel, rest it on her head, and Mom takes some more pictures. Then she gets one of me and Amber with Han, and he takes some of us with Nat, Mom, and Gil.

Gil's holding Natalie, and he says, "Say Papa! Pa-pa! Nat, say Papa!"

He's been going on like this for days, claiming Natalie can talk and her first word was "Papa." Apparently this happened when he was watching her and I was in the shower getting ready for work. No one else has heard her say it, though, and when I point out that he's her grandpa, not her papa, he tells me the whole word's too hard to say so they're starting small.

"Okay, smile," Han tells us.

"Pa-pa!" Nat says.

"I told you!" Gil crows.

He raises Nat in the air, and she yells, "Pa-pa-pa-pa-pa-pa-pa-pa-pa!"

He nuzzles the side of her neck, and she screeches with laughter. I hope Han gets some good pictures of them because I don't think I've ever seen him look so proud. I can't believe Mom and Gil are here at a school function, but they are. Mom's even wearing real shoes instead of slippers or dollar store flip-flops. And Gil has done something to what's left of his hair with styling gel. At least, we hope that's what he used. It could be Crisco.

We take one more picture where me and Amber hold up our empty diploma covers—they're going to mail us the real thing in a few weeks—and then we go with Han to wait in the cap-and-gown return line. I guess you have to buy them at most schools, but here they let us rent them, or else no one would come to graduation. The students at our school don't have money for stuff you only wear once.

"How come you didn't tell us you were getting an award?" Han asks me, smirking.

"I didn't know," I say. "If I did, I wouldn't have come. That was so lame."

Amber takes the framed certificate from me and examines it as we walk. "It *is* pretty geeky to miss less than fifty days in four whole years."

I couldn't believe it when they called my name. Me and two other dorks. When we were standing up there on the stage, my face probably as red as my hair, one of the guys told me that at other schools the award's for missing less than five days in all four years, but at Sacajawea they have to add a zero to the five in order to find anyone to give the award to. I don't know how this guy knew that, but he looked like the kind of nerd who would, so I totally believe him. I bet they don't do stupid shit like this at college.

I try to shake off the thought of college, telling myself not to think about that now. We have a party to go to. Gil knows someone who works at the VFW hall as a cleaner, and since graduation's on a Wednesday and not a weekend, he was able to get a discount on the rental. We're the first girls in our whole family to graduate. All my aunts chipped in to throw us a bash. We're making the room do double duty by having Natalie's birthday party at the same time.

After we turn in our rented clothes, we all pile into the Mustang and head for the hall. Since we only got four tickets between us, none of our other family came for the ceremony, and the party's already going strong when we get there. Inside the door is a table with a few gift bags for me and Amber on one end, but it's mostly piled high with colorful packages for the birthday girl.

There's a banner on one wall that says BABY'S FIRST BIRTH-DAY! and another one below it with CONGRATS, GRADS! in rainbow colors. Someone's used a Sharpie to add an *s* to the end of "grad" to make it plural. In the kitchen, our aunts put out tons of food from the bakery, and while we're all checking out Natalie's cake, Gil's brother, Tom, comes in with a stack of pizzas. Gil's right behind him with Jade's boyfriend and a couple of other guys I don't know, all carrying cases of beer and pop.

One of the advantages to the VFW hall is that it's in our neighborhood. We don't have to worry about anyone driving drunk because they can all stumble home. That and the fact that me, Aunt Ruby, and Jade's boyfriend are the only ones with cars anyway.

A couple of hours later, Han shows up. He had to go do the whole family thing with his parents before they'd let him come over here. Natalie's ripping paper off her presents—or more accurately, her cousins are "helping" her open the gifts while she chews on a bow. I can see that getting Nat's new dolly away from Lapis is gonna be a big problem later when it's time to go, but I decide not to worry about it now.

Han gives Natalie a pair of tiny silver starfish earrings for her birthday, which is really nice. She can keep them forever. They're babyproof ones, too, so we don't have to worry about her getting them out and choking or anything.

I considered inviting David, but then I chickened out. His mom and dad rented a banquet room at a hotel for his graduation party last weekend. Luckily, I had to work, so even though he sent me an engraved invitation, I didn't have to go. I gave him a used book on hot rods last weekend, and he got me a brand-new one on the history of Mustangs, and that was our big celebration.

Around eight, Jimmy and Betty stop by, and Jimmy gives me two presents. The first one is a joke: a can of Bondo, the putty you use to fix dents. He tells me he got it to remind me I don't need no "stinkin' college education" because aside from him, I'm the best body guy he knows. Sometimes I think I'm the son he never had.

The second gift is super heavy, and I think I know what it is before I open it. I pull off the classifieds he used for wrapping paper and find a red toolbox full of some really top-notch tools. "Wow! Thanks." I give him an awkward hug, maybe our first one ever, and I feel kinda teary, but then Betty chimes in with her usual chintziness.

"He won that at a car show a couple of weeks ago. I thought we should sell it on eBay, but the shipping would've been way too much for anyone to buy it."

Jimmy scowls, and I rush to cover her rudeness. "I'm happy to have it. Thanks."

"I knew you'd appreciate it," Jimmy says, giving his wife the look of death. Mercifully, Gil stumbles over at that moment, holding out a beer to Jimmy, who takes it and downs half of it in one swig.

By the time Natalie pounds her fists into her cake and everyone gets more pictures than we'll ever need, I'm beat. I find Amber washing frosting out of her hair in the kitchen. "Do you think everyone's drunk enough that we can leave and they won't notice?"

"Probably."

We consider sneaking out, but that's hard to do with an almost-one-year-old who's hopped up on sugar, especially when we have a load of presents we need to pry out of her cousins' hands. It takes an hour before we finally get out of there. By the time we do, I'm ready to drop.

Once Nat's in her car seat, she zonks out before I've even gotten her all the way buckled in. I slide into the driver's seat and we sit there in silence, letting the stillness wrap itself around us like a soothing blanket. I start to turn the key, and then I stop.

"Amber?"

"Yeah?"

"If I turn on this car and the radio's blasting, I will have to kill you. High school graduate or not."

She laughs and reaches for the knob, turning it all the way to the left until it clicks off.

"Good call," I say.

Later, Natalie's had a bath and is in her crib, and me and Amber are slumped on the couch, vegging out in front of the TV. A Hallmark commercial comes on, showing a bunch of "special graduation moments," and Amber reaches over and grabs my hand.

"We did it. Thanks, Crys."

"No problem." Then I laugh. "Well, maybe a few problems. But we made it."

The commercial ends, and in that split second of silence before the next one starts, Amber says, "If you promise we can come back in four years, I'll go to Kansas with you."

I wrap my arms around my sister and hug her hard. "I promise."

This is officially the best day of my life.

CHAPTER 23

One of the things on the list of stuff to bring to college is a computer. I call Han and tell him I need his help.

"What kind do you want?"

"A laptop. Something cheap," I say. "And new. I don't want a used piece of shit. It has to last me for all of college."

"Good luck with that."

"Really?"

"No, I'm kidding. Kind of. I'll find you something that'll last at least a couple of years."

"Cool."

He talks me into a refurbished one instead of new, which is really why I asked him for help in the first place — he knows about stuff like that. If you want to buy a car, you should ask me, but for everything else, Han's your guy.

A week later I'm the proud owner of a pre-owned shiny black laptop.

Now that school's over, Amber starts working most nights at the Glass Slipper and weekdays at Big Apple Pizza so she can make as much money as possible for the move. David's busy with a summer internship and I pick up a lot of his shifts at the station, plus it's busier in the shop, so I get to work in there on the weekends. We can still take Nat to the daycare at the school for the summer. The idea is to give new graduates a chance to either work full-time or find jobs if they don't have one.

We fall into a routine, but Nat still keeps us hopping. She wants to do everything herself. She won't let us feed her and grabs the spoon every time. Things that used to take ten minutes now take thirty. And she gets better at scooting and pulling herself up, holding on to the edges of furniture and moving so fast that we're always lunging after ballpoint pens and Gil's pipe before she can grab them and stick them in her mouth.

"God," Amber says one evening as she pries a lighter out of Natalie's chubby little hands while she screeches. "I didn't think we'd ever be as tired as we were right after she was born. But she's killing me."

I'm collapsed on the couch. "I know. Me too."

I take Natalie outside as much as possible so she can get fresh air, and she loves Bonehead, which is good. He follows her around our little yard, getting between her and the sidewalk if she starts to go too far and herding her back to where it's safe. Who knew he could actually be useful for something besides being a car alarm? While he watches her, I mess around with the engine of my car or take five-minute breathers in the sunshine.

Ever since Amber decided we could go to Kansas, things have been great between us. We haven't been able to find an apartment in McPherson yet, but we talk about moving all the time. It's like our old plan, except better, because after four years, we're gonna come back to Portland and I'll be able to make a real living. I haven't told anyone this, but I've come up with an even better idea than buying Jimmy's shop when he retires. I'm thinking the two of us should go into business together—sell the gas station and open a real full-service restoration shop. With his connections and the skills I'll learn, me and Jimmy'd be a great team.

I'm working at the station almost every day, and I can't help but see the price of gas going up, up, up. It's seventeen hundred miles to McPherson, and the Mustang isn't exactly known for its good gas mileage. This trip's going to cost us a lot. To help us cut down on travel expenses, Han finds us some secondhand camping gear so we don't have to stay in a motel every night. Amber's not sure a tent is a great idea with a baby, but I keep telling her it'll be an adventure.

The problem is, Amber's not acting like she wants an adventure. In fact, she's freaking me out a little. "If we can find a two-bedroom apartment," I tell her, "it'll be like a mansion.

Especially after the tent. Can you imagine Natalie having her own room?"

Amber looks at me and I'm surprised by the alarm on her face. "I don't want her to have her own room! I want to keep sharing with both of you. Promise me we'll get a studio."

"I doubt anyone will rent us a studio for three people. But we can get a one-bedroom if you want and all share."

"I do, Crys. I'm going to be alone enough as it is."

School doesn't start until the twenty-first of August, but as July flies by, we're getting pretty worried about finding a place to live. As usual, Han comes through for us. He drops by the station and follows me around while I'm pumping gas.

"It's a one-bedroom, the top floor of a house, right in town. You can walk to campus. I talked to the landlord on the phone," he says, "and she's okay with having a baby in the apartment, but you have to rent the place from the first of August."

"I was hoping someone would let us do half the month."

"I know, but she told me she's got a big waiting list of people who want the place, so you better take it."

I scrub the windshield of a 1999 Ford pickup while the guy goes inside to pay. "Okay. We're in. Thanks, Han."

Once the apartment's rented, we make a firm plan to leave on July twenty-eighth. I want to take it slow on the road. When Natalie was younger, she would've slept the whole way, but now we worry she's gonna be restless. Also, I've never driven so far, and I'm not sure how tired I'll get. We're also thinking that if we get to town ahead of most of the students, Amber can find a part-time job before all the good ones are taken.

I thought she'd be thrilled to hear Han found us such a nice place to live, but instead she gets all teary about leaving everyone behind.

"The heat's included in the rent," I tell her. "And an air conditioner, too."

"Yeah, I know . . . It's just . . ."

"Just what?"

"I don't know. Ignore me. I'm being stupid."

I try to stay excited about going, but Amber seems so sad all the time that I spend a lot of energy trying to think of ways to make the move easier for her. One day when Mom and Gil are out, I get Han to come over and help us set up Skype on my new computer. "So you can talk to Jade and Aunt Ruby whenever you want," I tell Amber.

Instead of cheering her up, that makes her look sadder, her face all worry lines and glistening eyes. "Mom doesn't have Skype."

Mom's the last person I thought Amber would miss. Aunt Ruby and Jade, yeah, but Mom? They get along okay, but they're definitely not close. "We'll get a phone," I tell her, hoping that'll make her feel better. "And I was thinking, maybe we could fly home for spring break."

She sighs, her chin drooping, and I look at Han for help. He shrugs.

"Amber? What's wrong?" My heart clenches when I say it. If she's backing out on me now, only ten days before we leave, I'm going to have a stroke.

She shakes her head and gives me a fake smile. "Nothing. Everything's fine."

Natalie yells to be picked up, and Han goes over and gets her out of the swing he found at a garage sale for ten bucks. "I'm gonna miss you, baby," he says.

"Han. Han. Han," Natalie babbles, smiling up at him.

"Did you hear that?" he asks. "She obviously loves me more than she loves you. I haven't heard her say Amber or Crystal."

"Yeah, whatever."

"You buy her so much crap," Amber says. "That's why she likes you."

"I only get her good stuff. Don't I, Nattie? I get you the most awesomest things ever, don't I?" She grins at him and pulls his hair until he squawks. "Hey! Let go, let go!"

We all laugh. I think I might actually miss Han once we're gone. He's kind of grown on me over the last year.

• • •

One steaming hot day about a week before we're supposed to leave, we're all out in the yard together. I offer a lick of cherry Popsicle to Natalie. She's whining in frustration and trying to peel my fingers off the stick so she can hold it. When I don't let go, she screeches at me and bangs her feet into my side, but I don't give in. I know she'll just drop it, and Bonehead's eaten enough Popsicles this week already. He's hovering, on full alert.

"I was thinking," Amber says. "Maybe I could come home for Thanksgiving."

"You want to come back that soon?"

"I'm gonna miss everyone. If I have something to look forward to . . ."

I'm about to tell her I'm not sure we can afford it when Bonehead lunges forward and snags the Popsicle out of my hand. Then Nat's screaming and Amber's doubled over laughing, and I'm chasing Bonehead, hoping to get the stick before he chomps it to pieces and chokes on it. Neither one of us brings up Thanksgiving again, but it hangs over us like a rain cloud.

The next week is made up of a bunch of "lasts." The Friday before we leave is the last time Nat goes to daycare. The weird thing is that she seems to know it, and when Mei-Zhen hugs her goodbye, she clings to her and cries when I take her.

"That was weird," Amber says when we get out to the car.

"Totally. I didn't even know she liked Mei-Zhen."

"I think she's nicer to the babies than she is to the moms."

"Probably."

Han takes us out to dinner that night, which he jokingly refers to as the "last supper." Me and Amber roll our eyes, but we've gotten used to his goofiness. He pretty much ignores us the whole time anyway, talking to and feeding Natalie, squeezing her toes to make her laugh, and holding her in his lap while we eat.

Sunday is Amber's last night at the Glass Slipper, and Aunt Ruby invites us to hang out after the bar closes for a little family goodbye. I don't really want to go, but honestly, I'm afraid to skip it. Jade's going to be there, and I know she's been trying to talk Amber into staying in Portland.

Around ten o'clock, I take Natalie over to Jade's. Her boyfriend, Teddy, is watching her girls and said it was okay if we leave Nat there too. I don't know him, but Amber swears he's a good guy. I give him a whole bunch of instructions in case Natalie wakes up. She'll probably sleep, but I leave Teddy two bottles, strained carrots, diapers, and toys.

After ten minutes of tapping her foot, Jade drags me out to the car. "He knows what he's doing. He hasn't killed my kids yet."

"A ringing endorsement," I say.

Teddy waves from the porch, smiling. I have to admit, he seems pretty responsible. In fact, it's like he's a grownup.

He's got to be close to thirty, and he has a real job with the phone company. His car is a spotless and boring 2007 Toyota Corolla, which reassures me because it probably means he's a little boring too.

I'm determined to get along with Jade tonight for Amber's sake. It's not like we hate each other, but we have never really liked each other, either. Once we're in the car, I say, "Your hair looks cool."

"Thanks." She's cropped it really short and spiked it up. I'm pretty sure the dark brown shade is natural, too, but I haven't seen her real color since we were kids. "After that red dye job it was pretty brittle, so I decided to start over."

"It looks good."

We're almost to the Glass Slipper when Jade says, "You know, Amber doesn't want to go to Kansas."

I get that familiar sinking feeling in my stomach that I've had for weeks every time I look at my sister. "Only because you keep telling her it's a bad idea."

"It is."

"No, it's not."

I slide into a parking spot and kill the engine.

"Maybe not for you, but it is for her. She likes her job, and she was totally committed to your 'plan,' if you remember."

I squeeze my eyes shut. "Look, Jade, can you just let us do this? Please? We've worked it out, and the last thing I need three days before we leave is you giving her doubts."

She opens the car door. "She's already got them. And if you cared about anyone besides yourself, you'd know that."

Inside, the bar's still open, so I hang out in the dish room with Amber. Jade's twenty-one, though, and she goes off to play darts with a couple of regulars. Amber's wearing rubber gloves and has her hands deep in a sink full of soapy water.

She looks up at me, her eyes big and sad. "These are the last pots I'm ever gonna scrub here."

"If it was me, I'd be happy about that."

She gives me a fake smile. Is Jade right? Is Amber only doing this for me? When we'd first talked about getting our apartment in McPherson, she'd sounded totally committed, like once she'd decided to go, she thought it would be exciting, but lately . . . well, I'm not so sure.

I try to cover my worry with cheerfulness. "So what's the plan for tonight?"

Amber shrugs. "I don't know. I guess Brad's gonna make all my favorite foods—veggie burgers and onion rings, cheesecake—and we're all going to hang out."

"Sounds fun."

"Yeah."

Okay, kill us now. That would lighten the mood in here. My stomach tightens into that familiar knot.

"Hey, chickens," Aunt Ruby says, sticking her head through the dish window. "It's totally dead out here tonight, so I'm closing early. Finish up and let's party!"

I pull on an apron and help Amber with the last of the pots and pans. I try to get her to talk about our road trip, but she barely answers. I start thinking maybe we should leave for Kansas tomorrow instead of Wednesday. The sooner I get her out of here, the better.

Half an hour later, we're all sitting around a table piled with food. The weird thing is, Brad's the only one drinking alcohol.

"You can have a beer," I tell Jade and Amber. "I'm driving."

"That's okay," Amber says. "I'm not up for one, and Jade doesn't drink anymore."

I look over at my cousin. "Really?"

"Don't act so surprised," Jade says. "You hardly know me."

That's true. Still, out of all my cousins, she's always been the biggest partier.

We're a sad little group, and I tell myself it's because we're all going to miss each other, nothing more than that. Amber picks at her food but doesn't eat much, and I don't either. The knot in my stomach makes it impossible.

After about an hour of small talk, Aunt Ruby takes out two envelopes. "One for Crystal. And one for Amber."

"You go first," Amber tells me.

Inside is a check for five hundred dollars. I look at Aunt Ruby. "Seriously?"

"College is expensive. I'm sure you can use it."

"Wow. This is amazing. Thank you so much." She shrugs like it's no big deal, but I'm thinking this will buy a lot of gas on the road.

"Now you, Ambie Pambie," Aunt Ruby says.

Amber's envelope is a lot thicker than mine, and when she opens it, she pulls out some papers stapled together in the corner. We all wait while she scans them. And then her face breaks into the biggest, widest smile I've ever seen.

"Is this for real?" she asks Aunt Ruby.

"Yep."

"Oh my God!" Amber jumps up and throws her arms around our aunt. "Thank you so much. Thank you. Thank you. Thank you!"

"What is it?" Jade asks.

"Aunt Ruby's given me ten percent of the Glass Slipper!" Amber says. Tears are streaming down her face, and she's bouncing around the table like gravity can't hold her.

The knot in my stomach cinches even tighter. "What do you mean? You're a partner now? But we—"

"Don't worry, Crystal," Aunt Ruby says. "I just wanted to give her something to look forward to in four years. I'm not asking her to stay."

I relax a tiny bit, but after this gift, Wednesday can't come soon enough.

CHAPTER 24

There's a cruise-in at Mikey's Diner the next day, and when I ask Amber to come along, she says, "That's one 'last' I can live without." I drop her at the salon where Jade works. It's closed on Mondays, but she's going to give Amber a trim.

"Don't let her dye your hair blue."

"As if."

Me and Nat go to Mikey's and a bunch of the hot rodders surprise me with a card and a wad of cash they've collected. A big meaty guy who goes by the name of Stick wraps his thick arm around my shoulder. "Do us proud at that school, Crystal. And then come back here and fix up the dings in Jack's car. It's a mess."

We all laugh because Jack has the nicest ride of any of us, a low-to-the-ground '33 Ford Victoria, all black, all the time. And everyone knows, if you're painting a car black, the body has to be perfectly straight or any flaws will show. His car is gorgeous.

I have to admit, I'm a little teary when it's time to go. Ever since I got my license, I've been meeting up with these guys to show off our cars and talk mechanics and body work. Most of them are grandpas, and they tell me they wish they had granddaughters like me. I'm gonna miss them all.

We swing by Jade's house to pick up Amber, and she meets me on the porch and says she's staying over. I want to talk her out of it, but I don't try. I know she's going to miss Jade. Instead, me and Nat leave her there, and I try not to think about the ten percent of Aunt Ruby's business that's now Amber's, or what Jade might be telling her.

It's hot tonight and Natalie's fussy, so I drive around for a little bit with all the windows down, but then I go home because I know Bonehead will start barking if someone doesn't feed him soon. Plus I need to get Natalie into her crib.

It's stifling in our bedroom and I feel sorry for Nat. Her skin's damp from the heat and she's got a rash between her thighs. I put some cream on her legs and leave her to sleep in a diaper. I'll put a light blanket over her later. Outside, I stand in the darkness, watching Bonehead eat.

"It's no big deal Amber is staying at Jade's, right?" I ask the dog. He snuffles into his food bowl, making a wet sucking sound as he inhales his dinner.

Gross.

I find Mom in the kitchen doing a crossword. I look around for something to eat besides the day-old doughnuts on the table next to her dirty coffee cup, but I can't find anything. "What're you doing home, anyway?" I ask.

"Even your old lady gets a night off from the chain gang."

"Oh, right."

She must be broke or she'd be at bingo. I disappear into our bedroom quick before she can hit me up for money. It's still so hot in here, I have to do something or me and Nat will suffocate. I go out to my car and get the toolkit Jimmy gave me for graduation. What I really need are bolt cutters, but there aren't any. Instead, I take a sledgehammer to the padlock Gil used to lock the overhead door when he turned the garage into our bedroom.

I'm standing outside in the driveway, bashing at it with all my worry over what Jade's telling Amber in every blow. It only takes about six good whacks before Mr. Hendricks is screaming at me from his porch to shut the hell up, and I can hear Natalie crying inside. Maybe this wasn't my best idea ever, but I've almost got it now. I give the lock one more hard *thwack,* it crumbles, and I'm able to get the chain free. I lift the creaky door for the first time in years, and it squeals, making Bonehead whine. Natalie's standing in her crib, her face pink and tears snaking down her cheeks.

"Sorry, baby," I say. "I didn't mean to scare you."

She stares at me with those huge blue eyes like I made her cry on purpose.

"I said I was sorry."

I look around at the mess I've made. I really didn't think this whole thing through. When I lifted the garage door, my mattress got showered with crud, dead bugs, and dirt. I don't have any other sheets and I'm too grossed out to just shake them. I'll have to sleep in Amber's bed tonight.

After I get Nat to lie back down and I stroke her hair until she falls asleep again, I put on a pair of shorts and a tanktop and climb under Amber's sheet. Streetlight and fresh air drift in, giving the usually pitch-black room a surreal feeling. I can't fall asleep, though, and after a while I decide it's because I'm too freaked out that someone might walk in and attack me and Nat. It's not the best neighborhood, after all. I get up and let Bonehead off his chain.

"You can sleep on my bed," I say, patting it, and he jumps right up like he owns it. I should probably figure out a way to tie him up—I don't want him to run away. But he looks so happy to be inside that I leave him alone. He scratches, turns around and around in a circle, and then curls himself into a tiny ball. Pretty amazing considering the size of him.

I lie awake for a long time in my sister's bed, missing her. I don't sleep much. That familiar pain has come back in my stomach. I curl up, almost as small as Bonehead on the other bed. It eases the stabbing in my gut a little, and after a while, I guess I drift off.

Tuesday's my last day at Jimmy's, and technically I'm not even working. I leave Natalie with Gil and go in to say good-bye and fill my tank. When I try to pay for the gas, Jimmy shakes me off. I hope no one tells Betty. I stand around for a few minutes, talking to Rosa and killing time until David's lunch break. I already know what route me and Amber are taking to Kansas, but he wants to show me some other road he says is way cooler.

"I got you a sandwich on my way in to work," he says after he punches the time clock.

He's a good man. His girlfriend's lucky to have him. We go to the break room and sit next to each other instead of across the table like usual. I unwrap my veggie delight sub while he opens a road atlas and spreads it out in front of us.

He points to the interstate on the map. "Don't tell me you're taking I-Eighty-Four?"

"Yep," I say. "East to Salt Lake City, on to Denver, and a straight shot to Kansas from there."

"Snoozefest. You should go south to Sacramento, then take Highway Fifty across Nevada."

I shake my head. "That'll burn a lot more gas. Some of

us aren't made of money. And I don't have air conditioning, either. Remember?"

"Chick-ennnn," he says, drawing out the last syllable and grinning.

"Yeah, I'd like to see you do it, Stanford Boy. 'Oh, my white polo shirt has perspiration stains!'"

"I'm telling you, you're missing the most awesome road in the entire United States. Highway Fifty's flat, straight, no cops. It's what the Mustang was made for."

"Maybe. But most of them don't have a baby in the back seat."

He tilts his chair back, shaking his head. "Oh, yeah. I forgot about that."

"Good thing I'm the one driving, then."

"Someday, College Girl . . . promise me someday you'll go that way."

"I promise."

We shake on it. And then I scarf my sandwich down and get the hell out before one of us tears up. I go to Big Apple Pizza to find Amber, but Tom tells me she called in sick for her last day. I swing by the house and pick up Natalie from Mom. Amber's not there, so I run over to Jade's, but no one's there, either. I think about going to the salon and telling Jade to butt out, but I don't want to make a scene where she works. She pisses me off, but her kids need to eat, and I get the feeling she's always on the edge of being fired for one thing or another, so I let it go for now.

Besides, I have something else I need to do. This morning, while Mom and Gil were sleeping, I managed to snag some money from them by going through their pockets. I know they'll never miss it. They can't keep track of what they have. I take the cash over to the landlord and tell him good luck, he's on his own from now on.

He says his woman left him anyway, so no one's nagging him to collect rent, but not to tell Gil and Mom. I promise him I won't. I don't know much about the guy, but he and Gil were in the army together and served in Afghanistan, so I guess that's the real reason he doesn't kick us out.

"If I get enough out of them to pay the property taxes every year," he says, "then that's all I care about. The house is a piece of shit anyway, and Gil's a real friend."

I'm kind of surprised to hear this, since I don't think they ever see each other, but it makes sense that they have a history. Anyone else would've evicted us a long time ago.

"Yeah, okay," I say. "Well . . . good luck."

"You too, Crystal."

I stop by the Glass Slipper on my way home, but according to Aunt Ruby there's been no sign of Amber. "Haven't seen her, chickadee," she says. "But give your old aunt a hug goodbye."

Later, I'm sitting at the table with Mom when the phone

rings. It has to be Amber. Finally! I run out to the living room and grab the receiver. "Hello?"

"Hey, Crys. It's me."

"Am, where are you?"

"I went to the beach for the day with Jade and Teddy and the kids."

"Why didn't you tell me?"

"Sorry. I stopped by the house, but no one was home."

"You couldn't have left a note?"

"We were in a hurry. I didn't think it mattered."

"Well, are you coming home now?"

There's a pause before she says, "I think I'm gonna stay over one more night."

"Amber? Is something wrong?"

"No," she says, real fast. "I'm just going to miss Jade. That's all."

"All right. But what about your stuff? Don't you have to pack?"

"It's all good," she says. "I'm ready to go."

I'm not convinced her staying at Jade's is a good idea, but she sounds fine, kind of happy even. "All right. I want to leave at seven tomorrow morning."

"I'll be there."

"Okay. Good night."

"Night."

I go back to the kitchen. It's the last time me and Mom

will sit here while she does a crossword, and as usual, she totally ignores me. There's a little pang in my heart when I think of her sitting here alone.

"Would you quit sighing like someone's hung you on the cross?" Mom says.

"Sorry."

"So what is it now?" she asks.

"I'm worried about Amber."

"You should learn to take care of yourself and let your sister live her own life."

"I guess."

I go into our bedroom and look around. It's pretty much the same as always, but I can tell Amber's been here. Instead of stuff piled on top of the Rubbermaid containers, everything's inside them. I guess she really is ready to go. I spend an hour going through my clothes, leaving the oldest ones on my bed. I've got the garage door open again, and Bonehead makes a nest out of a pair of jeans.

It's so hot I give Natalie a cool bath before I put her into her crib. "Last time, little girl." She smiles sleepily up at me, and I kiss her good night.

CHAPTER 25

At 6:48 the next morning I'm sitting on the steps waiting for Amber. Bonehead herds Nat around on the patch of dried-up grass and sits patiently when she throws her arms around his neck and says her version of "doggy" in his ear.

I said my goodbyes to Mom last night, and Gil actually went in to work for once, mumbling something about having to be there early to do the pizza prep, so he's gone already. I'm on pins and needles—tapping my feet, making myself count to five before I look down the street again, taking long, slow, deep breaths. Maybe I should've told Amber we were leaving later—she doesn't like to get up early.

I've already packed everything into the Mustang. We haven't got much, but the car filled up surprisingly fast. Nat's going to have to share the back seat with all the clothes Han got her and some of Amber's stuff, plus the cooler that I filled with baby snacks. We're leaving the crib and swing behind, hoping to find what we need in McPherson.

Natalie crawls over to me and pulls herself up on the step, Bonehead right behind her. I pat her head and scratch his ears, and the dog barks once in excitement. He wants me to unhook his chain and let him come along with us. Me and Amber talked about taking him, but what would we do with a dog when we got to Kansas? Technically, he belongs to Gil anyway. I hope he remembers to feed him.

"Sorry, buddy," I say. "You gotta stay here."

"Hey," Amber says. I look up and she's standing on the sidewalk. There's such a whoosh of relief, it shakes my body. Bonehead probably feels like this every time we pull into the driveway. By the time my sister walks across the scrappy grass, I'm standing and my heartbeat's going crazy, like my timing belt is out of whack. I kind of want to hug her.

Natalie's face lights up when she sees Amber, and she holds out her arms. "Amba!"

Amber leans down and scoops her up, holding her close. "Hi, sweetie." It hits me that this is probably the longest they've gone without seeing each other.

"She missed you."

"Yeah, me too." Amber kisses Nat's neck, making her giggle. "What did you feed her? I swear she weighs more than she did three days ago."

"I know. Every time I pick her up it's hard to believe she's that milky little lump we brought home from the hospital."

"No kidding."

"So I've packed everything and we're ready to go." I give my sister a big smile. It's a little fake. My heart's hammering in my chest. Until I get her in the car and we're on the road, I'm not going to relax. Amber looks around at the house and yard like she's actually sad to leave the dump. At her feet, the dog is head-butting her for attention, and she hands me Nat so she can give him a chin scratch.

"Is Gil here?"

"Nope. He actually went to work. I don't think he likes goodbyes. But Mom should be home pretty soon. We can wait if you want."

She doesn't answer. She walks over to the car and looks in at all our stuff, and the expression on her face is so sad that it hurts my heart.

"Amber," I say at the exact same time she says, "Crystal."

I laugh. "You go first."

The sadness in her eyes turns to fear, and she starts shaking her head. "I can't do this. I'm sorry. I can't leave. You're gonna have to go without me."

"What?" Deep down, I knew this was coming, but I'd told myself over and over she wouldn't do this to me. My arms and legs are jelly, and I set Nat on the grass before I drop her. "I can't go without you. Is this because of Jade?"

Amber goes to the open trunk and starts dragging containers out of the car. "Is this all mine?"

"What are you doing?"

"Is this my stuff or yours?"

"Stop it, Amber!"

"I'm not going with you, Crystal. I want to stay here."

"I've accepted my financial aid, quit my job, and rented an apartment. We're ready to go. It's too late to change your mind."

She doesn't answer. Instead, she separates her things from mine, tossing her stuff into the yard. I touch her shoulder. "Amber?"

She sighs. "I know I'm letting you down, but I can't go with you."

"You have to."

"You're not listening," she says. "You never listen to me."

"That's so not fair."

"Then why is college more important than the Glass Slipper?"

I knew it. I want to kill Aunt Ruby for making Amber a partner. "It's not more important. We're gonna do my thing, and then do yours. I promise."

"I don't want to wait! Why can't you understand that?"

The arguing is making Natalie whimper, so I lower my voice. "This is all Jade's fault. She's been filling your head with all this shit about getting on with your own life. But she wants to keep you here. She's always trying to steal you from me."

Amber runs her hands through her hair, tugging on it in frustration. "I'm a *person*, Crystal. I'm not something Jade can steal from you. You don't own me."

"I know, I just—"

"Please. Try to understand what you're asking me to do." She pulls the stroller out of the trunk, checking for more of her stuff. "Did I get everything?"

I move between her and the car, my hands on my hips. "So you're really gonna ruin this chance for me? For us?"

She sighs and picks up a Rubbermaid container, then heads for the house. I run after her and grab her arm. "Wait—"

When she turns on me, her eyes are full of anger. "Let me go." I drop her arm because she looks like she might slug me. "I don't want to fight with you, Crystal. Why can't you let this be easy? Let me say goodbye, and then you two should go. It doesn't have to be a big scene."

"Are you crazy? I can't take Natalie to college with me like she's a doll."

"Sure you can," she says. "You always have everything figured out, you'll figure this out, too." She abandons the container on the steps and walks around me to the back of the car, picks up the stroller, and starts to stuff it in the trunk again.

"Stop it," I say, pulling the stroller back out by a wheel. "What am I supposed to do with her in McPherson? Who's going to watch her? I don't know anyone."

"If college is that important to you, then I guess you'll do what everyone else does: find some daycare and let me live my own life."

"Fine." I crawl in the passenger side of the car and get three of Nat's bags out of the back seat. "If you're not going, nobody is."

"You're so wrong. You and Nat *are* going," she says. "I never said getting your degree isn't a smart thing. It'll be good for all of us. There is no way I'm letting you give up now or you'll end up blaming me."

I take two plastic bags of baby food out of the back seat and set them in the yard. "Well, that's because it's your fault! I was counting on you. I can't do it without you."

"Yeah, you can. And you're gonna have to."

When I turn around, Amber's trying to find room for the stroller in the front seat. It won't fit, and she's slamming it around like she wishes it was me.

"Would you stop putting stuff back in the car?" I yell at her as she bangs one of the handles against the dashboard. I grab the stroller and tug on it. "I'm not going anywhere."

She yanks it away from me and tosses it into the street just as a guy on a bike goes by. "Fine! Don't take the goddamned thing," Amber says. "I don't care. But you're still going."

"You crazy bitch!" the bike guy yells.

"Bite me!" I yell back.

I go get the stroller. Back at the car, Amber's strapping a whimpering Natalie into her car seat.

I drop the stroller onto the growing pile on the lawn. "Amber! Stop it!" I grab her around the waist and pull her out of the car. She lands on the ground and Bonehead immediately jumps on her, barking and licking her hair like it's some sort of game. I climb into the car and unstrap Natalie, who reaches out and grabs my ponytail, yanking so hard that I yelp, which makes her start crying for real. In the yard, Amber's yelling at Bonehead to get off her, and by the time I've got Natalie out of the car and my hair free, my sister's managed to get out from under the dog and has run inside the house.

I set a screeching Nat down next to Bonehead, who licks her face and makes her cry harder. Her piercing shrieks are too much for him, and he plops down and howls along with her, which gets Mr. Hendricks in on the action.

"It's seven o'clock in the goddamned morning! I swear to God I'm gonna call the cops if you don't shut the hell up over there!"

I'm too intent on unloading our stuff to tell him where

to stick his phone. Amber returns, sees Nat's clothes on the lawn, and puts them back in the car. I race around to the driver's side and pull them out. "Amber—"

"Save your breath," she says, scooping up Natalie and shoving her into her car seat like she's a stuffed animal or something.

I climb into the back seat from the driver's side and try to push Amber out the other door. The whole time, Natalie's between us, yelling, "No! No! No!"

"She's going with you!" Amber grabs the cooler, which I've managed to pull out of the back seat, and runs around and stuffs it in the trunk. I climb out, lifting Natalie as carefully as I can, and she slaps at my arms with her tiny hands, screaming. After I set her down, I snag the cooler while Amber shoves the Nordstrom shopping bags full of Nat's clothes into the trunk.

It's already hot outside, and her face is as red as her hair. Mine probably is too. Amber elbows me out of the way, hard, making me suck in my breath. I can feel sweat dripping down inside my T-shirt. "Would you stop it?" I slam the trunk closed so she can't put anything else in it. "I told you I'm not going, and even if I was, I can't take her with me!"

"You have to. She's *your*—"

"Don't say it!" I lunge, trying to get a hold of my sister, and she ducks out of my sweaty grip.

In a taunting voice she says, "Don't say what?"

"Amber, please? Please don't. Please?"

"What don't you want me to say, Crys?" I grab at her again, and her face is mean and spiteful. "Huh? Crystal? What?" I'm holding her now, my arms pinning her against me. She's struggling like a caught fish, but she still won't shut up. "You don't want me to say she's your daugh—"

I clamp my hand over Amber's mouth. "SHUT UP! SHUT UP! SHUT UP!"

She fights me off, biting my hand, pinching my arms, until I release her, and then she shoves me hard, sending me tripping over Bonehead, who yelps and starts barking again. Standing over me, her hands on her hips, she says, "You can't just walk away—"

"YOU PROMISED!" I scream, my voice breaking into a sob.

"What I promised is to *help* you, but you can't abandon her like this. Goddammit, Crystal, you're her *mother!* It's time you stop pretending that she dropped out of the fucking sky when the stork flew over our house by accident!"

Nat's cries have turned to whimpers, and tears are streaming down all of our faces.

"I called the cops!" Mr. Hendricks shouts at us.

Amber starts up again. "You have to take—"

"Please, Amber. Please? Please, I'm begging you . . ." In

the distance we hear the wail of a siren, which sets Bonehead howling again. I don't hear Amber's response over the noise. "What did you say?" I ask. My throat's choked with tears.

Amber looks at me, her face softening. "You know what? You're right. You can't take her with you. Just leave us. I'll take care of her. Go do what you have to do."

I lock eyes with her while all around us the world sounds like it's coming apart: Mr. Hendricks yelling, Natalie crying, Bonehead yowling, and the sirens getting closer and closer. When I don't move, she pulls me up and physically shoves me into the car, slamming the door. I sit there, gripping the steering wheel, wanting to stay, wanting to go. As much as I love Natalie, every time I look at her, I remember how I'm the one who screwed up the plan. How I'm the reason we almost dropped out of high school junior year. How I'm the fuck-up in this family, not Amber. And I can't deal with that. Not back when Nat was born, not now.

In my heart, I know Natalie's better off with Amber than with me. I start the engine, and before I back the Mustang out of the driveway, I look over at my sister. She's got her back to me, and she scoops up Natalie, unhooks Bonehead, and drags him into the house, shutting the door behind her, not even looking at me.

Fine. If this is how she wants it, this is how it's gonna be.

I peel out of the driveway. At the end of the street, I pass a cop car heading for our house. He's turned off his sirens now that he's so close, but his lights are still flashing. I don't even slow down, daring him to pull a U-turn and follow me, but he doesn't. For the first time in my life, I'm on my own.

CHAPTER 26

When I get to I-205, I decide to go south to California like David wanted me to. It's me and a car built for speed now, so what the hell? But as soon as I'm on the freeway, I'm stuck in rush-hour traffic. I turn up the radio until it shakes the car, trying to block out the words Amber promised me she'd never say. I could turn around and go back, but the police are probably still there and we all might get in trouble. I don't want to see her right now anyway. I'm so hurt she broke her promise.

As traffic crawls along, I'm able to slowly build up my wall of defense again. I've had so much practice not thinking about how we ended up with Natalie that after a while, all I hear, think, feel is the pulse of the music and the hum of the engine. Finally, after an hour and a half of creeping along, I reach I-5. Traffic's sluggish all the way to Salem, but then it picks up and I'm on my way. By now I'm not thinking about anything except driving.

The Mustang flies along and, for once, I have total control of everything in my life—the car, my thoughts, the future. All I have to do is stay on this road and keep heading south— the wheels eating up the asphalt, the open road ahead.

I'm a city driver and I've never driven much on the interstate. The speed of the highway is truly awesome, and the Mustang rises to the occasion, embracing the freedom as much as I do. I feel myself detach from my body and float above, watching myself drive, like when I play video games with Han. From my perch above the road, I see the Mustang weave in and out of traffic, passing semis, taking curves with the ease of a professional driver. The miles melt away, putting distance between me and Amber. And Natalie. The farther I go, the freer I am.

I drive.

And I drive.

And I drive.

Sometime in the afternoon, my ghost body registers that my physical body is shaking from hunger, and I float down and rejoin myself as I pull into a rest stop. I get out of the car— legs stiff, muscles tight—and try to shake off the tension. After I take a pee, I see some volunteers giving away coffee to help keep drivers awake, and I down two Styrofoam cups full of the sharp, bitter stuff. An old woman with lavender hair tries to talk to me, ask me where I'm headed, but I blow her off and go back to the car. The last thing I want to do is talk to anybody.

A couple of guys are checking out the Mustang, and when they ask about the engine, I answer by rote the questions that usually get my heart pumping with excitement. I open the hood for them and lean against the hot metal of the car, eating a slice of cold pizza from the box Gil brought home last night for our . . . my . . . road trip.

Eventually the guys run out of questions and my lunch is gone, so I get back into the Mustang and peel out, burning a little rubber to impress them. When me and Amber originally planned our route, we thought we should break it up into easy stretches. We'd never really been out of Portland, and it seemed like it might be fun to take our time and see some stuff. The trip was supposed to take six days to McPherson. Now I'm on my own and I don't have to stop for anything. I fly by Ashland, this little town that's so famous for its Shakespeare festival that even I've heard of it. I don't know how long it takes everyone else to get here from Portland, but I do it in four and a half hours. Go, me.

The next stretch is mountainous, big-tree country. The redwood forest towers overhead, but I hardly notice it. I zoom past landmarks. Past park entrances. Past lookouts full of minivans . . . without ever slowing down.

I drive until eight o'clock at night, and as the light starts to fade around me, I realize two things: 1) my eyes are stinging so bad that everything looks a little fuzzy, and 2) if I keep going at this rate, I'll burn out long before I get to McPherson. I pull into a rest stop north of Sacramento and do the whole routine from earlier all over again, minus the coffee— stretch, pee, pizza.

Then I get a sleeping bag out of the trunk. I don't bother with the tent—I'm sleeping in the car. There are signs all over saying NO OVERNIGHT CAMPING, but I'm too tired to worry about whether the back seat counts or not. At a rest stop earlier in the day, I'd moved the cooler to the front, but as I climb into the back of the Mustang I'm faced with Natalie's car seat. In all the yelling and arguing, I drove off with it, and now it sits there, condemning me. I'm the worst mother in the world. I always knew I would be, though, so nothing about the accusation surprises me.

I spend a few minutes undoing the buckles with trembling hands, and when the carrier's finally free, I put it in the trunk, which is practically empty without Natalie's stroller or Amber's containers. My whole body's shaking as I spread out the sleeping bag and climb in the back seat again, using a sweatshirt for a pillow.

Before I left home, I took the Mustang to the car wash and cleaned out the inside really good, but it still smells like Bonehead, and for some reason that gives me the only comfort I've had all day long. But as soon as I shut my eyes I see Amber in the yard picking up a wailing Natalie and walking away from me. I squeeze my eyes tighter, wanting to obliterate this morning from my memory. The seat's hard against my hips, and I wiggle around, trying to get comfortable. If I thought being away from Natalie all day while I was at school was bad, it's nothing like my loneliness right now. I haven't spent a night away from her since she was born, and my arms ache, not knowing what to do without her. I wrap them tightly around myself and I guess I fall asleep. The revving engine of a semi-truck wakes me when the edges of morning are still hovering. For a second, I wonder where I am, and then it all slots together and I know the hollow in my stomach has nothing to do with being hungry.

I hit the road at dawn, and stop in Sacramento for breakfast, an Egg McMuffin without the meat. I get that weird detached feeling again as soon as I'm on Highway 50 and up to speed. The power of the Mustang's V8 engine is my power, the mile markers flying past my window are my past, and the road ahead is unknown, like my future.

But the memories press in on me from every side, surrounding me, making my chest tight and my breathing shallow. I inhale deeply, but it's like right after I run a mile in PE and can't catch my breath. Thinking I'm not getting enough air makes my heart race with panic, and I grip the steering wheel tighter. Flashes of the last two years zip through my mind like a slideshow. The memories are trying to overtake me from behind, and I press the gas pedal to outrun them. But then they're coming at me over the horizon, images thrown at my face like asteroids in a video game. They crowd me from both sides and from above.

Traffic turns out to be what saves me. The closer I get to Carson City, the more I have to focus on my driving. There are a lot more cars here, and I'm able to shake everything bad that's been chasing me—the sense of failure, of shame, of abandoning Amber and Natalie. I stop for gas and coffee, but the whole time the tank is filling, my hands are shaking, and no matter how many times I suck in air, I can't seem to get that one deep breath that lets me relax.

David's promised road is nothing but desert and vast nothingness stretching out before me. It's when I'm finally free of worrying about traffic that the memories I've been fighting all morning catch up. They grab me and don't let go. I'm still driving, but my soul shrinks and sinks down, down, down, until I'm back in that black day. The wrenching pain, the soft encouraging words from Amber, the bright lights overhead. And then total blackness. And I'm in my bed at home, sore and achy, unable to pull myself out of the darkness.

"Come on, Crys," Amber says. "Try to sit up and eat something." But I can't. Shame has replaced hunger. Fear chokes thirst away. Apprehension, a word I never knew until now, overwhelms my lungs' capacity to take a deep breath. And the small bit of self-preservation that my body fights to ignite goes out inside me. All there is is dark. And hopelessness. And disgrace.

Hours later, or maybe days, Amber's there again, holding the baby's tiny white body out to me. "Take her for a minute," she says. And I do. There's no fight left in me. But the bundle is like a bomb someone has asked me to love.

"See?" Amber says. "Isn't she beautiful? She's perfect."

She *is* perfect. She looks at me with wide blue eyes I don't recognize and a tiny tuft of strawberry blond curls that I do. But I hand her back as soon as Amber will take her, and I sink into the depths of my mattress.

"You have to get up, Crystal. This has gone on long enough." Mom pulls the worn sheet off me, and I try to burrow under my pillow. She yanks that away too. "Grab her arm," I hear her say. Gil touches me tentatively, and when I don't fight him, he holds tighter to my elbow and helps Mom lift me out of bed. "Get these disgusting clothes off," she tells me. "Or we'll do it for you."

"Gil," I mumble, not wanting to strip in front of him. My voice sounds unfamiliar, cracked and dry. Mom shoos him out of our room, and as I peel off my T-shirt, sticky with sweat, and step out of the leggings I put on at the hospital, I see Amber sitting on her bed holding the baby and watching me.

"Now," Mom says, handing me a robe I've never seen before, "you're gonna shower, and then you're gonna eat something, and then we're gonna talk."

Who is this woman who never said more than "Seriously, Crystal? You? I thought it'd be Amber" when she found out what I'd done? Why does she care now? Why won't she let me sleep? Why won't she let me fade into nothing like I want to?

She marches me to the bathroom and doesn't leave until I'm standing naked under the shower. I let the water fall on me like sizzling rain until my skin turns pink. Then I shampoo my matted hair. By the time I've washed my body, trying to scrub off the shame, the water's running cold.

I wonder how long I've been in bed. My underarms are hairy, and so are my legs, but it's been so long since I could reach to shave them they aren't really indicators of anything. My belly is soft and squishy, instead of flat like it was before the baby, or taut like it was during my pregnancy.

When I come out of the shower, I pull on the robe and notice for the first time it's got that weird geometric print of hospital clothing. Probably Mom stuck it in her purse. Or maybe they sent me home in it. When I get back to the bedroom, Amber's put the baby in a basket propped up on our storage containers, and she's waiting for me with the special comb we use to untangle our curly hair. She sits me down and starts to work on the mess.

When she's done, she leads me out to the kitchen, and I'm shocked to find that Mom's actually cooked. There's a mushroom lasagna and one of those salads that come in a bag with a packet of dressing and croutons. Pepperidge Farm garlic bread. All my favorite foods. Amber sits me down, and Gil and Mom take chairs while my sister gets us drinks. We eat a meal together for maybe the first time in my whole life, not counting holidays, which are usually at the Glass Slipper anyway. No one says a word, and the chewing and slurping sounds are magnified by a thousand. Amber puts Jell-O pudding cups in front of us and we peel back the wrappers, all licking the chocolate off the foil at the same time.

"So," Mom says, once the little containers are empty. "Are you depressed? Like baby blues? Or are you feeling sorry for yourself because you're human and you fucked up?"

I stare at her. "I . . . I'm not sure. Is there a difference?"

"Amber made you a doctor's appointment to find out," she says. "Tomorrow."

"Okay."

Ahead of me on the highway, lightning flares against the desert sky and the flash snags my attention, dragging me back to the present and the road. I look at the speedometer, and I'm surprised to see it's holding steady at eighty-nine miles an hour. I can't register the speed. It doesn't feel like anything at all—even the wind tearing through the open windows means nothing to me—and I keep my foot down. David was right. There's nothing out here. No one but me, my overwhelming shame, and a couple of birds flying in circles in the hazy sky. I'm surprised by how much darker it's gotten without me noticing. A storm plays out in front of me, lighting up the clouds like someone striking a match. God . . . I wish I had a smoke. It occurs to me for the first time that if I'm living in Kansas and Nat's in Oregon, then there's no reason why I can't start smoking again. I vow to buy a pack at the next gas station. If there is such a thing. It feels like there's nothing anymore.

Just me and the car and this long, flat road with the mountains so far in the distance that they don't even seem to be getting closer. The storm's on the horizon, and I keep driving toward it, thinking that maybe when I'm in the middle of it, it will lift me right off the ground and spin me around, dropping me in Kansas like Dorothy. Except I doubt it's a tornado in Nevada. And that's not what happened to Dorothy anyway.

My foot presses harder on the gas pedal and my mind drifts away again. The doctor Mom made me see asks me a lot of questions like "Do you want to kill yourself?" and "Have you considered harming your daughter?" I'm totally shocked. I haven't had any of these thoughts and I would never hurt her in a million years.

I'm the one who screwed everything up. She didn't do anything. My face burns with humiliation at the idea that I would ever injure that helpless little girl. I know I've failed everyone—Amber, my parents, the baby who spent nine months inside of me—but I'd have to be a monster to want to get rid of her. When the doctor asks me those questions, I know for sure what everyone thinks of me. I'm a horrible, disgusting slut who can't be trusted to do the right thing.

The fact that the doctor decides I'm not clinically depressed doesn't alleviate my disgrace, but it makes Amber and Mom feel better. He tells me I should try to get into a routine and maybe do some exercise, to come see him again if I think I'm going to do anything rash.

I drive on toward the storm. Overhead the sky is getting darker but no rain falls, and I keep the gas pedal down, trying to outrun all the anxiety fighting for attention in my head. But the rhythm of the tires on the pavement and the repetition of the scenery make it too easy for my mind to drift away from the road, and the demons gain ground again.

Amber finally gave the baby a name because I wouldn't. Couldn't.

Natalie after a doll we'd had as a kid, *Sapphire* because everyone in our family would freak if she didn't have a jewel or precious stone in her name, and *Robbins* because it was ours, and we had no idea who the father was anyway.

Amber made all the doctor's appointments and the ones with social workers to get food stamps for formula. Sometimes she even posed as me, saving me from tough questions. And she found out about daycare at the high school and enrolled Natalie. She acts like she's not good at organization, but she can totally do it if she doesn't panic. That's why Aunt Ruby thinks my sister will be able to run the Glass Slipper someday. Amber arranged our schedules so one of us was always free to watch the baby, and we didn't have to count on Gil or Mom for anything. She filled out forms, deposited my paycheck once I went back to work, and gave me her tips so I had money to fix up our car. The Mustang was what kept me sane and she knew it. Slowly, methodically, we did what the doctor ordered, and we developed a routine.

Why did everything have to get all fucked up now? Why did I lie? Why wouldn't Amber forgive me? Why couldn't she understand that I knew I was asking a lot of her, but that it was for all of us? The Glass Slipper would be there in four years. We could've made a new life for ourselves that was better than anything we'd ever dreamed of. Why did she have to say out loud that I was Natalie's mother? Why didn't she stick to our agreement?

Why, why, why? The words race around in my head, making me dizzy. My foot presses harder on the accelerator. The engine roars. I am so close to flying. That's what this car was made for, and that's what I want to do . . . to take flight. If I could go a little faster—a little bit more gas should do it—I'm sure I can get liftoff. So close. I'm so close!

Ahead of me, lightning flashes like fireworks, ripping apart the sky. Thunder crashes overhead, muffled by the roar of the engine.

Behind me lights swirl and whirl.

Red.

Blue.

Red.

Blue.

Around.

And around.

And around.

The siren rips through the trance I'm locked in, yanking the part of me that is floating over the car back into my body, and I release the gas, pumping my foot on the brake so I won't go into a skid. After what seems like miles but is probably only a couple hundred feet, the Mustang stops and I turn off the engine. My head falls forward to rest against my hands on the wooden steering wheel.

I'm so . . . so . . . so tired.

CHAPTER 27

She runs my license and plate number to make sure the car isn't stolen.

She examines my insurance.

She makes me take a Breathalyzer and walk the line.

Satisfied I'm just an idiot in a powerful car, she writes me the biggest ticket anyone's ever gotten and tells me to have a nice day.

After the cop leaves, I sit there staring at the paper in my hand but not really seeing it. And then a tear falls onto the citation—one big splotch. I'm probably not the first person to cry on a ticket. Pretty soon there's another fat drop. And then another. After a minute, the tears are falling so fast I toss the ticket onto the passenger seat before it disintegrates.

I slump forward, sobbing. My body shakes and convulses, shuddering, causing my head to bang against the hard wood of the steering wheel. It's been over a hundred degrees outside all day, probably hotter in my car, and yet I'm shivering. I rock myself back and forth, the shame cascading off me in salty tears, the humiliation pouring out through my sweat glands, self-righteousness dripping under my arms, soaking my tank-top, the smell of failure stinking up the car.

After years of berating Amber for sleeping around, of threatening to abandon her if she ended up pregnant, of dragging her home screaming when she was too drunk to say no but not too far gone to fight me, of covering her up with my flannel shirt after she'd danced a striptease on a table, after all that, I was the one who messed up our lives. And did she abandon me?

No.

Did she let them take Nat away when I said they could?

No.

Did I ever thank her for that?

No.

And if I hadn't had Amber that first month, what would've happened to Natalie then? Or to me? What no one knew is that while I was in bed refusing to acknowledge my daughter, I was also trying to convince myself she was actually Amber's child. I was a traitor even back then, and the whole time, my sister took care of the baby anyway. She fed her and changed her and whisked her out of the room when she cried, so I could sleep.

And then Amber came up with the idea that saved us all. She offered to raise Nat with me. She told me we'd graduate, meet new people, and after a while no one would even remember I was the one who'd given birth. We'd never mention it. Natalie could call us by our first names, as if we were both her aunts or something. For hours, days, weeks, Amber sat by my bed, telling me how we could do this. And slowly, over that summer, we remade our plans. And how did I thank Amber? I applied to McPherson, lied about it, and ran off, leaving them both the first chance I got.

After a while, I realize my tears are drying up, but I feel like I might barf, so I pull myself out of the car and stumble around to the side of the road. I kneel on the still-hot ground, dry-heaving. When did I last eat? A bean burrito at Taco Bell this afternoon? Or was that last night?

The storm is still in the distance when I first collapse in the dust, but after a while I notice the air has gotten cooler and the sky is almost black. I try to stand, but my knees buckle and I have to lean against the fender. There are bits of gravel and glass embedded in my shins, and I gingerly brush them away. Little spurts of blood appear and there are deep, angry imprints in my skin. Nothing less than I deserve.

Back in the car, I sit there as the rain starts to fall, plopping onto my windshield and leaving streaks through the dust and grime and dead bugs splattered across it. The weather is getting really cold now, and my throat is dry and scratchy.

The half bottle of water I have left is tepid, but I drink it anyway. I need to find food and somewhere to sleep. After driving along the deserted road for another hour, I see a roadside motel and pull in. I've given up on camping because of the rain. The motel's like the one in that old movie *Psycho*. Perfect. Maybe if I'm lucky someone will jump into the shower and stab me to death. I get a room from a woman in the office who never takes her eyes off the TV, which is good because mine are all puffy and red, making me look like I'm stoned.

There aren't any restaurants around, so I get a couple of candy bars from a dusty vending machine and two more bottles of water. My room's actually nicer than I expect— clean and with a Southwestern theme. Lots of cactuses everywhere . . . on the sheets, the bedspread, the towels, the wallpaper.

I stretch out on the bed and eat the candy and drink the water. My mind is swirling, a hot mess of emotions and memories. But I can't take any more tonight. I stare at a black-and-white photo of a cactus silhouetted against the setting sun until I can't see the picture anymore . . . it's a blob of blankness and forgetfulness and nothing.

I'm hot and sweaty, and sometime during the night I've gotten under the covers. I kick them off, but they cling to my sticky legs, confusing my dreams. The room is warm and stuffy, and it's like a drug to my body. I can't wake up, and I don't want to anyway, so I roll over, pulling a corner of the sheet over my eyes to block out the light from around the curtains.

I'm having those weird half dreams where I'm up and awake, but then I realize I'm still on the bed and sink back into sleep until it happens again. I think my eyes are open, but they're not, and down I go again.

And again.

And again.

A jolting rap like a car with serious engine knock penetrates my murky sleep. And then there's the sound of a key turning and a door opening. I roll over and manage to pry my burning eyes open. A short, dark woman with streaks of gray in her black hair is peering through the three-inch gap the security chain allows.

"You are okay?" she asks in a sharp voice.

"Yeah, just tired."

I stumble to my feet and open the door for the stranger, who comes into the room all bustle and efficiency. She tells me she's the owner of the motel and that checkout was at eleven. It's now three-fifteen. The maid didn't show up today and I'm the only guest, so no one realized I was still here until they noticed the Mustang.

"No see car from office," she explains. "My nephew come with mail and ask 'Whose car?'"

"Oh." I'm still kind of out of it, and my eyelids feel hot and swollen from crying and sleep.

"He love cars."

"Yeah. Me too."

While I've been standing there in a daze, she's come in and made the bed. She even picks up the candy wrappers I left on the end table, tossing them in the garbage can, making me feel like a total slob.

"Can I stay another night?"

"Yes. *No problemo*," she says. "You are hungry?" I'm weak with hunger, and she can see it, so there's no point in denying it. I nod. "Come with me."

I slip on my shoes and follow her across the parking lot. She leads me into the little lobby where I checked in the night before and through a door marked PRIVATE. It's like another world in here. Her apartment is small, tidy, and covered with crocheted afghans. There are dainty little cups in a china cabinet, and everything is spotless. Dust doesn't even float through the shaft of sunlight coming in the kitchen window.

She sits me down at a round wooden table, deftly dropping a placemat, cloth napkin, and silverware in front of me. "*Agua?*" she asks. "Water?"

"*Sí*," I say, smiling. "Please."

It's cool in here, the air conditioning whirring away in another room, and I relax a little. After a few minutes, she puts a plate in front of me. "My nephew," she says, "he eat all the *carne* — meat. Sorry. But here is chile rellenos. Is good too."

"Oh, that's okay. I don't eat meat anyway."

She raises her eyebrows at me. *"Vegetariana?"*

I nod.

She purses her lips and studies me like she's considering something. "I make vegetable tamales for your dinner."

"Oh, no," I say. "You don't have to cook for me again. This is great."

"No restaurant here," she says. "You eat with me and Ramon."

The food smells so delicious, and I can tell there's no point in fighting her, so I give in. "Umm . . . okay. Thanks." I take a bite of the steaming chile rellenos and cheese slides off my fork. It's so good I almost start crying again. And then the spicy heat hits me like I've swallowed fire, and my eyes start streaming.

"Too hot?"

"No, no." I gasp, trying not to cough. "It's great." Because it *is,* but *oh my God.* Every cell in my mouth's screaming in pain. I try to hide my agony by smiling, but she can totally tell, and she rushes to get me a big glass of chocolate milk.

"This help."

I drink half of it down without stopping, and she laughs. But she's right, the sweetness cuts the heat, and I'm able to breathe again. She tries to take my plate away, but I say no, I want it.

"You are sure?"

"Yeah." The food is killer, but it's really delicious.

She brings me some salad to help cool down the dish. While I eat, we talk. She tells me she's Mrs. Gomez, a widow, and she owns the place with her nephew. I give her the sanitized version of my story: I'm Crystal, driving myself to college, just another student on the road. She gives me a lecture on driving so far without sleep, and I meekly apologize. It doesn't stop her from sending me back to my room for a nap, though.

I'm not sleepy, but I do stink, so I take a long, hot shower. By the time I get out, the window air conditioner has kicked in and it's icy cold in my room. I watch TV so I don't have to think about anything real. Around seven o'clock, someone knocks on the door. For one crazy moment I think maybe it's Amber, that she's tracked me down, and I leap off the bed and race across the little room.

Of course it's not Amber, but I've already flung open the door and now I'm face-to-face with a guy who's about my height, which makes him pretty damn short, but he's also stocky and barrel-chested with huge muscular arms. God, I'm so stupid sometimes! What was I thinking opening the door? My body tenses, ready for a fight. He's also a lot older than me . . . maybe forty? His black hair and eyes are shiny, reflecting the light from my room. I'm freaking out inside, but then a tiny bit of relief seeps in because he's smiling at me.

"Hey," he says. "You're Crystal, right? I'm Ramon. The nephew. It's time to eat."

All the tension dissolves, and I hope he hadn't noticed I was afraid at first. "Oh, right. Okay."

When we go through the lobby, the lady at the desk—the one who checked me in the night before—has her attention glued to the TV again and still doesn't look up. We walk into the private apartment and sit down at the kitchen table. Mrs. Gomez sets a steaming plate of tamales in front of me.

"Good?" she asks after my first bite, which isn't spicy at all.

"Amazing. Thank you so much."

Ramon asks a lot of questions about my car, and we're already eating our ice cream before he runs out of things to say. It's still light when we go outside and I open the hood, letting him check out the engine. I can tell he wants to go for a ride, but I can't do it. After last night, I'm too scared to get behind the wheel. What if I lose control and try to fly again? I think I might have to stay here, at this motel, for the rest of my life. Or at least until my money runs out.

I ask Ramon if he's got a license and he says he does. I let him drive my car. No one but me has ever driven the Mustang, except for the time Han took us to the hospital, but for some reason, I don't even care. It doesn't seem that important anymore. I sit on the curb, waiting for him to come back.

He's only gone about twenty minutes, and when he gets out of the car, he's grinning like Bonehead does when Amber brings him a bit of steak from work. I let Ramon go on and on about the Mustang's power for a few minutes, and then I interrupt and ask about the motel's Internet. Until a little while ago, I'd forgotten about my computer and email. Maybe Amber's changed her mind and wants to come with me.

"Internet? Sure," he says. "Free in all the rooms. You got a computer?"

"Yeah."

He can tell I want to go inside, so he thanks me again and adds, "It was really cool to drive your car."

"No problem."

He goes back to his aunt's, and I dig the computer out of the trunk and carry it into my room. It takes me a while to figure out how to get online, but once I do, I'm super excited. There *is* an email from Amber! Han must've let her use his laptop.

When I open it, there isn't any message, just a bunch of attachments. I click on them one at a time. They're all pictures of Natalie. The very last one is of the three of us. Me and Amber are in our graduation caps and gowns and Nat's gotten a hold of my tassel. I guess Mom did get that picture after all.

Amber's laughing, looking up at Nat. Our baby's eyes are wide and full of spark, and I have a look of surprise on my face that's turning into laughter. As I sit there on the bed more than six hundred miles from my baby, my mind fills with more images of Natalie. It's like one of those montage videos on YouTube. First she's tiny and red with a scrunchy face and baby acne. In the next memory, she looks like a totally different kid. She's got milky white skin, so pale you can see the veins underneath. Amber's dressed her in a tiny jumper with strawberries for buttons. My sister holds Natalie out to me, but I refuse her, turning my face away. She must've been a few weeks old by then.

After that, it's a blur of images playing across my mind. Smiles and spit bubbles, screams and whimpers. Poopy diapers and bare-naked legs kicking in the air. And then I remember last winter when we had the flu and I was afraid we'd die and she'd never know how much we . . . I . . . loved her.

I quickly try to replace that memory with something better, and a picture of her in that awful red velvet Christmas dress Han bought her makes me laugh. God, she looked horrible in it! I giggle a little, remembering.

"Look at you," Han had said. "Aren't you gorgeous?" He held her up over his head, and she smiled down at him, her big blue eyes wide.

And then a wave of nausea rushes over me as I remember Han looking up at her with those exact same eyes. Immediately, I want to run to the bathroom and throw up the tamales, but I can't move. My legs are like lumps of iron weighing me down. I swallow back the vomit.

"No . . ." I say into the pillow I'm suddenly clutching to my chest. "No, no, no, no, no, no, no, no, no." But the memories won't stop now. It's too late to block them. Once the thought of Han's blue eyes has slipped through a gap in the brick wall I've put up, it starts to crumble fast. Big chunks fall, hitting me in my most tender spots.

An end-of-summer party at our cousin Jade's house. Me and Amber walk. It's only a few streets away and that way we can both drink. It's hot and she talks me into being a girly girl for once. I borrow a denim miniskirt and a lacy tank-top. We're all in the dark backyard—me, Amber, Jade, Han— drinking beer, smoking pot and cigarettes.

And then I'm waking up in one of the dank rooms in Jade's house. And . . .

Oh God, oh God, oh God, oh God . . . This can't be true. But I know it is. And Han has known it all along and never said a word. *He never said a word.* He let me say I didn't know who the father was. And the weird thing is, I'm not sure I did know. I mean, I must've because we weren't that drunk. But until this very moment, I couldn't remember that night at all. In my head, it's been dark, and black, and a mystery.

And then I missed all those periods. One after the other. By the time I was three months gone, I knew, but I kept it a secret until I was almost five months pregnant. One day Amber walked in on me in the bathroom as I got out of the shower. After years of berating her for being easy, I was the one who had carried on the family legacy of getting pregnant in high school. Amber had counted on me to get us out of the family rut, to build us a new life, but I'd let her down.

I hold the motel pillow as close to me as I can, squeezing it, wondering what to do with this new information. After a long time, some of the shame recedes and I think I know. I fall into a dreamless sleep.

I wake up in the morning on top of the cactus bedspread, disoriented, hot, and thirsty. I have no idea when I fell asleep or what time it is now. The bedside clock has stopped at 2:45. I know what I have to do, and oddly, now that I've decided, I'm okay with it.

I pick up the phone, and it takes me a minute to figure out how to get the operator. Once I do, I give her the number and wait.

He answers on the first ring. "Yo?"

"I have a collect call from Crystal Robbins," a computer voice says. "Will you accept the charges?"

"Yeah, of course."

"Go ahead."

"Hey," I say, unsure where to start. "I'm in trouble."

Like he's done every single time I've asked him for help, he doesn't even hesitate. "Tell me what you need."

CHAPTER 28

Whenever we've needed something for the baby, Han came through. All this time I told myself he was just a nice guy who liked the challenge of scoring stuff for cheap. Now I know why he's been hanging around, and I owe him, but before I can do anything to make it up to him, I need his help again.

"Where are you?" he asks.

"Somewhere in Nevada. In a motel."

"Did something happen to the Mustang?"

"No. Something happened to me."

"Shit! Are you okay? If anyone—"

"No, it's nothing like that. I'm okay physically. But . . . I can't drive. I don't trust myself."

"I don't understand."

"I know. I'm not making sense, but I need your help. I need you to come and get me. Please?"

"Yeah, of course," he says. "I'll get there. What's the name of the place where you're staying?"

I look at the sheet of guest rules and regulations by the phone. "It's called the Three Cacti Motel. I'm in room eight." I can hear his fingers tapping on a keyboard and then he says, "Okay. I've got their website up. Stay right where you are and I'll call you back in ten minutes."

"Okay. And, Han?"

"Yeah?"

"Thanks."

"No problem. I'll call you back."

I sit there by the phone, waiting and feeling stupid. Ten minutes go by, and then fifteen. My underarms go all prickly, and it's not from the heat. It's cool in the motel room. My discomfort is more from embarrassment. What was I thinking? I'm about to call him back and tell him to forget it, that I'm fine, when the phone rings. I grab the receiver fast.

"Do you think you can drive yourself to Reno?" Han asks.

"It's not that far."

"What's in Reno?"

"My mom's cousin works for the airline, and she can get me a stand-by ticket for thirty-five bucks."

I take a deep breath and let it out slow. "Yeah, I can do that."

He must hear the doubt in my voice. "If you don't think you can, I'll get to you somehow."

"No, it's okay. I can do it."

"I don't know when I'll be able to get there, but I booked you a hotel room in Reno for tonight. It's cheap, but the reviews say it's safe."

"Thanks."

"Stay there and wait for me."

"I will," I say. "And Han? Don't tell Amber, okay?"

"I won't. I promise."

He emails the hotel information so I don't have to write it down, and we hang up. After I check out, Mrs. Gomez gives me a packet of foil-wrapped tamales for the road. "Drive careful," she tells me. "Let me know you get to Reno okay." I promise and she gives me a strong hug.

The drive to Reno is hot and slow. And startling. When I was driving before, everything was a blur, distorted by emotions and memories. But now, for the first time, I really see the landscape around me, and it looks as strange as if I've landed on the moon . . . dusty, barren, unfamiliar. The desert stretches in every direction like an abandoned blanket—muted browns, golds, and pinks, lonely and bare, but hauntingly beautiful, too. The vast emptiness adds to the ache I already have in my heart.

I stay five miles under the speed limit and listen to music, making myself sing along to 1950s pop songs so all I can think about are the lyrics and not what's going to happen when I meet up with Han. I drive so slow and careful that by the time I reach the hotel, Han's already waiting out front, baking in the heat. I worry he's a mirage at first, but he waves to me and I know he's real.

"How'd you get here so fast?" I ask him once I've parked.

"The first flight I tried had a seat." He acts like he's going to hug me, but I step back, afraid to touch him, and he drops his arms. "Let's check in," he says.

He's only booked one room, but it has two beds, and I toss my stuff on one and he throws his bag on the other. We sit there looking at each other. I guess he's waiting for me to talk, but I'm not ready.

"We could hit the road now," I say.

"Maybe we could chill for a day. I've never been to Reno."

"Sit by the pool?" I ask, half smiling.

"Why not?"

I can't imagine having time to sit around a pool. I always have so much to do—work, school assignments, the baby.

Oh, God.

Natalie.

I miss her so much the hole in my heart opens wider. "How's Nat?"

"She's good. I saw her yesterday."

"How come?"

"Amber called to tell me they stayed."

More like to tell him her side of the story and win him over. Me and Han sit there for a while, lost in thoughts and awkwardness. I know why he's here, but I didn't really explain myself to him over the phone.

"So how far are we from Kansas, anyway?" he asks.

I shake my head. "I'm not going to school."

"What do you mean?"

"I need you to drive me back to Portland."

"But what about college?"

"I don't know if I'm still going. I have some things to do at home first. And then . . . maybe." Tears well up, threatening to spill over.

"Let's get some food," Han says, jumping up, his face panicked. "I'm starving."

We spend our "rich people's day of leisure," as Han starts calling it, in air-conditioned shopping malls and at all-you-can-eat buffets. For a skinny guy, he can really pack away the food. I don't do too bad myself. Everything's really cheap in Reno because they want you to gamble, but we're too young to get into the casinos. There are slot machines everywhere, though, even in the grocery store where we go for pop.

"You know what I'm gonna do?" I say. "I'm gonna play ten bucks for Mom."

We pick a slot machine and Han watches while I play. I've never gambled before, mostly because Mom does enough for all of us, but also because it always seemed stupid. At least until I start winning, and then it's kinda fun.

"No wonder she likes this."

"Yeah, it's great when you're winning."

"And I'm gonna keep it that way." I'm up to eighty bucks before I start losing. I quit when I'm forty-seven dollars ahead.

"The lady wins," Han says. "Take that, Reno!"

"Mom'll be able to tell everyone she won big in Nevada now." I head to the register. "Unlike if she was really here."

Mom doesn't end up getting her winnings, though, because when I try to cash out, the clerk wants ID to prove I'm twenty-one. I don't have it, and he tries to confiscate my ticket, but Han and I run out of the store, laughing, the paper clutched in my fist. I'll give it to Mom and maybe Aunt Pearl can get her money on her next trip.

"It's the thought that counts," Han tells me.

"Yeah. Whatever."

That night, we hang out by the pool. There are NO SMOKING signs every ten feet, but no one's around, so we risk lighting up. God, it feels so good to smoke again. At least, right now. I don't miss the hacking cough in the morning. I think most people have to smoke for years before they develop a cough, but me and Amber got it almost right away. We've always had trouble with our lungs. Mom says it's 'cause we were preemies, but I think our bedroom's too damn cold in the winter. After my first drag, some of the tension I've been carrying around in my shoulders eases, and ironically, I get that deep breath I've been needing for days.

I exhale the smoke, relishing the rush like a guy on death row. We're heading back to Portland tomorrow, so I won't be smoking much longer. I inhale again and let out the breath real slow. It's time to say what I need to say. I didn't get Han here just so he could drive me home.

"Hey." I try to keep my voice light. "You're gonna have to quit smoking."

"Me? Why?"

"Because you're Nat's father, and No Smoking's one of the rules."

Next to me, Han sits up straight on his lounge chair, but I stay frozen, afraid to look over at him. "Her father?" His voice breaks on the word. "You mean it?"

"If you want to be," I say, carefully casual. "It might be good."

"I thought you didn't . . . didn't know. That's what Amber told me."

"Yeah, well . . ." I can feel my face flush. "I didn't remember it was you until last night. It's like I blocked it or something." I can feel him looking at me, and my heart rate speeds up. "I don't know exactly what happened at that party. Some of it's coming back, though. And I realized . . . you and Nat have the exact same eyes."

"Yeah. We definitely do." I can hear the smile in his voice. "Wow. I wasn't expecting this. But this is great. I love that kid."

"Me too. And she really likes you."

"She said my name," Han reminds me.

"I know." I can't help laughing at how proud he sounds.

Someone comes out of the hotel and turns off all the lights. "Pool's closed," he calls to us.

"We're not swimming," I call back.

The worker goes inside. The only lights on now are the ones underwater, giving the pool area a nuclear glow. Above us you can see the faint trace of stars in the darkening sky. Searchlights crisscross overhead, making me feel like I've landed in the world's biggest car lot.

"I don't want you to think you have to—"

"I thought you hated me," he says.

I shake my head. God, this is so hard. Me and Amber haven't even discussed it. Every time she tried to bring it up, I refused to go there. "I never hated you."

"That makes me feel a little better."

I want to stop talking, but Han deserves more. I go on. "The day after that party I convinced myself I hadn't done anything." My voice is shaky, and I hope he can't hear how nervous I am. "And then, well, I was pregnant . . . so I kind of had to admit something must've happened. But I felt like such an idiot. I couldn't think about it. I was supposed to be the responsible one. I swear I didn't remember it was you until last night."

"You're making my performance feel very memorable," Han says, trying to crack a joke, but it falls flat.

"I'm sorry. But I want you to understand I wouldn't have shut you out like that if I'd remembered. You've been so good to us. You can't even imagine how much I hate myself right now for what I did to you."

"Don't."

We sit there, smoking in the semi-darkness, not talking for a while. I guess Han has a lot to think about now too. But there's one more thing I have to know about that night.

"Did you know it was me?" I ask.

"As opposed to . . . ?"

"Amber."

Han's body shoots up in the chair again. "I'm not stupid. I've always been able to tell you two apart."

But there's still a big gap in my memory, and if I can't remember it, then he's going to have to fill me in. "I know," I say. "But then . . . why'd we do it? We were never like that . . ."

He stands and paces next to the pool's edge, rubbing his hands over his face, hard, like he wants to peel his skin off. "I always liked you. Not Amber."

"Oh, please. You were all over her for two years."

"I pretended to like Amber so I could get to know *you*. You're not that easy to make friends with."

I can't believe this. But why would he lie? "Really?"

"Really."

Wow. "So what happened that night? Did you make a move and I said yes?"

He's still standing by the pool, looking up at the sky. "The thing is . . . if you really don't remember . . . it's just, Crys, that night was so fucked up. I never should've let it happen. I mean, I wanted it to, but not like that."

A wave of dread washes over me. Memories fight to surface, but I'm not ready. Not here. Not while we're outside with the endless sky already making me feel small and scared. "You know what?" I say, jumping up off the lounge chair. "I'm shot. Let's go to bed."

"Sounds good," he says without an argument.

I watch the clock change from 1:21 to 1:22. We've been in our separate beds for fifty-seven minutes. Han is out cold, but I'm wide awake. I don't want to make him tell me his version of what happened that night. I need my own truth, and so I force myself to try to remember. I think about waking up naked in Jade's house. Han is there beside me. And we're on the floor. I refused to do it in her bed. And I'm freaking out.

"Oh my God!" I whisper-yell at him in case other people are around. "What the hell did we do?" I throw clothes at him. "We've got to get out of here."

"Crystal—"

"Don't talk to me," I say. "This never happened. Never."

"But—"

"Han, promise me this never happened!"

I don't wait for him to say it. I'm in my clothes now—not mine, but the skanky ones I borrowed from Amber so I wouldn't have to listen to those guys call me a dyke all night.

She works on a car like a grease monkey.

She dresses like a guy.

I bet she likes girls.

One night with me and she'd change.

The voices follow me as I run the four blocks to our house. It's three in the morning but no one's home, and I jump in the shower, washing off everything—the stink of cigarettes and pot, the beer oozing out of my pores, Han's sweat as he . . . as he . . .

Why did I listen to those guys? Why did I let them torment me into trying to prove something? The truth is, I'm not a cold bitch like they say. I just . . . don't really like guys. Or girls. I mean, I think I like guys more, but everyone I know is an idiot. Someday I'll probably fall in love, once me and Amber have our new life, but right now I'm too busy to screw around with high school boys. And then Han had been there. And he'd heard them as they walked by us.

"Is that Amber?" one of them had said.

"Nah. She's with Rick inside. That's the frigid one."

"Good luck, dude," the first one said to Han.

"Ignore them," he told me.

But those assholes, or some version of them, had been harassing me all summer. And at that moment, I was sick of it. I threw the joint I was smoking on the ground and grabbed Han and kissed him hard, for everyone to see. At first he was too stunned to respond, but I kept at it.

His mouth was warm and tasted like beer and smoke. It wasn't fun, but I was determined, and the longer and harder I kissed him, the more he got into it. We made out right there in the backyard, my hands snaking under his shirt, feeling his ribs through his skin. His fingers in my hair, our bodies pressing together, our lips making smacking sounds. Finally someone shouted at us to get a room, and we broke apart. I remember forcing myself to smile big as I took Han's hand and led him right past those assholes and into the house, their catcalls following us.

The rest is still a blur, but that's enough. That's all I need to know right now. My body's shaking under the covers, and I let the memory fade away and force myself to focus on the clock here in Nevada, tears sliding down my face, soaking the pillow.

"I'm sorry, Han," I whisper. "I'm so sorry."

He mumbles something in his sleep, and I hear him roll over in his bed.

What have I done? Will he ever forgive me?

CHAPTER 29

In the morning, I feel oddly light. I mean, there's still a sense of dread. I know we're not done talking about this, but I'll save that conversation for the road. We decide not to rush out of town. Instead, we eat a huge breakfast for $2.99 each, and then we go looking for presents. At a souvenir shop, I find a T-shirt for Gil that says I LOST EVERYTHING EXCEPT THIS SHIRT IN RENO, NEVADA. The one we find for Mom is in the back where they keep the triple-XL shirts. It's light blue and says: WANNA BET?

"You can see through that material," Han says.

His worried face cracks me up. I know what he means, though. No one wants to see Mom's gigantic boobs coming at them. "Don't worry, she'll sleep in it. You'll never have to see her in it." I giggle at his obvious relief.

We don't find anything for Amber, so we go to the next

shop over and they have the perfect top: a black tank with RENO written across it in rhinestones. While I'm deciding if I should get it big in case it shrinks, Han nudges me. He's holding up a toddler-size shirt. In block lettering it says MY PARENTS WENT TO RENO AND ALL I GOT WAS THIS LOUSY T-SHIRT.

To be honest, it kinda freaks me out. But then I shrug. "Why the hell not? It's true, isn't it?"

"I'll pay for this one," Han says, grinning all the way to the cash register.

After the shopping spree, we hit a lunch buffet and then walk back to the car. Now that it's actually time for Han to drive, I'm not so sure I need him after all. Letting Ramon take the car out the other night was a moment of weakness, but I think I'm over it.

I clutch the keys in my hand tighter. "Maybe I'll drive after all."

"Forget it. I didn't come all this way to be a passenger."

"But I think I'm good now."

"Actually, you're a control freak," Han says, laughing. He takes the key from me and opens the passenger door. "Get in the car already."

I climb in, but I'm not happy. He gets behind the wheel and my nerves ratchet up tenfold.

"See?" he says, backing out. "This isn't so bad."

"Watch out for the guy on the bike!"

"Chill. He's across the road, Crys."

"Not that one!" I shout as he almost takes out someone in yellow spandex on our right side.

"Oh, yeah, sorry. Didn't see him."

Han pulls into traffic, making my heart start pumping harder. We go about four blocks before he changes lanes without signaling and a couple of guys in an SUV come unglued, honking and swearing at us as they swerve out of the way.

"Oh my God."

"Will you relax?" he says. "You're making me nervous. You didn't freak out like this when I drove your ass to the hospital last winter."

"I felt like dying that day. Now I'd like to live."

"*You* called *me*, remember?"

"You're the only one I know with a driver's license."

And I'm starting to wonder how he got it.

"Very funny."

I wasn't trying to be, but I keep this to myself. While it's true, I did call him so he could drive, I also knew we needed to talk, and I knew if I waited until I got back to Portland, I might chicken out. I can already tell we won't be discussing anything serious while Han is driving, though, or we might not survive the trip.

We finally get out of Reno, which makes things a little better. There are semi-trucks whizzing by us, and Han putts along like a little old lady, but at least he's staying in one lane.

"It's a muscle car," I remind him. "Put your foot down a little so you don't embarrass Mustang owners everywhere."

"I'm gonna ignore that, Miss One-Hundred-and-Twenty-Miles-an-Hour-in-a-Sixty-Five-Mile-an-Hour-Zone."

"Yeah, well, I'd rather die speeding than get creamed by an eighteen-wheeler for going too slow."

"Why do we keep talking about dying?"

"Mostly it's your driving."

"Ha-ha."

But a small part of me is worried about dying because I'm afraid I'll never see Amber and Natalie again, and not because of anything real, like Han's sucky driving. It's more like I know if I die, the last thing they'll remember is the huge fight on the lawn and the cops coming, and that would be really horrible.

"Did Amber get in trouble with the police after our big fight?" I ask.

"Nah. She told them it was an old boyfriend picking up his stuff and being an asshole about it."

That's one good thing, anyway.

We drive in agitated silence for a while. Well, I don't think Han's worried about anything, but his driving really is scaring the crap out of me. I wonder how long I have to wait until I can take over without any more control-freak comments.

"We can switch off anytime," I say.

"I've only been driving for an hour."

It seems like way longer. "Okay, well . . . it's about nine hours to Portland so . . . you know . . . I'm good to drive a long stretch."

He doesn't answer, and after a while I notice he's relaxed a little. At least his knuckles aren't white anymore. And he's going the speed limit, which is better than granny pace. Maybe he's right and I was making him nervous. I vow to shut up and let him drive.

It's almost five o'clock when we get to Red Bluff and pick up I-5, heading north. Han's been driving for about four hours, and we stop for coffee and switch places. We don't talk much, and I don't know what he's thinking about, but I've got something on my mind and I want him to weigh in.

"Han? What would you think if I took Natalie to Kansas?"

"I thought that was the plan."

"I know, but that was before you had any . . . claim on her."

I see him smile, and that old familiar knot in my stomach tightens. "I think you should go to college," he says, and I relax a little.

"Really?"

"Yeah. Of course. You belong there."

"But won't you miss her?"

"I was always gonna miss her. That's why I was planning to visit."

"You were?"

"Yep."

"Oh. Cool." We drive on for a while, the hot wind blowing in through the open windows, tossing my curls around my face.

"So you're still going?" he asks. "Without Amber?"

"Actually, when I called you to come and get me, I wasn't planning on it. But I've been thinking about it a lot while you were driving. Something Amber said to me before I left makes a lot of sense."

"What's that?"

"She told me that if I really want to go to college, then I'll have to suck it up and do what everyone else does: find daycare."

"Oh, I'm all over that," Han says. "I'll find you the best daycare in the whole state of Kansas."

I laugh. "Sounds expensive."

"You know what?" he asks. "I'm gonna pay for it."

"I didn't mean—"

"I know you didn't. But I'm serious. I'm her dad. I should pay for it."

"Really?"

"Definitely. You can count on me."

"Wow. Thanks."

I can't believe it. This is so great. Maybe college will happen after all. Classes don't start for three weeks, and I need to do some stuff at home to make things right with Amber, but we already have an apartment lined up . . . If I get my shit together fast, and if Han helps me, I think I might be able to pull this off.

"Uh, Crystal?" Han says, snapping me back to the present.

"Yeah?"

"You're going eighty-five."

I ease up on the gas pedal. "Sorry. I was getting excited about college again."

"That's good. But I don't think you can afford another ticket."

"Yeah. No kidding."

Somewhere outside of Weed, California, traffic slows and I tap my brakes. Cars trickle to a standstill, and I kill the engine a few minutes later so we don't overheat. After an hour of sitting there, we see people getting out and standing by their cars to talk, so we do, too. Everyone else seems to know what's going on because they all have cell phones. Han weaves through the parked cars and asks someone what's up. He comes back and tells me it's an eighteen-wheeler, jack-knifed, blocking all lanes.

"But it happened around four thirty," he says. "So hopefully it's almost cleared."

The sun's getting lower, but it's still beating down on us, and we climb back inside the stifling car to get out of it.

"God, this feels like our bedroom at home," I say.

"How do you sleep?"

"You get used to it, I guess."

It's seven o'clock before traffic starts moving again. By the time we pass the crash site, about five miles up the road, all that's left is a mangled guardrail and piles of gray ash from the flares. As soon as I see the wreckage, I decide not to let Han drive anymore. Natalie needs her parents.

Just before we get to the Oregon border, we pull off at a rest stop and have a cigarette.

"Well," I say, inhaling deeply, "last one for me."

Amber will undoubtedly smell the smoke on my breath anyway, but I might as well try to get it out of my system now. Han looks at me, takes a last mournful puff, smashes the butt under his shoe, and tosses the rest of the pack into the garbage can.

"Really?" I ask.

"Once Amber finds out you're letting me be Nat's dad, I won't have a choice."

"I'm not *letting* you," I say. "You *are* her dad."

"Well, yeah. You know what I mean."

He's smiling, but I feel so bad. Sure, he's been around the house a lot, but only on the fringes of Nat's life. By being so ashamed, so self-centered, I've kept him from his daughter for over a year. I really suck. Somehow I have to make it up to him.

CHAPTER 30

Han insists on driving again, so I reluctantly let him. Honestly, I'm so tired, I haven't got any fight left in me. It's getting dark, and we're outside of Medford when a loud whapping sound startles me awake. I hadn't even realized I was sleeping.

"What'd you hit?" I ask.

"Nothing. I swear."

"Pull over."

"I am. I'm not stupid." He eases the Mustang onto the shoulder of the road. I'm out of the car instantly. I have a feeling I know what's up, and sure enough, I'm right. The rear passenger tire's flat.

"I know I didn't hit anything," Han says, coming around to look.

"It's all right," I tell him. "Relax. It's just a flat. We

probably picked up a nail somewhere. Go turn the hazard lights on and get me the keys."

"What do we do now?" he asks when he comes back. "We don't have a phone."

I look at him as if he's nuts. "We change the tire."

"You know how to do that, right?"

"I'm a *mechanic*."

"Oh, yeah. Duh. Sorry. I'm kinda tired."

I've got the trunk open, and I start unloading my crap onto the side of the road. Once I get the cover off the spare, I loosen the hold-downs and lift out the tire. It's pretty heavy, so I say, "Feel free to help me, here." Han grabs one side of the spare, and we set it on the grass.

"Find me a rock to chock the left back wheel and then maybe light some flares?" I say. "They're in that road safety kit."

I pop the hubcap off and loosen the lug nuts before jacking up the car. The nuts are impossible to get off once the vehicle is raised. Plus, the car could fall. Then I find the sweet spot for the jack and begin to lift the Mustang. Han is back now, staring at me in the fading light.

"What?" I ask as I lift the flat tire off and roll it to the side.

"It's just . . . I'm impressed, is all."

"Please tell me you know how to change a tire."

"No idea."

I shake my head in disgust. "Seriously, you shouldn't even be able to get a license if you can't change your own tire." I was already doubting he should have a driver's license anyway, but now I know they should take it away. "You saw what I did?"

"Yeah, I guess."

"Okay, so now we're gonna put on the spare. Grab it like this. Got it?"

"Uh-huh."

We lift the tire together and slide it into place. "And then you put the lug nuts on. You want to tighten them with your fingers while the car's still jacked up. First you do this one, and then the one across from it. In a star pattern."

I'm still having trouble getting over the idea that Han can't change a tire on his own. What kind of a dad is he gonna be for Nat if he can't teach her the basics? But then I think about all the things he's helped me with: buying the computer, finding all those clothes and the car seat online, and getting a cheap ticket to Reno to bail me out. I'll be there to teach Natalie everything she needs to know about cars.

I watch while he tightens the lug nuts. "Han?"

"Yeah?" he says, concentrating on what he's doing.

"How come you never . . . you know . . . said anything before? I mean, you must've known you were Nat's dad."

He keeps his eyes on the spare tire. "Uh . . . well, Amber said you didn't want to talk about it."

"You told Amber?"

"Not exactly . . . but I asked her if she knew who the dad was."

"Oh."

It seems like a pretty big deal for him to just drop it because my sister told him I didn't want to talk about it, but who am I to judge?

"What do we do next?" he asks. And for a minute, I think he means about me and him and Nat, but then I realize he's talking about the tire. "We lower the car, tighten up the lug nuts all the way, and we're ready to go."

"Wow," he says, letting the jack down. "That's pretty easy."

I laugh. "Yep."

In Medford we find an all-night tire place and go in and have the original one plugged. Just like I thought, we'd picked up a nail. At least I didn't have a blowout and have to buy a whole new tire. Still, it was after hours, so it set me back a pretty big chunk of change, considering I could've fixed the tire myself at Jimmy's. But we are still almost three hundred miles from Portland and I don't want to risk driving on the spare that far.

We stock up on burritos and pop before hitting the road

again, and I sit back and let Han drive. He wants to prove to me the flat tire wasn't his fault, which is stupid, because I already know that. I could've driven over that nail before he even flew down to meet me. Sometimes you can go a long time with one in your tire and not even know it.

I look out my window at the reflective mile markers as they fly past, trying to use the darkness to block out the one thing I've never had to worry about before today—Natalie's father coming into the picture and wanting joint custody. It seems like Han would've made his move a long time ago if he wanted that, though.

"I know you said I should take Natalie to Kansas, but did you mean it?"

"Yeah, definitely."

"You're not going to try to take her away from me, are you?"

Han looks over at me for way too long.

"Eyes on the road!"

"Sorry," he says. "Why would I do that?"

"I don't know . . ."

He reaches out and touches my knee, then squeezes it in what he probably thinks is a reassuring way. Personally, I think he should have both hands on the steering wheel, but I manage to keep my mouth shut.

"You probably could take her," I say. "I abandoned her."

"You didn't abandon her. You left her with her aunt and grandparents so you could go to college."

I'm pretty sure Amber has a different take on that. "Why're you being so nice?"

"Don't take this the wrong way," he says, "because I'm not *in* love with you, but I do love you. And Natalie, too."

"If you really love me," I can't help saying, "you'll put both hands on the steering wheel."

He laughs and grabs it tightly with two hands. "Better?"

"Much." We drive in silence for a while. I'm not totally sold on what I'm about to say, but I make the offer anyway. "You could come to Kansas with us."

Han sighs. "I actually thought about it. But my dad's business is in the shithole right now." He laughs. "No pun intended."

"Yeah, right." I've heard all of Han's plumbing jokes before. He loves them.

"Seriously, though, I need to stick around Portland for a while and help him out," he says. "But you're coming back, right?"

"In four years."

"And maybe for visits?"

"Yeah. I hope so."

I look over at him. The headlights of the oncoming cars

swing across his face, lighting up the peach fuzz on his chin. He's a good guy, and for the first time I realize how lucky I really am. "I could put your name on Natalie's birth certificate. Or register it on her records or whatever you do."

He looks over at me. "I'd love that."

"Eyes on the road!"

He laughs and makes a big show of bugging out his eyes and staring straight ahead. God. He's right—I am a control freak.

"Han? I don't want child support. This was my fault—"

"Crys? We can work that out later, okay?" he says. "I need to concentrate on my driving here."

I can tell he doesn't want to stress me out by arguing, so I say okay.

At three in the morning, we pull up in front of Han's house.

"Thanks for coming to get me."

"You and me are in it together, Crystal. For life."

Whoa. He's right. "Yeah. I guess we are."

He's got his hand on the door, but he's not getting out. I'm afraid of what he might say, but I make myself stay quiet and wait.

"It's not true about Amber," he finally tells me.

"What isn't?"

"The reason I didn't ask you about being Nat's dad? It's

not because Amber told me not to, I mean she did, but . . . the truth is, I was chickenshit."

"Oh." That I can understand.

"I was afraid of my dad finding out. You know what he did to my sister."

Everyone knew. Brittany was hooking up with an Asian guy and their dad told her to break up with him, but she wouldn't, and so he threw all her stuff out in the yard and changed the locks. She was only fifteen. It's been two years and no one knows where she is anymore.

Han locks his eyes onto mine. "He told me from the time I was ten that if I got a girl pregnant, he'd kick my ass and then throw me out." I nod. I believe it. "Anyway, I convinced myself that if that happened, I'd never be able to support Natalie, but if I laid low, eventually he'd drink himself to death and I'd get the plumbing business and maybe be able to take care of her."

"Makes sense to me."

"I guess. But it's still bullshit. I should've just manned up."

"I don't know . . . it's hard." He sits there, his head hanging. "Han?"

"Yeah?"

"We'll figure it out. But not tonight, okay?"

"Sure." He gives me a quick one-arm hug and gets out of the car. I drive the last little bit to our house on autopilot.

Bonehead hears the Mustang and is barking his head off by the time I pull into the driveway.

"Shut that fucking dog up!" Mr. Hendricks yells from his bedroom window, and I laugh, letting out the breath I feel like I've been holding for days. It's good to be home. At least until I look up and see my sister scowling in the open doorway.

Then I'm not so sure.

CHAPTER 31

Amber steps aside to let me in, but before I can say anything, she says, "You have to sleep on the couch."

"Jeez, Am—"

"I'm not being a bitch. It's because of the fleas."

"Fleas?" I'm in the living room now, and it's packed full of all the stuff from our bedroom, including Natalie, who's sleeping in her crib. My heart grows a couple of sizes when I spot her—yeah, exactly like the Grinch's. It's hot in here. The windows are open for once, which helps a little, but there's a faint chemical smell hanging around too.

"Somehow our room got infested," Amber tells me. "The whole house had to be bombed, but our room's where we put the can. It was the worst."

That would be my fault. But I'm not stupid enough to mention that it was me who let Bonehead sleep inside those two nights before I left. Obviously no one's noticed I broke the lock open. Maybe tomorrow I'll pretend to undo it to get some air in there.

Amber's already claimed one end of the couch, and I stand over Nat's crib, unable to take my eyes off her. Light from the kitchen spills into the room, shining on her red hair. The need to pick her up is so strong that my arms ache along with my heart, but like they say, you only wake a sleeping baby once because she's cute, and then you learn your lesson: she'll cry for hours. We already learned that lesson a long time ago.

I take my chances and stroke her head, though. All she's wearing is a diaper, and she's kicked off her blankie, so I straighten it. A few tears might stray down my cheeks, but I tell myself it's sweat and wipe my face.

I look over at Amber. I know her well enough to see she's only pretending to be asleep. "Am, I'm sorry. I'm really, really—"

"I can't do this tonight," she says, keeping her eyes closed. "I have to get up early for work."

"But I want to say—"

She opens her eyes. "Not now, Crystal. Pick me up at the Glass Slipper at three thirty tomorrow. It can wait."

"Okay."

She tosses me a pillow and closes her eyes again. I'm

anxious to tell her that I'm taking her advice and going to Kansas with Natalie, but she's turned on her side, her back to me. I realize I'm exhausted too. I head for the bathroom instead of pushing the matter.

When I come back, Amber murmurs, "She missed you."

I want to let my sister know I'm back now and I won't ever leave Natalie again, but the words are stuck in my throat.

The sound of someone slamming the kitchen door wakes me up. Amber's gone and I'm twisted in a blanket, my body already sweaty from the heat. Mom comes into the living room in her work uniform and takes a hard look at me.

"The prodigal daughter returns, huh?"

"Hey, Mom."

I sit up and stretch. Natalie's still asleep, which might be some kind of miracle. The clock by the TV says seven thirty. I get up and stand over her crib, looking down at her. I think I wake her through sheer willpower, because she opens her eyes, sees me, smiles, and holds out her arms.

"Kwis! Up!"

I almost die of joy when she says my name. She's been saying "Amba" for a while now but couldn't seem to get mine. My sister must've taught her while I was gone. Now I have to teach her "Mama." I scoop Natalie up, my baby warm against my chest, and for the first time in five days, my body totally relaxes.

"So are you here for good?" Mom asks.

I snuggle my face into Natalie's soft curls. "Nope. A few weeks. I'm still going to Kansas."

"And you're here to talk Amber into it?"

I shake my head, smiling. I can't take my eyes off Natalie. "No. Just me and my daughter." My heart's hammering at the words, but I did it. I said them. "Han's gonna help me work it all out."

If Mom's shocked that I called Nat my daughter, she doesn't show it. When I finally do look up at her, she's standing there, nodding her head. "You know, Crystal, I might be a crappy mother, but in my heart, I knew I did okay with you girls."

"You're not a crappy mom."

"Yeah, well . . . I was young when I had you two. I did the best I could."

"We're all gonna be fine."

"I think you're right." She takes a step down the hall. "I'm going to bed."

"Oh, wait. I have something for you." I find my jeans that I left crumpled on the floor last night and dig the receipt from the slot machine out of one of the pockets. "Your winnings."

"From what?"

"They wouldn't let me cash out, but I played ten bucks for you in Reno before they noticed I was underage."

She examines the paper. "Excellent! You're charmed. You should go to bingo with me sometime."

"I'll pass. I have this for you too." I get her Reno T-shirt from the white plastic bag and hand it over. She takes it, reads it, and laughs. "You can wear it to bed."

"You betcha. Thanks." She trundles off down the hallway.

Nat wiggles around in my arms. "Babababababa!"

"Are you hungry, little girl? You want to eat?"

"Yes!"

That's new too. Normally all she says is no. We go to the kitchen, and I give her a bottle and pour some cereal for myself. I'm one hundred percent positive Nat has grown bigger since I saw her last. She definitely weighs more. After giving her a bath, I consider putting her in the Reno shirt, but I decide maybe I'll wait until after I've talked to Amber about Han. I don't want her to freak out.

Around noon, Gil comes stumbling out of the bedroom, his eyes bloodshot and what's left of his hair sticking out at all angles.

"Heard you were back."

"Yep."

"Good to see you."

"Thanks."

He tells me it's been three days since the flea bomb, so

we can move back into our room anytime. I open the garage door to let in some air while I shift our crap. I have to keep Natalie in her swing, but I put it in the shade of the world's scraggliest plum tree in the yard. I swear, it makes Charlie Brown's Christmas tree look awesome. Nat's okay there for a while, but pretty soon she wants out, and when I don't get her right away, she screams at me. The thing is, she can crawl so fast, even Bonehead can't keep track of her anymore unless I let him off his chain, and then I'd have the two of them to chase.

"Okay, okay," I tell her, abandoning the bed I was trying to drag back into place. She sticks her arms straight up in the air and breaks into a big smile, making my heart go all warm and gooey. I set her on Amber's bed, which is against the back wall, and she plays with her toes for a while, gurgling and babbling. It doesn't last, though, and out of the corner of my eye, I see her scooting toward the edge of the bed.

"Okay, big girl. Let's you and me get out of here. It's time to pick up Auntie Amber anyway." Auntie Amber. That sounds so weird. But I'm determined to do this right. Nat's not going to grow up confused about who's who, like we're embarrassed to acknowledge her or something.

Natalie squirms the whole time I strap her into the car seat, but I know she'll be happy once we get to the park, so

I try to ignore her squeals of protest. I run inside the house, leaving the car doors open and Bonehead on duty, and quick as I can, throw some snacks together for her. There's pizza on the table, but I'm not *that* hungry. I'll have to share Nat's Cheerios.

Bonehead almost loses his mind when I unhook his chain and let him into the back seat. I hear Nat shriek as I go around to the driver's side, and when I look in the back, Bonehead's licking the piece of banana I gave her. I take it away from her and give it to the dog, and then I make him get in the front seat with me. She's screaming now, mad at both of us, and I grab a handful of fish crackers and put them on the tray of her car seat. She immediately stops yelling and stuffs them in her mouth with both hands.

Amber's waiting outside the Glass Slipper.

"Get in the back," she tells Bonehead, pushing him until he climbs over the seat.

"Is the park okay?" I ask.

"Whatever."

There's a fenced area for dogs where we can let Bonehead run. He's not fixed, though, so if there are any other dogs, we'll have to keep him on the leash, because he either fights them or humps them. None of the other owners like this very much, but the dogs don't seem to mind.

"It's your lucky day," I tell him when we get to the park

and no one's around. Once we're inside the fence, I let him loose and he goes absolutely crazy. He jumps, runs, barks, back and forth, back and forth. I don't even need to throw a ball to keep him busy. He's so excited it's contagious, and all three of us laugh. Me and Amber each hold one of Nat's hands while she toddles around, giggling and screaming happily.

As we walk, I tell Amber that Han flew down and drove back home with me.

"He did? How come?"

"I kind of freaked out. Being away from Natalie . . . and what you said . . . calling me her mother. I was driving like a crazy person, like I could outrun the truth." I explain how I wanted to fly.

And when I tell her how much my speeding ticket is, she hits me in the shoulder. "Crystal!"

"I know, I know. I can't even think about what it's going to do to my insurance." Then I tell her about sleeping in the cactus room and the chile rellenos and how I called Han because we had to talk about Natalie.

"Really?" Amber drops Natalie's hand and stands there, staring at me. "You talked about that?"

"We had to."

"About friggin' time."

"You knew it was him, right?"

"Well, I figured," she says. "I mean, who else could it have been? It's not like you were going around having sex with a bunch of strangers."

I cringe at the word "sex." I've let myself remember the who and the when, but I'm still blocking the details.

"Doggy! Doggy!" Nat screams, and Bonehead runs over, licks her face, and knocks her over.

Amber sets Natalie back on her feet and I push the dog away. "Go. Run. Get out of here or we're going home." Bonehead takes off, covering ground in leaps and bounds. "I want you to know," I tell Amber, "I wasn't faking it. I really didn't know Han was the one until the other night when I kind of lost it and everything came back to me."

"I never thought you were lying. I could tell you didn't remember. But don't you think it's weird you didn't know all this time?"

"Yeah, I guess, but it's also like . . . the thing is . . . as soon as I forced myself to try to remember, I did. But before that, I refused to go there."

"You blocked it," Amber says. "It's PTSD. Like when a girl gets raped."

"Han didn't rape me!"

"Duh," she says. "Chill. I know. I just meant that people can block stuff out if they want to forget."

"I'm pretty sure that's what happened." I can't even admit

all of it to Amber, though. While I was never afraid I'd been raped, I *was* terrified that maybe I'd slept with one of my tormentors, just to prove them wrong. How sad would that have been? If one of those assholes was Natalie's dad, I think I'd want to kill myself.

Nat's face is turning a little pink, so we lead her over to some shade. "You should go on one of those talk shows," Amber says.

I laugh. "Forget it. I can barely even admit the truth to you."

The three of us sit down on a patch of dry grass. "I could pretend to be you," Amber offers.

Natalie climbs into my lap and leans against me. "Can we change the subject now?" I try to think of something that doesn't make my stomach churn. "So what's new with you?"

"Aunt Ruby made me the assistant manager."

"Wow. Already? Cool."

"Yeah. I'm really excited. I have a lot of ideas."

She tells me about her plans for the tavern for a while, but ever since I picked her up, we've been talking around me going to college and we both know it. Now it's time to tell her I'm gonna do it, and Natalie's going with me. I wait until there's a pause in the conversation, and then I take a deep breath, which does absolutely nothing to eliminate the queasiness in my stomach. "You know when we were having that big fight in the driveway? Before I ran off?" I ask.

"What fight?" Amber says, all innocent, and for a second I'm confused, but then she laughs. "Oh, you mean that all-out screamfest we had the other day where we shoved things in and out of the car, including our baby. That fight?"

I nudge her shoulder with mine. "Yeah . . . that one."

"What about it?"

"Well, you said something . . . You said that if I really wanted to go to college, I'd do what everyone else does and find a daycare, not ask you to give up your life."

"Oh, that."

I smile at her. "So . . . you're right."

"I am?"

"Yeah. And that's what I'm gonna do. Me and Nat are going to Kansas. And Han's going to help me find someplace for her to go when I'm in class and working."

Amber puts her arm around my shoulder. "I think that's great," she says. "I know I never told you, but I'm really proud of you for getting into college."

"You are?"

"Of course. My sister, the college graduate. I like the sound of that."

"Yeah, well . . . it'll be a while." Natalie's fallen asleep in my lap, and I stroke her sweaty hair. "God, I love this kid. I have no idea what I was thinking when I took off like that."

"I knew you'd be back," Amber says.

"I'm glad one of us has faith in me."

"I have enough for both of us, Crys. We'll all be okay."

We sit there in the shade, our little threesome of a family. Things are changing, but I think Amber's right. We're gonna be okay.

CHAPTER 32

On Saturday morning I bundle Nat into the car. We're
going to a car show in Banks, Oregon. Amber has to work,
but she made sure I knew she'd be giving it a miss even if
she had the day off. "You're never gonna get me interested in
cars, Crys," she said. "But have fun."

Bonehead practically yanks his stake right out of the
ground—he's dying to go along. He looked so happy at the
park the other day that me and Amber decided he needs a
new home, one where he can run around. We asked Han
for help, and in two hours flat, he found a woman who lives
out in the country and takes rescue dogs. She said she'd be
happy to have Bonehead if we got him neutered first. After I
take him to the vet on Monday to get snipped, he'll probably
never want to get into the Mustang again. Today, I decide to
let him have his own "last."

As soon as I let Bonehead off the chain, he lurches to-ward the car and I have to grab his collar and yell at him to calm down. I make him sit before I let him inside the Mus-tang so he doesn't trample Natalie in his excitement. When I finally open the door and push back the seat, he hurtles him-self into the back and starts licking something off her face, making her laugh.

At the show, I pay my registration fee and find my spot, and then I get Nat out of her car seat and into the fancy stroller. I wheel her onto the grass about ten feet behind the Mustang and tell her I'll be just a minute.

"No," she says. "No, no, no!"

"Don't worry. You can still see me." I tousle her straw-berry curls and head back to the car.

"No!"

"I'm right here," I tell her while I do all the stuff you do at a show, which is kind of like a cruise-in except there are hun-dreds of cars here, plus judges and trophies. Mostly it's the same guys and cars I see everywhere, but it's still fun. I take all the junk out of the inside of the car and pile it by Natalie.

"See? I didn't go anywhere."

"Up!"

"In a sec." I prop open the hood and trunk and run a chamois over the chrome. I keep the car pristine, but you always do the basics anyway.

A couple of hot rodders are walking by, and Stick notices

the Mustang and comes over. "I thought we seen the last of you."

"Almost. False start. But I'm leaving soon."

"Good thing or we'd want our money back," he says, giving me a big wink.

"No chance of that."

He wanders off and I get Bonehead out of the car. I've got the choke chain on him—it's the only way to keep him under control—but he still drags me behind him. When we get back to the stroller, I stake the dog to the ground. Two car widows are cooing over Nat and she's smiling up at them.

"Who's this?" one of the women asks me.

"That's my daughter, Natalie."

I hear a funny noise behind me, like a gasp, and when I turn around, David's standing there, his face full of surprise. "Your *daughter?*"

I want to be brave enough to look him straight in the eye, but instead I bend over Bonehead and scratch his ears. "Yep. My daughter." The words still feel weird in my throat, like I'm choking on a hazelnut in one of those coffeecakes Mom brings home from work. But they feel good, too. I'm proud of Nat.

"But . . . all this time I thought she was your sister's kid."

"Yeah, well . . ."

The two women give each other raised-eyebrow looks and wander off.

David's staring at me. "That's so weird. Why did I think that?"

I want to say it was his mistake, but I can't do that anymore. "I kind of let you think she was Amber's."

"Okay. Now I don't feel so stupid. But why?"

I take a breath and let it out with a little self-conscious laugh. "Because I was ashamed of being dumb enough to get knocked up. Can we leave it at that?"

He looks confused as well as a little embarrassed. "Sure." He leans over and squeezes Natalie's bare foot and she squeals. "Hey, Nattie baby."

I've been dreading telling him. He probably already thinks I'm a bigtime liar because of how I kept McPherson a secret from Amber. It's pretty clear I'd misled him about Natalie, too, but he's acting cooler than I deserve, and I try to relax.

All around us are the sounds of hot rod engines . . . that sort of loud lion's purr of hard work, sweat, grease, and love. Car doors slam, guys with beer bellies call out greetings to other hot rodders, and 1950s music blasts over the loudspeaker. These are the sounds of summer, the sounds I love so much.

"I was hoping I'd see you," I tell David. "I stopped by Jimmy's to talk to you yesterday, and he said you were coming here."

"Yeah, he told me. Why aren't you in Kansas?"

"I forgot something," I said. "Had to come back for precious cargo. But I'm still going. I have to do a few things first. Like make you an offer you can't refuse."

He snags my folding lawn chair. "Sorry, I'm taken."

"You wish. It's better than that, anyway."

He grins. "Ooh. Sounds promising. I'm listening." Bonehead sticks his head into David's crotch, and Stanford Boy laughs and shoves him away. But then he scratches Bonehead's ears and wins a new friend for life. The dog relaxes, falling in love for sure and settling at David's feet on the grass.

I take a deep breath. I can't believe I'm going to do this, but I've thought about it constantly for the past two days, and I know it's the right thing to do. It'll be hard, but as an old hot rodder once told me, "Darlin', we don't really own these cars. We just steward them for a while and pass them on to the next guy."

I pull a FOR SALE sign out of the diaper bag. "So . . ." I say, holding it up. "Should we put this in the Mustang or your Chevelle?"

David looks horrified. "Why would I put it in the Chevelle?"

"Me and Amber own the Mustang together, and she's staying here, which means I need to sell it so I can give her half the money. Do you want to sell the Chevelle and buy my car or not?"

His look of horror turns to confusion. "Huh?"

"I've gotta sell the car," I explain. "And I'd rather sell it to you than to a stranger."

"But what would I do with it?"

"Finish restoring it. You keep saying you want to learn how to do stuff. You need a project car for that."

"But—"

"Look, I know I've already done most of the fun stuff— the body work and the engine—but there's still the interior to do. And it needs to be painted. Maybe you could learn to spray cars."

David looks at me like I'm crazy.

"Up! Up! Up!" Nat screeches, and I take her out of the stroller and let her toddle around on the grass, holding her hands so she doesn't fall.

"I'm going to Stanford, remember?"

"So drive it like it is this year," I say. "And then come back in June and get some help from Jimmy."

I can tell he's totally considering it. "I don't know . . ."

"Or better yet, skip the high-powered internship next summer and drive the Mustang to Kansas to take some of the short workshops at the college."

I can see him debating the pros and cons. Finally he says, "My parents would kill me if I sold the Chevelle."

"But it's yours, right? I mean, you've got the title in your name, don't you?"

"Well, yeah . . . but they would be so freaking mad."

I smirk. "Bonus, if you ask me."

He smiles. I play patty-cake with Nat, giving David time to think things over. His parents might run his life, make him go to Stanford, insist he study pre-med, all the clichés . . . but there's a car geek inside him, and if you're born with that gene, it can't be suppressed.

"How much should I ask for the Chevelle?"

I know I've got him now. "How much did you pay for it?"

"I'm not sure. My parents got it for me for my sixteenth birthday."

I roll my eyes. I knew it. "Well, I did a little research . . ." I give him a price, and he chokes on his bottled water.

"Holy shit! That much?"

"Probably. Maybe more at auction."

"And what do you want for the Mustang?"

"I need to get twenty thousand out of it." This isn't exactly true. I'm hoping for sixteen, but you always start high so there's room for negotiation. "Even paying me what I want would leave you with a bunch of cash to work on it."

"Okay," he says, nodding. "Let's do it. You've got a deal."

I shake my head and let out a noisy sigh of disgust. "You rich boys. Don't you know anything?"

"What?"

"You can't just accept my asking price. You've gotta ne-gotiate or you're gonna get taken for a ride. Besides, whoever buys your car's gonna talk you down too."

"Oh, I'm not selling mine."

"What do you mean? I thought you said you were going to buy my car."

"I've got the cash. Don't worry."

I slug him hard.

"Ow! What was that for?"

"Taking my shifts at work all year when you didn't need the money."

David's face turns a little pink. "Oh. Sorry about that."

"Whatever. So you really want to give me twenty for the car?"

"Don't I?"

"You know I'm overcharging you, right?"

"You could use it for college."

"I'm not taking charity. Negotiate or no deal."

I wait for him to counteroffer, but he stares at me blankly. "I'm not really good at this stuff," he finally says. "Whenever I go to Mexico I just pay whatever those street vendor guys ask for."

"Even *I* know you're not supposed to do that."

"Could you walk me through it? Since we're friends?"

"Oh my God. You're pathetic." I'm sitting cross-legged on

the grass, and I fall back laughing. He looks like he's about six years old, afraid of being wrong or messing up. Man, his parents have done a number on him. Natalie laughs because I do, and then she plops herself down next to me and leans against my arm, putting her thumb in her mouth.

"Yeah, okay," I tell him. "But pay attention." I cross my arms and look him up and down. "I want twenty thousand for the Mustang. Not a penny less."

"I thought we were negotiating."

I stare at him, amazed. "And they're gonna let you be a doctor?"

He finally realizes I was leading him through the negotiation like he asked. "Oh, right. Sorry. Okay. So what do I say?"

"I don't know . . . Something like: 'It's a sweet car. But that's a little too rich for me. I could give you . . . maybe . . . fifteen?'"

He repeats what I tell him, word for word.

I shake my head. "No can do. Can't go lower than nineteen five."

"Okay," he says.

"Oh my God. You are so bad at this. Forget it. Give me seventeen and we'll call it good."

"Thank you. I really hate haggling. I'll get you the money on Monday."

After we shake, I tell him that even sixteen was probably

a little high, but he doesn't care. I can see the excitement in his eyes, and I'm glad that if I have to part with it, then at least it's going to a good guy. Kind of a nerd, but still . . . he'll treat my Mustang right. And with the kind of money he has to put into it, the car's gonna look awesome when he's done. I can hardly wait to see it. Maybe he'll even let me drive it someday.

CHAPTER 33

David shows up in a cab on Monday afternoon with two checks, one for Amber, one for me. It's the only time he's been to our house, but I've decided that's one more thing I can't be embarrassed about. I live here, at least for another week, and that's how it is. I hand over the keys to my other baby, and he hugs me.

"I promise I'll take good care of it."

"I know." I swallow the lump in my throat and squeeze my eyes shut tight so the tears don't leak out. "You can go now. Before I change my mind."

"Okay. See you at Christmas, or maybe in Kansas next summer."

"Go, okay?"

"I'm going, I'm going."

After he drives away, I hand Amber her check. She shakes

her head in wonder. "I can't believe we got so much, Crystal. We only paid three thousand for it!"

"Yeah, but I put about three thousand hours of work into it, too. Remember?" Probably a slight exaggeration, but maybe not. One of the reasons we'd gotten such a killer deal in the first place was because the car had been in a hailstorm in North Dakota and had about a million tiny dents. Also, the motor was shot.

"Yeah, true. Plus all your wages before Natalie."

Amber had tried to talk me out of selling the Mustang, but I had all my arguments lined up and ready to go. First of all, she owned half of it, so it wasn't fair for me to take it with me. Second, I wasn't sure I could drive all the way to Kansas with Natalie by myself; the Greyhound just made more sense. And third, Amber would need a car once I was gone. Jimmy was already looking for something reliable for her.

I also didn't think I'd really have a use for a car in Kansas, but if I do, I can buy some junker for cheap and get it running. At school, they have a project car for us to work on as a class, so not having the Mustang won't be that bad. I can get my car fix there.

"Han told me he'd teach me to drive," Amber says as we go inside.

"Yeah, he told me that too, so I signed you up for Sears driving school."

"Seriously?"

"Seriously. He's a scary driver. Don't do anything he does."

"Okay. I wish you had time to teach me."

"I'll give you a few lessons." And then with a sinking feeling I remember I can't — we sold our car.

We go in our bedroom to check on Nat, who's having a nap. She's still asleep, and I nod to Amber to come out into the kitchen. "I want to talk to you."

"Uh-oh. Sounds ominous."

"No, it's not. It's about living here. You need some of that Mustang money for the car Jimmy finds you, but I think you should get an apartment. I'd feel better if you were in a safer neighborhood."

Amber grins at me. "Don't worry. I've got a plan already."

"You do?"

"Jade and Teddy are moving in together, and the house they leased has one of those mother-in-law suites upstairs. I'm gonna rent it from them."

I'm about to say, "Are you out of your mind? You can't live with Jade. She's a terrible influence." But the look on Amber's face is so hopeful. I know she wants my approval, and she's been so good to me, so I keep my real feelings to myself. "Cool. Where is it?"

She breaks into a huge smile. "Over on Twenty-First and Weidler."

At least that's a good neighborhood. I still can't help but

say, "Are you sure, Amber? I mean, I think you should get your own apartment, but Jade's . . . she's . . . well . . ."

Amber puts her arm around my shoulder. "I know you and Jade don't get along, but she's changed a lot since she met Teddy. She doesn't drink anymore. And she even quit pot."

"Really?"

"Really."

This actually makes me feel a lot better. And the fact that Amber would have her own place, but there'd be family right downstairs, is probably exactly what she wants if we can't live together.

"Sounds good," I say. And it doesn't even cost me much to admit it. I'm not a big believer in fate—not like Mom anyway—but maybe this is how it was all supposed to work out.

On the eighteenth of August, Amber drives me, Natalie, and Han to the Greyhound station in the little Honda Fit that Jimmy found for her. She's only got her learner's permit, but she can drive with me or Han in the car. She's already a better driver than Natalie's daddy. I refrain from telling him that, though. I don't want to hurt his feelings.

"I can't believe you're leaving me," Amber says in the parking lot. I can tell she's trying not to cry.

"Stop," I say. "Or I won't be able to go."

"Sorry."

I wait until she's out of the car, and then I quickly turn the knob on her stereo so the music will come on full blast when she gets back in. I won't be here when it happens, but it gives me a little thrill anyway.

Up until this minute, I've been super excited. I've gone over my courses online about a million times, and Han found a daycare that's not only clean and cute, but accredited and not too expensive. He's already paid for the first month, too. But now, here at the bus station, all my enthusiasm vanishes. How can me and Amber possibly live so far apart that we won't see each other every day? The first time I left for Kansas, I was too mad to care, but now . . . now, I'm not sure how I'll survive without my sister. And what about Nat? I know she's going to miss Amber, and she'll probably think I'm really mean for taking her away.

Han holds Natalie while me and Amber lug my stuff into the station, and I see he's whispering in her ear. And I'm taking Natalie away from her dad, too. God. I am so selfish.

"You know what, Am? This is a stupid idea. I should stay here."

"Forget it. You're going."

"You just said—"

"You're going." She walks up to the counter and tells the lady my name.

"Yeah, okay." I really do want to go. But no one told me it would be the hardest thing I've ever done.

Amber squeezes my hand while the lady consults her computer. Me and Nat are only taking the essentials on the bus: one suitcase, which we check; a diaper bag; a car seat; and my backpack full of snacks. Amber helped me ship everything else yesterday. Once I'm all checked in, we join Han and Natalie on hard plastic chairs in the waiting room. Natalie's starting to fade in his arms.

"Don't let her go to sleep!" I practically screech, startling her awake. Me and Amber have kept her up all day so she'll fall asleep as soon as we get on the bus. She's cranky and whiny and I'm sorry this is the way Han has to say goodbye, but I don't want to be the passenger everyone hates because my kid is screaming.

He bounces her up and down, and she looks at him like he's a traitor, like "How can you do this to me when I'm so tired?" She screams and Han pulls her close, wiping at her tears with his thumb. A little lump gets stuck in my throat.

"I'm glad I'm not getting on the bus with you," Amber says, nodding at the people around us who are already glaring.

"You'll be a good girl, won't you, Nattie?" Han says. "Yes, you will. You'll sleep for Mommy, won't you?"

I like the way it sounds when Han calls me Mommy. Weird how fast I've gotten used to it. I doubt Natalie will be able to sleep for almost two whole days, though, which is how long it'll take us to get to McPherson. But I'm also not going to give her baby Benadryl like Mom suggested. I checked the Internet, and while the medicine is supposedly safe, a lot of pediatricians say not to do it. It's still a drug. Sometimes I think it's a miracle that me and Amber made it to adulthood. I did take Rosa's advice, though. When she heard we were going by bus, she said, "Been there, done that. Spend the extra money and buy two seats. Just because you *can* hold her in your lap for free doesn't mean you want to."

The four of us sit there in silence, me fingering our boarding passes, Amber fiddling with her hair. And then Han comes to life. "Oh, man, I almost forgot." He hands Natalie to Amber and runs out to the car. A minute later, he's back with a plastic bag. "One for Mommy," he says, giving me a brand-new cell phone. "And one for Auntie Amber."

"Wow." I examine it. It's no iPhone, but it's pretty nice.

"I have one for me, too," he says. "They're all charged up, and I've programmed our numbers into them."

"I thought you said you'd kill yourself before you got one of these," Amber teases him.

"That was before Nat. I got us the family plan. We can talk as much as we want."

"Thanks."

"Yeah, this is great, Han. Thanks."

He's looking pretty proud of himself. And he should be, too. He still hasn't told his dad about Natalie because he's getting his plumber training from him and needs the job, but he came clean with his mom. She promised not to tell, and we took Natalie to the restaurant where she waitresses and they got to meet each other. Now Natalie has two grandmas.

Before I'm really ready, they announce our bus. Panic rushes over me. "Oh my God," I say. "What am I doing? I can't leave you guys."

Amber steers me toward the line at door number six. "We've already covered that. You'll be fine," she says. "Go on."

"But—" Tears are spilling over onto my cheeks. Amber and Nat are crying too. Even Han looks teary.

"Aunt Ruby says I can have two weeks off next summer," Amber reminds me for the thousandth time. "I'll drive out and see you both."

"Me too," Han says. "I mean, I'll go with her."

"You guys promise?"

The line's moving forward now. "We promise," Amber says.

"But don't let him drive," I tell her.

She rolls her eyes and hugs me hard. Then she takes Natalie from Han so he can hug me while she says goodbye to her niece. When Han lets me go, I give Amber another hug, squeezing Nat between us until she squawks. Then I'm being herded through the door, out into the hot August night with Nat on one hip, the backpack and diaper bag slung over my shoulders, and the car seat in my other hand.

"Send lots of pictures!" Amber yells after us.

"Call every day!"

"We will."

Me and Nat make our way onto the bus and up the stairs, squeezing down the aisle, dodging elbows and swinging luggage as people try to put their stuff in the overhead bins. A few people give us wary looks, but Natalie coos and gurgles at them and their grimaces turn to smiles. At least for now.

I get the car seat buckled down, then settle Natalie into her seat. We can't see Amber or Han, but I tell her, "Say bye-bye to Auntie Amber. Bye-bye to Daddy."

She opens and closes her chubby fingers, her version of waving. "Bye bye bye bye bye!" She keeps repeating it as I strap her in, and then I sit down next to her and fall back against my seat, totally exhausted. Maybe we'll both sleep.

I look over at her, my pale-skinned, blue-eyed, strawberry-blond daughter, and I feel a surge of love come from somewhere so deep inside me that it makes me shudder. "Well," I say to her as the bus pulls out, "it looks like it's you and me, kid."

She waves at the window. "Bye-bye."

"Hey, Nat," I say, and she looks up at me. "You ready for our very first road trip together?"

"Yes!" she yells.

I laugh. I doubt she actually understood the question, but her enthusiasm makes me happy anyway. This might be our first road trip, but it definitely won't be our last. And someday we'll be doing it in an extremely cool car I restored myself. I take Natalie's tiny hand in mine and squeeze gently. Our future stretches out in front of us, and for the first time in my entire life, I'm looking forward to it.

Thank you to Karen Grove, my lovely editor, for her insight, for being my sounding board, and for her all-around fabulousness. And to Michael Bourret for making the writer-editor match. *Merci!* Your faith knows no bounds.

Thanks to Papa for teaching me about cars, instilling in me the love for the cool ones, and most important, for checking this book for errors (if there are any, we need to talk . . . Just kidding, they're all mine).

Big hugs and lots of chocolate to my early readers: Eileen Cook, Alexa Barry, and Iain Lawrence. Thanks also to the best cheerleaders a writer could have: Zac Brewer, Joelle Charbonneau, LJA, S. Barney, Bill Cameron, and Suzanne Selfors. And to Karilyn McEnroe for the Spanish help.

Love to K.B. and the Berthelot family for sharing something important and personal, with special thanks to Nicole.

And even though he'll probably never see this, thanks to Jay Leno, for first bringing this program at McPherson College to my attention and making me want to write about it. Also to Joshua Hubin in the automotive restoration program for answering my questions about the admissions process, which apparently changes year to year!

Husbands always seem to get thanked last, but we all know why: They make writing books possible, so there's a lot to say. Thanks, darling, for the input, the cups of tea, and all the egg sandwiches when I was too busy to cook for real. You're my shining star.